Praise for *Sex Is*

"Assured. Accomplished. Memorable . . . Parks gives us a glimpse of the titanic struggle of meditation, of the mind's fluctuations under restraint, observing itself."—*Kirkus Reviews* (starred)

"It's a cracker—clever, funny, and insightful, with complicated, conflicted, and totally convincing Beth at its heart."—*Daily Mail*

"Parks writes with detachment, wit, and intelligence, and the troubled voice in Beth is entirely convincing."—*The Times*

"A wry and subtle story about what happens when the Western self tries to lose itself."—*Prospect*

"An eminently readable and thought-provoking novel that teases you to the last page, and possibly beyond."—*Spectator*

"Tim Parks is very good at rubbing beliefs up against each other, which leads to subtle, unsettling questions. . . . Full of observations that are quirky, witty, and deep."—*Sunday Herald*

"A thrilling novel by a master of the inner monologue who deals with his themes with great care and irony."—*Der Spiegel*

"Highly entertaining."—*Süddeutsche Zeitung*

"Impressive."—*Die Zeit*

Sex Is Forbidden

TIM PARKS

Sex Is Forbidden

A Novel

ARCADE PUBLISHING • NEW YORK

First North American Edition

Arcade Publishing books may be purchased in bulk at special discounts for sales promotion, corporate gifts, fund-raising, or educational purposes. Special editions can also be created to specifications. For details, contact the Special Sales Department, Arcade Publishing, 307 West 36th Street, 11th Floor, New York, NY 10018 or arcade@skyhorsepublishing.com.

Arcade Publishing® is a registered trademark of Skyhorse Publishing, Inc.®, a Delaware corporation.

Visit our website at www.arcadepub.com.
Visit the author's website at www.tim-parks.com.

10 9 8 7 6 5 4 3 2 1

Library of Congress Cataloging-in-Publication Data

Parks, Tim.
  [Server.]
  Sex is forbidden / Tim Parks.
    pages cm.
Originally published under the title "The Server"
ISBN 978-1-61145-907-4 (hardcover: alk. paper)
ISBN 978-1-62872-534-6 (paperback: alk. paper)
ISBN 978-1-62872-308-3 (ebook)
1. Buddhist centers—Fiction. 2. Spiritual retreats—Fiction. 3. Self-actualization (Psychology)—Fiction. I. Title.
PR6066.A6957S47 2013
823'.914—dc23

2013022508

Printed in the United States of America

Enough of worldly affairs! I shall concentrate my mind in meditation, dragging it from false paths.

The Bodhicaryāvatāra

Sex Is Forbidden

Sex Is Forbidden

Sex is forbidden at the Dasgupta Institute. That's one of the big advantages of working here. Of course I'm a volunteer, they don't pay me, so I don't mean *really* working. I'm a server, officially. Harper says it's unusual for anyone to serve for more than three or four retreats in a row. Which makes sense. Parents don't put you through school to have you spend your life cooking and cleaning for free. They have ambitions for you, they have their plans. It's hard to disappoint.

All the servers here are young, or youngish, between things anyway. I suppose, if you think about it, people are always between things, there's no other way to be. But you know what I mean. Summer jobs, gap years. Sometimes I wonder what things I'm between. I suppose it should be pretty easy to say what the stuff behind you is, how you came to be here and so on. Most people's worries are about the future. But the longer I stay at the Dasgupta Institute the less certain I am about what happened before. In the early days here, when I first sat and tried

1

to meditate, the past hammered on in my head. Everybody gets that. You sit and close your eyes and the thoughts start barking like crazy dogs. They used to, and I haven't forgotten. Just that nowadays I'm not so sure any more what it added up to. Perhaps, churning over and over, the old thoughts have worn themselves out. The torment has faded. Perhaps the truth is I'm not between things at all at the Dasgupta. I'll live here for ever maybe, or if I go, the Dasgupta will live with me.

This morning I felt very lazy. The gong sounds at four. Servers don't have to start preparing breakfast till six, so I usually sit in the first hour and a half of meditation and leave when the chanting begins. This is definitely the best part of the day. Why? I don't really know. Nothing hurts before dawn. You walk to the meditation hall through the dark. The morning air feels soft, everything's damp and dewy and it's very quiet. If you are one of the first, you'll see rabbits in the grass. There are stars, and the stars are bright here. Chilly. People wear fleeces with hoods and look like monks or ghosts. Everything feels kind of ghostly and on hold. In the hall your cushion and blankets welcome you. The lights are dimmed. You close your eyes and listen to the others coming in, snuffling and fidgeting and coughing. That can drive you mad. A voice starts in your head: Hey, I didn't get up so early to listen to your coughs and farts, thank you very much. I get enough stink cleaning loos. Then you realize these sounds are cosy. They protect you. That's a strange thing. You're going crazy with someone for constantly blowing her nose and you feel protected and humbled too. This person is making a big sacrifice coming to the Dasgupta and trying to change her life. Who are you to be so critical? In the end it's good to feel humbled and say to yourself, Stop bitching about the poor woman's snuffles, Beth

Marriot. You've no idea the shit she may be going through, or the bad things she's between.

So I let the coughs and snuffling be. I accept them, like an itch or a cramp, or the crows scrabbling on the prefab roof. Those crows can make quite a racket. I love the morning session. It's the best. But today I felt lazy. When the gong sounded I didn't get up. Something must be changing. *Anicca.* Feel the change. *Ahneechaaa, ahneechaaaa, ahneechaaaa.* I love the way Mi Nu says that word in her singsong Asian voice. Feel the pulsing in your wrists, Beth, feel the tingling in your cheeks. Change. *Anicca.* Maybe it's the same change that made me pick up a pen. Today, on impulse, I picked up a pen. Writing is another thing that is forbidden at the Dasgupta Institute. Writing and sex.

Not that I ever minded the writing ban. The only rule that really got to me when I first came to the Dasgupta was the Noble Silence. No talking. No singing. For me there are moments when it just seems natural to say right out loud—Good morning, folks! Could you pass the water jug? Hey, you've forgotten to take your shoes off! Or other moments when I *have to* burst out singing, *When the working day is done, Girls just wanna have fun!* I just have to rock and shake and stamp my feet. So silence was hard for me. In fact what's nice about being a server is that you can talk a bit, at least in the kitchen. No, you *have to talk* to get your job done. Though never to the meditators of course. The meditators mustn't be disturbed.

Actually, I tell a lie. The no-smoking rule drove me crazy too. I'd brought three packs to get me through the ten days and smoked them in the bushes at the bottom of the field. People must have seen. But I never finished them. Eight months later

I still have half a pack. You'd think this was a major event in my life, chucking smoking. God knows, I'd tried often enough, with Carl on my back. But now I can't even remember when it happened. Meditation does that. We live in a trance at the Dasgupta. An endless *jhāna*. I like that word. One day I found I wasn't smoking. One day I realized I had stopped thinking, of Dad and Mum and Jonathan and Carl and Zoë. I'd stopped thinking of Pocus, stopped thinking of the future. So the Dasgupta technique does work. I had grown in Dhamma. Except now here I am all of a sudden writing this down. Me who never wrote anything but songs in the past. Actually, I still don't mind the no-writing rule. I mean, it was nice smoking when I wasn't supposed to smoke. I didn't stop because of the rule. And it's nice writing now and knowing I'm not supposed to write. It's made me feel pretty intense this morning. Intensely Beth. Maybe I'm about to switch from being a model Dasgupta server to a crazy, bad-girl rebel breaking all the rules. Then they'll chuck me out and I'll find out what things I've been between all this time.

One of the male servers has a BlackBerry. I was pretty mad when I saw it. Ralph. He's German. Servers get to be around members of the opposite sex when they're cooking. There's only one kitchen and we cook the same stuff for everyone, men and women, new students and old, though there are some things old students are supposed to renounce, of course, like cakes and afternoon fruit. I came in a few minutes early for the breakfast shift and Ralph was sitting on one of the counters bent over the little screen. Ralph is proud of being a server. His cute face goes smooth with devotion. He likes to think of the good he is doing. Without us the meditators wouldn't have the freedom to live in silence, they wouldn't be able to offload their bad karma and *sankharas* and start purifying themselves. Well, first he tried to slip the thing in his apron pocket, then when he saw I'd seen what he was up to, he asked if I'd like to check my email. He wanted to make me a party to the crime. I nearly reported him. Maybe I should have. 'That's really against the spirit of the Dasgupta,' I said. 'You should be ashamed of yourself. What's the point of us creating this pure atmosphere here if you're polluting it looking at porn on your BlackBerry?'

That upset him. It was pretty funny. How could I think he was looking at porn? he said. He has a strong German accent. 'Why do you zink zat?' I was struggling to keep a straight face. 'All men look at porn,' I told him. Which is the truest thing on earth. 'Why did you try to hide it otherwise?'

But if I had reported Ralph, to the Harpers, or Mi Nu, they would have been sterner with me for telling tales than with him about his BlackBerry. At the Dasgupta each person must obey the rules *because they want to*. So long as they're not disturbing someone's meditation, rule breakers don't need to be reprimanded. I suppose I could have made out that Ralph was disturbing me, but I'm not sure a server counts. As an old student, a server is supposed to be above being disturbed. Otherwise why did we learn the method? Still, it *does* disturb me. It itches, thinking of him having access to the net, thinking of what it would be like to open my email again. Or Facebook. Christ. Perhaps now I've got pen and paper I could write an anonymous note. RALPH HAS A BLACK-BERRY. HE SURFS FOR PORN. Perhaps now I've started writing, I'll start smoking again too. I could finish what's left of that last pack. Then Ralph could report *me*. I'd let him get a whiff of smoky breath while we were scrubbing carrots. They'd ask me where I got cigarettes from, since I haven't been out of the grounds for months. I'd confess and say I was sorry. To Mi Nu maybe. Mi Nu Wai. I'd like to have a reason to confess some stuff to her. I could tell her I skived off to the pub some nights. But I don't think Ralph would report me. Ralph likes me. He's always there to help scrape the plates and pull the gunk from the plughole after lunch. Perhaps he let me see his BlackBerry on purpose. Ralph likes me, but he's too young, too sweet, too *German*. I never went for sweet boys. There must be dozens of more attractive men here. And women for that matter. It's a good job sex is forbidden at the Dasgupta. Maybe there are good reasons for forbidding writing.

I didn't go back to sleep again when I stayed in bed. The others got up with that lovely submission we all have in the morning. They went to meditation. But I lay in bed thinking. After about ten minutes Meredith came back to ask me if I was ill, but since even servers are only supposed to speak when they have to, I didn't answer. Meredith's a chubby kid, rather pretty, I suppose. She has a pretty smile. She's going to start at Cambridge at the end of summer, so she says. I didn't answer. I didn't even shake my head. Now she'll be wondering what's up or what she did to offend me. Jesus. Why am I so mean? I don't know. I enjoy it. I enjoy being nice and I enjoy being mean. I think Meredith deserves a bit of meanness. She definitely needs to lose some weight. If I ever had a chance of going to Cambridge, I blew it way back.

So I didn't go back to sleep but lay there thinking. It's been a while since I did this. In the past when I lay in bed thinking I'd be planning planning planning, I'd be anxious and excited. I'd be writing songs in my head, sorting out practice sessions, rehearsal space, gigs, emails, the website, money. But when I arrived at the Dasgupta I'd jump out of bed as fast as I could because the

6

thoughts were *horrible*. The moment I woke up my head was pounding. No, that's not right. There'd be one split second of peace before the thoughts came down like an avalanche and buried me. Then I'd curse that second of peace for making the avalanche so much worse. You've got to get over these thoughts, I kept telling myself. Got to got to. You have to kill these thoughts before they kill you. Kill kill kill. The Dasgupta is a great place for killing thoughts. I understood that. I realized at once how lucky I'd been to come here. I'd have died. But those days are gone. They've faded. This morning I just stayed in bed to think about yesterday's find. I wanted to enjoy thinking over something new that's happened, the first in months. Yesterday's find has started me writing. I should be careful.

In one of the men's rooms I found a diary. While the meditators meditate, the servers clean. The male servers clean the men's side and the female servers the women's. Every day the toilets, every other day the showers and the washbasins. Replenish the loo paper, the paper towels, tampons and sanitary pads, replenish the hand soap and the bio powder for people washing their socks and panties. Fish out the hair blocking the plugs. There are still people who chuck tampons in the loo. I don't mind, the day passes. It's weird how easily you can slip from meditation to washing floors, as if it was the same thing. But we had run out of disinfectant. Of course I'm not supposed to, but I went round to the male side. I hate to leave a job half done and the meditators were all away in the hall. Ralph and Rob were digging weeds from the path. 'Cupboard at the end of the corridor,' they said. 'Dormitory A.'

I got the disinfectant, then, walking back down the corridor, I pushed open a door to see what the men's rooms were like. Why do I do stuff like this? Someone could have been in there, meditating alone, and I would have offended him with my female form. Or even masturbating! You never know with men. Mrs Harper would have a heart attack.

It was a single room, so for someone elderly or disabled, or important somehow. No way I ever had a single room. A suitcase was open on the bed and it was full of red exercise books, which is against the rules. There were pens too, half a dozen biros. I picked up one of the exercise books. Just seeing the handwriting made me feel anxious. It was tall and very slanted, like a strong wind was blowing along the lines, bending the tops of the letters, pushing them towards the edge of the page. I read a few words and knew at once this guy was in serious trouble. *Since evidently you're incapable of deciding who you are you may as well become nothing.* Stuff like that. *Since you've destroyed everyone you've had anything to do with, don't you owe it to them now to destroy yourself?* No, it was more stylish than that. I can't remember the exact words. Or more pompous. Definitely an oldie, I thought. Or maybe not. What do I know? Maybe a pompous handicapped kid or a teacher's pet. One notebook was only half written and the last pages had this week's date and stuff about arriving at the Dasgupta and only realizing when it was too late that he wouldn't be able to get back to the locker where he'd left his mobile. *No mobile for ten whole days.* I smiled because the same thing had happened to me the first time. Happens to everyone. It's a trick they play. *Why do I always write as if this were for somebody else?* he'd written. That got me weirdly excited.

I took one of the notebooks and brought it back to the female side. Not smart. While the others were in the hall this morning I read it. I mean I flicked through it. The handwriting

8

is terrible and I'm not sure I care that much. Then in the next hour of Strong Determination, when the coast was clear, I took it back, with the disinfectant, before hurrying to the hall. We all have to go to Strong Determination, servers and students alike. It wasn't smart because after reading it I couldn't concentrate on my meditation. Suddenly all the old thoughts and memories were shouting and screaming and stamping their feet again. Suddenly I'm wondering whether all my time at the Dasgupta hasn't been completely wasted.

Total Surrender

Every ten days there is a changeover at the Dasgupta. The vow of silence is lifted before lunch. The meditators chatter like crazy for an afternoon, make their donations while they're still excited and leave the following morning. Retreat over. So if I don't go back to look at the diary for another eight days it will disappear with whoever wrote it and I'll be safe. Another group will arrive and I'll sink back into Dasgupta ways. I've already managed one day. I'm feeling better, my equanimity is returning. I can tell by the tension level in my thighs when I'm sitting. Of course I've no way of knowing who wrote it because I can't be on the men's side when people go back to their rooms. Even then I'd have to be right in the dormitory corridor to see who went to that door or right outside the room when he came to the window to draw his curtains. I don't really know which women are in which rooms. Why should I? There are so many. We don't clean the bedrooms during the retreat, but at the end when you sweep under all the beds it's amazing the stuff you find. Cigarette packs, food wrappers, Cadbury's, Mr Kipling.

A brandy bottle once. People look so solemn when they walk to the Metta Hall before dawn with their hoods over their bowed heads but nearly all of them have stuff they shouldn't in their rooms.

'What we are asking of you for the next ten days,' Harper says, when people arrive, 'is total surrender.' It's the only time he actually makes a speech and he keeps it downbeat and straightforward. 'You must put yourself totally in our hands. That is the only way you will get results.' People look solemn and accepting. They've read the spiel on the website, so it's hardly a surprise. But they all hold something back: a magazine, cigarettes, an MP3, something of themselves to hang on to through ten days of silence. Once I found an anal massager. That upset me. It made me laugh. I showed it to Harper. I get pretty angry when people break the rules. You can see they're exchanging looks when they shouldn't. Noble Silence also means no eye contact, no intimacy, no sniggering. You think, Why should I bother, if they're not going to? But it makes me smile too and I'm glad they do it. After all, I talked a fair bit myself the first ten days I was here. There was a nice French girl in my room who hugged me when I cried and gave me mints. She was sweet and very soft. I forget her name. Carl and I used to talk a lot about giving yourself. He said with love the only way was to give yourself absolutely, totally and completely. That's what love was. I said it wasn't something a person could just decide yes or no. Some people gave totally when they didn't want to and others couldn't give when they did want to and that was the same with music and with anything that needed commitment. You did or you didn't, you could or you couldn't, depending on you, depending on the situation. It wasn't a decision you could take. Now I've started sneaking looks at the men in the Metta Hall wondering which one it could be. Why do I want to know? Two days ago I would have taken refuge in the triple gem. *Buddham saranam gacchami. Dhammam saranam gacchami. Sangham saranam gacchami.* It was a pleasure just to say those words. I take refuge in the Dhamma. But not now. I'm not going to now. Something has changed. *Anicca.*

Three refuges and also three places on the site where you can check out the men. It's amazing how sly the Dasgupta people are about separating the sexes. When the first-timers arrive, in their cars, or ferried from the bus stop in the minibus, they have the impression they're walking into an ordinary old farm building. There's a porch and a corridor—everybody is chatting, laughing—then a locker room on the left. You put your things in a locker, like at the swimming-pool, your money, books, pens, phone, laptop. Then when you turn the key, it pops out in your hand, so you don't feel you've lost touch with your stuff. You have the key. You can go back any time. You think.

Next there's a huge room, an old barn it must have been, or cowshed, with rows of tables for eating, and the women go to register on the far right, the men on the left. Then while Harper's saying his piece about total surrender the locker room is locked up and the door leading back to the entrance and the outside world is shut and placed out of bounds. And as he's winding up his speech, wishing everyone a good retreat, two servers quietly unfold a partition wall down the middle of the dining hall between the men's and women's tables and bolt it into place. And that's it. You can't get back to your stuff in the locker room, or out to the road, and you can't talk to the other sex any more. The only way out of the hall now leads to the bathrooms, the dormitories, the meditation hall and the recreation field, all strictly divided into male and female.

Sometimes, when there are couples, someone gets upset. They knew they were going to be split up, but they haven't had time to say goodbye. I remember one pregnant woman getting really hysterical. There's always at least one couple expecting a child, always their first child. They want to feel holy and consecrated. They're in awe about creation. This woman rushed over as we were pushing home the bolts. I quite like rolling out the partition. I always volunteer. She started shouting and banged a fist on the screen. 'Goodbyes are overrated,' I told her.

After this separation there are three places where you can get a look at the men, or more likely see them trying to get a look at you. The wire fence that runs from the bathroom block to the Metta Hall isn't completely covered with climbers yet. There are gaps. So we're talking about seeing the opposite sex through wire netting and breaks in jasmine and dog roses, you walking, them walking. With a bit of luck you might get a glimpse of a nice hippie type, but mostly it's gloomy, gangly boys or older blokes shambling about with their heads bowed over their paunches. It must be tough for older guys at the Dasgupta. They've had more time to pile up their bad karma and *sankharas*. I bet their thighs and ankles burn like hell through the sittings of Strong Determination. Girls get through their shit younger, I suppose. By thirty I reckon I'll be purified or dead.

Beyond the hall there's another fence dividing the big field, then the wood. There is no ivy or anything on this fence, but the paths are miles apart and the grass either side is left unmown, so it's deep and wet. If you turn your head while you're taking a walk round the field you can maybe see a guy stepping slowly along in his loose meditation pants and shabby top. We're all shabby at the Dasgupta. Or maybe there's someone sitting on the bench at the top of the field looking out across the countryside. People sit and stare without really seeing. But that's about it. Of course, if you pressed on across the field and into the wood, then left the path and fought your way through the brambles to the fence, theoretically you could talk face to face with a man there. I bet some couples do that. If you were desperate you could even climb over and kiss. It's not so high. Couples have to sign a special clause at the Dasgupta saying they won't speak to each other or touch each other for the whole ten days of the retreat. But why am I thinking of this? I shouldn't. I shouldn't be thinking of lovers promising they won't even try to look at each other. What a luxury! Imagine a couple, in love, she's expecting a baby, he's in adoration, and they make a solemn vow not to speak to each other or even look at each other for ten days. For ten precious days of her pregnancy they will be silent and devout, sitting in meditation and purifying their minds to be ready for the birth of their firstborn. They're quite near to each other, physically—the Dasgupta is not exactly huge—but they don't try to make contact in any way, except of course in their heads they will be sending constant whispered messages of affection and encouragement: I love you, Treasure, I love you, I really do, our baby will soon be born strong and beautiful and I will love him all the more, or her, because she will be our baby, I will love you in him, or in her, and of course both these parents-to-be are safe in the thought that even though they're not actually in each other's arms, the other can't be cheating on them, it's impossible, how could anyone cheat on anyone at the Dasgupta Institute? so for the whole ten days they'll be feeling so pure because they've abstained from talking and touching and at the same time completely secure in the knowledge that the moment they're home, still feeling clean and holy and chattering about all their weird and wonderful meditation experiences, they're going to jump straight into the sack together and make the most loving and delicious love.

I knew I shouldn't have started thinking about this. I shouldn't have started writing. One thing leads to another when you think and write your thoughts down. False empty fantasies, painful formations of the mind, *sankharas*. These couples know exactly what things they're between when they come for their ten days at the Dasgupta Institute. They're between kisses and caresses. No wonder they don't bother with the brambles in the wood. It would just spoil the fabulous time they're going to have when they get their purified selves or non-selves back between the sheets. No condoms since she's already got their baby in her belly. So much for renouncing attachment. So much for overcoming cravings. I knew I shouldn't have started thinking about this. The time Jonathan came back from Australia. God. The mind is fire. That's a true thing Dasgupta says. Words are sparks. Ideas are fireworks. You light the blue touchpaper and it's always too short. The ideas blow up in your face. But I wouldn't want their happiness. Really. Or their baby. No, I wouldn't. They will let each other down soon enough. Be sure. All of them. They will live in fear of being let down, in horror of letting down. Or both. Love is waiting for betrayal, doesn't matter which of you is guilty, then the turmoil, then the emptiness. So much for equanimity. The guy with the diary knows this. But I don't want their illusions. I don't want to write songs about their illusions, or their disappointments. A song about happiness is always a song about disappointment in the making. The more the happiness the more I hear people crying. I don't want to write about them or imagine them. Or their baby. Mummy and Daddy. Still, I wish them well. I do.

15

I try to. May they be fully enlightened, may they be filled with happiness and sympathetic joy, may their child grow healthy and beautiful in the path of Dhamma. May all beings be happy and peaceful, may all beings be liberated, liberated, liberated.

The third place, I was saying, where you can see the boys is the Metta Hall itself. They're on the left, we're on the right. Seventy mats their side, in rows, all with blue cushions and grey blankets. Seventy mats our side with blue cushions and white blankets, or sort of off-white. With a broad aisle between. The men with their video screen high on the wall up front. Us with ours. Our gazes mustn't tangle when we watch Dasgupta's talks. A man is a distraction for a woman and a woman is a huge distraction for a man. Of course, if you came into the hall a little late for the hour of Strong Determination, then you'd be able to check out all the men in a single glance across the other side as you walked to your place. But my mat is quite a distance from the aisle and I have no excuses for going closer. I like it that way. What do I need to look at men for? Unless I faked some reason to go and kneel before Mi Nu Wai, some special request.

People coming into the Metta Hall take their shoes off in the porch, men in their porch on the left side, women in our porch on the right. They pad into the hall in socks or barefoot, go to their designated mats, fuss over their cushions and blankets, settle themselves, close their eyes. No one looks around, except the teachers and their assistants. Two male assistants, two female. They are checking us in. They have lists. The recording won't start till we're all in our places. They check your clothing too. I got sent back once because I'd forgotten my bra. That was a long time ago. My T-shirt was tight, they said. I was embarrassed, but pleased too. On the way I stopped in the bathroom

16

to look in the mirror. They were right. You could see the nipples. Anyway, today I glanced up and across to the left for a moment as I was walking between the cushions. But because the teacher's assistants are always watching you, you can't really check out the other sex. You'd be noticed. And without my glasses, what would I see anyway? I'm not going to start wearing glasses to meditate. In the end I don't care who the diarist is. He's another troubled man. A pig or a loser. Maybe both.

When I've settled on my mat the only person I look at is Mi Nu Wai. Meeee Noooo Waaaiiii. She sits up front on a broad, low stool, almost a table, with a white cushion, in loose white trousers and blouse. Her shoulders are slim as a bird's, and when she pulls her shawl around her it's as if her dark hair were the top of a pale triangle floating a little above us. Her back is straight but not vertical, she leans forward slightly, towards the meditators, and her face is upturned in earnest serenity. She is so still, so pale, so timeless, so almost not there that you can't help but gaze at her, the way you stare at something on the horizon about to disappear. I sit and pull my ankles into my crotch. I want to be like Mi Nu Wai. I want her stillness, her ghostliness. Beth Marriot is too fleshy and fidgety with her big thighs and her big tits squeezed in their bikini top under her fleece. You're a giggle of tits, Betsy M, Jonathan said, a gaggle a giggle a gurgle a goggle a google of tits. I always preferred bikini tops. I don't need support. Just to hide the nipples. Drove him nuts. To his nuts.

Stop.

Breathe.

Observe your breath.

The in-breath, the out-breath.

The left nostril, the right nostril.

Breathing is so beautiful, when the faintest back and forth just tingles your lip.

How does Mi Nu sit so still? In a single move she settles and gathers herself and right away she is still. Not like something turned off or dead, switched on more like, luminous and alive. Her stillness glows like the moon. I can feel it from five yards away. Mi Nu is the moon, leaning over me from her raised seat, pale and bright and still. A faint smile lifts the corners of her mouth. I must become like her. Sometimes I think she is rocking a little, just barely, back and forward, like she wants to sink herself deeper into stillness and silence. Or maybe it's me. I'm in a trance watching Mi Nu. My eyes are half closed. A slow, stoned tenderness wells up in my chest. Then I can't say if it's her rocking, very slightly, or me. We are fastened together, the way your eyes fasten to the moon at night, or the endless stars, on your back on a beach. 'Are you moonstruck or what?' Carl asked. 'What are you thinking about, Beth? For Christ's sake. Talk to me!'

I keep my eyes on Mi Nu. What is behind is behind. I must become like her. I love her black hair spreading on the whitish shawl. She never fusses when she settles. The soft white wool gathers round her and falls still. I love it when she wears her hair in a ponytail. Her skin and shawl melt together, ghostly and softly glowing. The air is a halo for Mi Nu. She is a cone of light. She is a cone of pale light gathering the room around her stillness. But already the chanting has begun. Only five minutes to go. Mi Nu has tied me to her stillness for a solid hour. I haven't suffered or fidgeted at all. No strong determination required. Only adoration. Her face doesn't respond to Dasgupta's throaty voice, opening the chants. *Buddham saranam gacchami.* Not even a flicker of reaction. The smile floats, bright and quiet. The moon sails through time in quiet stillness. I love Mi Nu Wai.

Then the recording is over and in a single move she is on her feet. The shawl slips from her back. She rises in one quick, slinky move, like a snake from its basket. Not a trace of stiffness. She looks around and grins, pretty sassily actually, and tosses back her hair. Oh, I adore Mi Nu. I adore her flat chest. I want to be like her, sit beside her, eat beside her, meditate opposite her. I want to be on stage and sing with her, bump hips with her. I want to have my periods when she has hers, share the same bathroom, the same bed, share our clothes. I want to smell her breath and tie up her hair for her. Who gives a damn about sick men and their pompous diaries? Who needs their tales of misery and woe? Mi Nu has no story at all. She is a flow of stillness. Not like zinged-up Zoë, popping pills and lining up lovers. All the same, getting to my feet, I cast a glance towards the men. I can't help it. They are stretching their stiff legs and shuffling and groaning. I'd need my glasses to make out much at this distance. A guy with a red bandana. Not him. One hefty oldie has built himself an arm-chair of cushions. But there are seventy guys over there. I want to spend my life with my eyes fixed on Mi Nu.

Dukkha

I love noise and I love silence. I ruined my hearing with head-phones and amps. I miss my piano, my guitar, my wah wah. Not really though. I don't really care what happens to the band without me. I gave up everything for the band then I gave up the band for nothing. I gave up Carl. I didn't go home, or apply to college or university. I haven't contacted Jonathan. Or looked for a job. May all beings be free from all attachment. May all beings be liberated. You like to think you miss things, Beth Marriot, but you don't really. Not even singing.

Can that be true?

This morning I was up at four. I was out before the others were awake. I lay in the wet grass in the field beyond the hall. Today I am going to look at that diary again. I haven't actually taken a deci-sion, but I know I will. Like when you used to think you'd stopped smoking but in another part of your mind you knew you hadn't, you knew sooner or later you'd light up again. Then it was a pleasure to think how much you'd enjoy the first ciggie. And shameful too.

Yet again you'd failed to make a decision. Couldn't decide to live with Carl, couldn't decide to leave Carl, couldn't decide to give everything to the band, couldn't decide to leave the band, couldn't decide to go to university—which university? to study what?—couldn't decide about a job at Marriot's, couldn't decide to look elsewhere, couldn't decide anything at all. Nothing. But that first ciggie will be great. The first puff. Of course, as soon as you know you haven't stopped, you actually put off lighting up so as to enjoy thinking about it. Hmmm. It's wonderful lying in the wet grass among the molehills, before dawn. There is nothing to decide here. The cold seeps into you. I can feel it spreading up my back. It starts at the base of the spine and climbs to the shoulders. Cold can be so good. The sky is grey, hushed. It's too early for birds. There's mist on the hills. Listen. The silence whines. Closing my eyes, I hear surf. It's far away. Surf crashing on the coast, sucking the shingle. In the waves it's cold, it's truly cold.

Stop.

Breathe.

A DROWNING ACCIDENT, JONNIE. I'M IN INTENSIVE CARE.

Stop.

PLEASE COME. PLEASE, JONNIE.

I CAN'T, BETH. I CAN'T COME NOW.

Dukkha, Jonathan. All life is *dukkha.* Suffering and dissatisfaction. That's a true thing Dasgupta says. Even happiness is *dukkha.* Yes. It's fantastically cold on my back in the wet grass. My head is going numb. Except there must be an animal in the bushes behind me. Scrabbling. A rabbit or a hedgehog. Spring is coming. I'm going to look at that diary again.

Mi Nu Wai doesn't join the early-morning session till six, when the chanting starts. I sat for an hour then went to the kitchen,

pulled out the pans, filled them with jugs from the boilers, measured out the oats. I love the kitchen at dawn. Five and a half litres
of oats to twelve of water. That's for the men: four and a half to
ten for the women. I love moving around, switching things on,
quietly, alone. In their bin the oats are soft and dry and sweet.
Oaty. Everything is very itself in the morning. Everything is just
there, not waiting for my fingers to light lights and shift plates.
Just there. Very still. The cooker, the matches, the ladles hanging
from their rail, gleaming.

While the water was coming to the boil, I laid out the breakfast stuff in the female dining hall, replenished the cereals and
the sunflower seeds, opened the tubs of jam, the peanut butter,
the honey, the hummus. That sticky smell always gets me, always
puts me in a breakfast state of mind. There was milk to fetch,
dairy and soya. Teabags. The first rule for a Dasgupta server is
never to imagine you are indispensable. 'If you feel stressed and
can't work in a spirit of love, stop at once.' That's the rule. 'Go
to the Metta Hall and meditate.' Better no server at all than
someone spraying negativity about, multiplying *sankharas*.

Except I *am* indispensable. I'm always here before the others,
whatever the rota. The fact is Mrs Harper leaves a lot of the
responsibility to me these days. I know the routines, the menus,
the recipes. The others come and go. She never said in so many
words she was delegating to me, I've never officially been kitchen
manager, they wouldn't trust me, but that's what she's done. This
session's manager couldn't fry an egg. And he's a snacker. Bean-
pole Paul. I hate snackers.

Meredith appears half asleep.

'Your apron?' I ask. 'Your hat?'

22

Rob's making chai for himself.

'Has anyone put the prunes on? Is the men's side laid out?'

I've always been indispensable. To the band, to Carl, to Dad, always. There would have been no gigs without Bossy Beth. We'd never have arrived on time, never have got paid. How would my parents have stayed together if I hadn't been around to listen to them moaning about each other?

'There's no point in making the toast yet,' I tell Ralph. 'Just get the oven ready and the bread on the trays. No one wants cold toast.'

Ralph is the only server working hard. To impress me.

'Your back is vet, Bess,' he says.

I'm frowning. I'm not going to answer.

'Why zo, Bess?'

Right speech is usually no speech. No speech, no eye contact. Noble Silence. Then the chanting pipes up—*Ananta pūnyamayī*. It's time to get the oats in the water. *Ananta gunyamayī*. Everything is in a state of constant change, the Buddha said. *Anicca, anicca*. Arising and passing away. Pains, pleasures, relationships. Arising and passing away. But every day at the Dasgupta Institute the chanting clicks in at six sharp in the Metta Hall and in the kitchen too. They've piped it through. *Ananta pūnyamayī*. In the hall the new students with their sitting pains know they only have another half-hour to hang on and the servers know they have to hurry up to get the food on the table.

'You must be freezing,' Ralph says.

'*Ananta gunyamayī*.' I like to hum along. I've learned whole sections now, even if I've no idea what it means. Like when Pocus did a number in Japanese. People told me I was pretty convincing in Japanese.

'Vat happened?' Ralph rabbits on. 'You are zoaking, Bess.'

Soaking was Jonathan's word. 'You're soaking, Betsy M. You dirty little girl. Sopping soaking poking wet.' I was never indispensable to Jonathan.

'Put the fruit out,' I tell Rob. 'Make sure the apples and pears are washed.

Ralph says, 'If you vant to go and change your shirt, Bess, I'm doing porridge.'

'This is the first time you've been a server, isn't it, Ralph?'

'Yes.'

He smiles. He's got me to say something.

'Remember what it says on the website, right at the beginning? The page about Dhamma Service?'

He really does have a cute face. Big full lips.

'It says, "Being a server is an opportunity to grow in Dhamma by helping others, not a chance to socialize."'

Bavatu sava mangelam.

It's funny but I've never figured where the loudspeakers are, in the kitchen. It's as if Dasgupta's voice oozed from the oven vent or the drains. He's reached the final blessing now. But he loves to drag it out. Three times. Each one longer.

Baavaatuu saavaa maaangelam.

May all beings be happy. I checked the porridge in both pans, grabbed the oven cloth.

Baaaaavaaaaattttuuuuu saaaavaaaa ma-angeh-laaaaaaaaaaaaam.

Dasgupta stretches it for ever in a last twist of torment to test the sitters' equanimity. I think he has a sense of humour. Now the meditators are only three slow *sadhus* from relief, three amens from breakfast.

Ralph said: 'Zat pan's too heavy for you, Bess. I do it.'

'Evidently not,' I said.

Saaadooo.

I heaved the pan for the women's side off the burner and banged it on to a trolley.

Saaadooo.

'And for Christ's sake it's Beth, Ralph, Beth, th th th, not Bess. Can't you pronounce a 'th'?'

'Bess.'

Saaadooo.

Finished. They're free. They're hungry.

I slammed the trolley through the swing doors into the corridor then the door to the female dining hall and hoisted the pan on to the table. I love its sudden hard heat against my chest. When you take off the lid the steam rushes up with a hot, homey smell. I was shivery, my clothes sticking to my back. I bent over the pan letting the heat come up in my face. But people were already at the door. Only day three and already a group of early birds has formed. They must have left meditation early. They're making sure they get a banana. I told Mrs Harper that by having only enough bananas for half the meditators we were creating a situation where some people would be producing bad karma for themselves by rushing to grab. The kiwis and oranges don't attract anything like the same attention and there are apples galore. 'Maybe we should drop the bananas altogether,' I told her. You'd see people giving up their place in the porridge queue to go and grab a banana, then joining the back of the queue again, content to wait, fruit in hand. Before I wrote the notice, ONLY ONE BANANA EACH, some new students took two.

'Why are you watching them?' Mrs Harper smiled. 'It's not for us to calculate their karma.'

25

If only I was having this conversation with Mi Nu, but she never comes to the dining hall. She eats alone in the female leader's bungalow. Mrs Harper is a wonderful person. She's very slow and full, almost swollen, very kind and vague, and she seems to move on wheels rather than walk, turning very slowly, in loose, ankle-length dresses. Perhaps there *are* rubber wheels hidden down there, driven by a silent motor. With only one speed. Snail's pace. It's fantastic how slow she is. But I like that. She never flaps. When I see Mrs Harper's big pale face and self-cut fringe I think of words like 'matronly' and 'Mothers' Union' and when I talk to her I always notice how her wedding ring has sunk into the puffiness of her finger. You could never imagine her twisting it off and throwing it in her husband's face. 'Fuck off, you two-faced, cheating bastard!' If I'd been brought up by the Harpers I'd be completely different. They are so calm together. I doubt they make love, though. I doubt they have children. When I showed Mr Harper the anal massager, there was such a look crossed his face.

'Do you think,' I asked Mrs Harper, 'that the servers should be eating the bananas, I mean with there not being enough for all the meditators?'

She smiled. She has a slight American accent. 'Elisabeth, dear, if you feel like eating a banana, please do. No one wants you to go without.'

Her eyes are always surprised, in a generous way. Her voice drawls and coos. On the other hand, she's always reminding us that the servers mustn't eat before the meditators have finished, we're here to serve them, so if we wanted bananas we would have to put them aside for ourselves *before* laying the fruit out. Which is not in the spirit of the Dasgupta, is it? The spirit of the

Dasgupta is that we cook for the meditators and eat their left-overs. We don't cook for ourselves. Those are the rules. We come second. 'If you want a banana,' I told Ralph, and I tipped him a wink, 'you'd better put one aside before the hordes arrive.' He was carrying out the toast tray for the men and his eyes fell. He'd already put a couple of bananas aside. I knew. Good job I loathe the things or there'd be a serious shortage.

I opened the dining-hall door and the meditators pushed through. There's a sink in the porch to wash your hands, but nobody does. It's six thirty and they've been up since four. They haven't eaten since lunch yesterday, at eleven. People are always pleased with themselves after the early-morning session. We feel virtuous meditating before breakfast and at this hour virtue seems worth having. It brings peace of mind. I remember my first peace of mind at the Dasgupta came during a morning session. It was the first moment I caught myself feeling good after months of misery. As soon as I noticed, of course, the feeling went. I was straight back to the torment and confusion. But I had experienced it for a moment, and that gave me hope. Later I realized you must never tell yourself you're at peace. This is a weird thing with the Dasgupta. You can learn to be calm here. You sort of *perform* calmness. You can make yourself serene and very slow so that you feel like you're actually mixed up with the things around you. Your body *is* the rabbit in the dew at dawn, or the sycamores behind the hall when the wind shakes their leaves. I can't explain. But the moment you *notice* it and congratulate yourself, the spell breaks and you're in trouble again.

Often, especially in the early days, it seemed to me that this business of losing the calm and balance I'd been working towards always happened at mealtimes. In the Metta Hall, surrounded by a hundred and fifty people wrapped in blankets, sitting still, breathing quietly, you could settle yourself in a wordless trance. Where there are no words, there are no decisions, no names, no plans, no pain. Even your body grows transparent, like it was made of air. Then you're happy. No. Happy is wrong. You're easy, unworried. You are floating in a cool river and the water carries you down.

Then the gong sounds and you have to eat. You have to get up from your cushion, put on your shoes, walk to the dining hall. You have to decide what to eat and how much. You start wondering whether it's better to be served first when the porridge is piping hot or later when the banana mob have grabbed their loot and gone. You start to watch the others, to think, to criticize, to calculate. You want to eat frugally, to be virtuous, but then your food is finished and you're still hungry, no, you're hungrier than before. You go back for a second bowl of porridge, pile up your plate with toast, slabs of butter, spoonfuls of jam, two apples, two oranges. Stuffing yourself, you remember the pig-outs after concerts, beer and biryani, joints and whisky. Then you see yourself four in a bed in some slum hotel or hostel. Doncaster. Dortmund. Or huddled together in sleeping bags in the van. Carl, Zoë, Frank. *A huge hand for Frank Halliday on DRUMS!* Suddenly you realize how peaceful you were ten minutes ago in the hall on your cushion and how completely that peacefulness has gone. It's gone. The porridge is poisoned. The apples are sour.

Don't eat, Beth. Stop eating.

I skipped meals. It's never been a problem for me not to eat. It's harder for me to eat moderately than to cut out food

28

altogether. One thing or the other, that's me. Gluttony or starvation. But you have to eat at the Dasgupta, the same way you have to meditate. Not eating is not allowed. The same Dhamma workers who count you in for the hour of Strong Determination are there to check that you go to lunch. Course managers is their official name, though they don't really manage anything. They have their registers and clipboards. You have to meditate with the Dasgupta method and you have to eat Dasgupta food at Dasgupta times. Vegetarian. Six thirty and eleven a.m.

'Elisabeth.' Mrs Harper took me aside. 'You're not eating.'

This was before I became a server. I'd been here a month maybe, sitting one retreat after another. They're free after all. Obviously they'd realized I was a case.

'I'm off food. I want to purify myself.'

Mrs Harper smiled. She was firm. 'Fasting is not allowed at the Dasgupta, Elisabeth. You must go and eat now.'

And she meant that to be the end of the conversation. Fasting is not allowed, that's what it says in the Dasgupta Institute rule book, so there is no need for discussion. Whenever you talk to the people who count at the Dasgupta, they close the conversation quickly. It's not that they don't want to help you. They have a whole schedule of times when you can go and talk to them. One day when I've thought of the right question I'll go and talk to Mi Nu. But they always close the conversation quickly. There's a rule, so obey it. Things are clear at the Dasgupta. Discussion would inflame the mind. They identify your problem and provide the solution: meditate. If you're in pain, make an objective note, say to yourself, Pain, pain, not *my* pain. If distracting thoughts keep churning in your head, say, Thoughts, thoughts, not *my* thoughts. And that's that.

29

They see you are breaking a rule and very politely they remind you not to.

'Fasting is forbidden, Elisabeth. Now let's be silent again.'

'Why is it forbidden?'

I do want to be like them. I want to have what they have, to sit stiller than still, like Mi Nu. Only someone perfectly peaceful inside could sit so still for so long. But I need to provoke them too. I want to make them squirm.

'Tell me why it's forbidden.'

Mrs Harper was smiling her surprised smile. She's like a headmistress with a favourite who's got into mischief.

'We're not masochists, Elisabeth. We don't believe in punishing ourselves. That's not the way to purity.'

'I eat like a pig,' I told her. 'I hate myself.'

She cocked her head on one side.

'Look, I've done some bad stuff,' I went on. 'But *really* bad. I don't want to be reincarnated as a pig!'

I meant it, but then I couldn't help laughing. I spluttered. Mrs Harper said nothing.

'You've no idea,' I wailed. 'I'm sure I'll be better if I don't eat for a week or so. Just let me starve for a week. I've got to do something about myself. I want to be pure.'

Mrs Harper said, 'Not eating after noon every day is purification enough, Elisabeth. The important thing is to learn to eat with moderation. Starving yourself will only lead to pride and self-importance.'

'But that's the point,' I yelled. 'I can't do anything with moderation. I just can't.'

I burst into tears. She said nothing, but I knew she was watching me. I stopped and snuffled. She offered a tissue.

'You see,' I told her, 'I'm such a drama queen.'

'You'll learn,' Mrs Harper said. 'That's what the Dasgupta's for. Actually, you are already learning, Elisabeth, you're already changing. Now you want to speed up that change. You want to purify yourself all at once. That's understandable, but it is a mistake. Change comes at its own pace. Meditate and observe, Elisabeth. Develop your equanimity. Observe yourself as you are and as you change with an equanimous mind. There is no hurry.'

If Mi Nu had told me this I'm sure I would have found it very beautiful. I was furious.

'I killed someone,' I told her. 'That's why I came here. Someone died because of me. Maybe more than one. That's why I've got to purify myself. OK?'

Mrs Harper sighed. Her shapeless chest rose and fell in her grey dress. She thought for a moment then said: 'I am not your confessor, Elisabeth. There is no God seeking to punish you. There is no priest to absolve you. For the moment it's enough for you to know that fasting is forbidden at the Dasgupta Institute.'

Lunch was almost over. She pointed the way and led me to the dining hall. I filled my plate with curried pasta, helped myself to a mountain of apple pie and ate like a hog.

Your Pain Is a Door

My diarist wishes he hadn't come. He's angry. He hates the evening videos, the Dasgupta discourses. He can't sit still. His legs and back are killing him.

Ninety minutes. And the man's so damn smug. As if we were in a Bombay Rotary in the sixties.

That made me laugh. Dad was a Rotary fanatic. The diarist is looking for an excuse to leave.

You chose the worst time to come here. You were running away. Too bad you can't run away from your thoughts.

These few words filled a whole page. He really scribbles sometimes, like he's writing in a big hurry. Actually, you can't run away from the Dasgupta either. Not easily. They won't let you have your mobiles and credit cards back without an almighty grilling. 'Leaving now you are putting yourself in danger.' I've heard Harper say that. 'You came here to change the way you think and live. You made a solemn vow that you would stay the whole ten days. Strong in that knowledge, we began a delicate operation on your thought processes, an operation that penetrates to the core of your mind. Going now is like walking out in the middle of brain surgery.'

Harper sounds pretty convincing when he says this stuff. And it's true your mind changes here, deep inside. The diarist keeps talking about his GREAT DILEMMA. He can't concentrate on his breathing. He can't *want* to concentrate. *Your life has come to nothing. One bad decision after another.* He hates himself. *UNFINISHED BUSINESS.* The capitals are huge.

I flicked back and forth through the pages but couldn't find what the dilemma was. There's stuff about a company going under, someone called Susie throwing away her talent. *Flushing it down the toilet.* Two people he talks about with initials T and L. I reckon L must be his wife. Laura? Linda? Lucy?

Actually, I love the scenes when someone tries to bail out of the Dasgupta. Harper & Co. do everything they can to stop the other meditators noticing, but sometimes there's real drama. 'You're all fucking loonies!' one guy yelled, right in the middle of Strong Determination. He stood up and kicked away his cushion. Fantastic. Sometimes I think if all the first-timers could share how bad they felt trying to sit cross-legged all day, I mean if there wasn't the Noble Silence and they could all just shout it out, 'My ankles are killing me, my knees are killing me, my thighs are torturing me, my back is on fire, my thoughts are pile drivers,' maybe we'd get a stampede and a hundred and forty people would break down the door and grab their stuff and get the hell out.

Why does it cheer me up imagining that? Sometimes I grin and chuckle and hum an old favourite, 'The Kids Aren't Alright'. '2 Minutes to Midnight'. Why, though? I'm not a prisoner here. I can walk out any time I want. Servers don't take a vow to stay.

We're here of our own free will. Some only stay the weekend, to help out and meditate a bit, or they come whenever they have some time off, then go when they want. There's no pressure. We have free access to the locker room, to any stuff we've stowed. The truth is I never dream of leaving. Maybe this is the question I could ask Mi Nu: Why do I love imagining trouble if I know I'm better off when everything is quiet?

I stayed in his room about fifteen minutes. I was too flustered to read carefully. They'd definitely ask me to leave if they caught me here. It's more than against the rules. Last month they asked a guy to leave when he told Harper he was attracted to one of the girl servers and wanted to invite her out after the retreat was over. He hoped she would become his wife. They sent him packing the same day. 'There is no place for sentimental longings at the Dasgupta,' Harper told him. I thought 'longings' sounded weird. The girl was Italian. Aurora. What a great name. When she found out, she said, 'Why he must tell Mr Harper if he is wanting to marry *me*? What an *idiota*!' We giggled for days.

I should have grabbed one of the exercise books and got out. Or not gone at all. It's dumb running risks like this. What for? But if I take the one he's writing in now, he'll know. And that's the one I want to read. I want to see what he thinks of the Dasgupta. What he thinks about the servers, about the food. Maybe he's mentioned me.

People must be profoundly sick to want to sit through all this pain, listening to all this claptrap. He wrote that last night, after the second video, the one about the noble eightfold path, *sila, samādhi, paññā.* On the next page there was just one sentence written quite small. *It's you that's profoundly sick, mate. You you you.*

34

But aside from the diary I just wanted to sit in his room for a few minutes. There was an aura. Maybe it's a smell. He'd left the bed unmade. A sheet and three blankets. He must have asked for an extra. Probably feels the cold. Like Jonathan. Like dad. Older men. Jonathan loved it when I took risks, flashing my tits in the pub or peeing between parked cars. The time we made love in the cinema! *Match Point*. What a yawn of a film. 'You're breathtaking, Beth!' He kept shaking his head. It was the risks excited him. I took more and more. The evening together with Carl! He loved how self-destructive I could be.

This guy leaves his clothes all over the floor too. Dark blue underwear. Pretty large. Tracksuit pants. I sat on the bed and breathed deep. Not *anapana,* but a big deep sigh. All this men's stuff. Dirty socks on the radiator, a heavy coat over the wardrobe door. Nail parings on the bedside table. Breathing deep, I began to feel an electric current of happiness and unhappiness. Bethness. Something about his coat tells me he's a smoker. I stood up to smell. Yes. I went back to the bed, clicked his biro, turned a page and wrote, 'Your pain is a door. Go through it.'

Blessing

I love washing rice and kichada beans. The rice is milky white, the beans bright yellow. 'Mix together rice and beans in equal amounts in eight oven trays and rinse clean.' I use lukewarm water. The steel trays fit neatly over the sink under the tap. Three rinses, the recipe says. I never do less than four. If you use cold water your fingers freeze and you can't enjoy it. In the warm water the grains feel delicate and friendly, you can imagine you're moving your fingers in someone's hair. Stupid. The thing is not to imagine anything, just to be happy with white rice and yellow kichada beans. As soon as you run the water in the tray everything goes milky. The rice disappears and the tiny beans lose their yellowness. The water turns soft and slippery on your fingers as you run them back and forth through a sludge of grains. Tip the pan gently to drain and the white and yellow come back, but changed, softened.

At the second rinse, the cloudiness is thinner, like muslin curtains, or mist when you're in a plane and the ground shows pale beneath. When we went to Berlin. No. Like itself, like nothing but itself. Water rinsing rice. The third time you have to work hard to bring out a few wisps of milkiness. Probably the recipe's right and a fourth rinse is unnecessary, but I like to watch the clear water run over the clean wet grains.

Since it's an odd day today, a day of blessing, when I got to the fifth or sixth tray I remembered to bless the rice and the beans. I was trying to be a hundred per cent present with the soft feel of the grains between my fingertips and the water going from transparent to milky to transparent again. Matter changing in my hands. *Anicca.*

There is something specially lovely about seeing things through clean water, even if they're not lovely in themselves. Carrots, celery, even turnips. Like when you've meditated for two hours straight, all the thoughts and mental mess have settled, your head is clear, and when you put on your shoes again and step out of the Metta Hall every blade of grass, the leaves on the trees, even people's clothes on the washing line have a transparent underwater weirdness.

Then you wish your mind would stay like that for ever, which is a mistake, because it won't, it can't, so you're setting yourself up for disappointment. *Dukkha.* Maybe wishing things would stay as you're seeing them is actually the first step away from the experience, the way saying 'I'm happy' is definitely the first step back to being unhappy. You've got to look at the rice and beans as things you enjoy but don't need in any way. You love washing rice and kichada beans, but if you don't wash any more rice or any more lemon-yellow kichada beans for another ten years, another lifetime, it won't make a jot of difference. That's how you should have treated Jonathan. That's how you should have treated everything.

I couldn't. I was enjoying the rice and beans, sort of, but I couldn't bless them. I started to mutter, 'From the bottom of my heart, I bless you, rice and beans, rice for your milkiness and beans for your bright yellowness.' Stupid. The whole point of blessing days is to bless things *without words*. You see something positive and your heart goes out to it, but free from any desire. When you need words, you're performing, you're forcing yourself. You don't love the beans at all, Beth. You're just trying to get your head back to where it was before you found that diary. I finished rinsing the rice and beans and went to put the oven on to preheat.

Vikram, the mind behind the kitchen, drops in once or twice each retreat and gets upset because people are improvising: they're not following the recipe book to the letter. Usually it's the foreign women; they want to show off how much better their French or Spanish or Indian cooking is. They come to a place where we're supposed to be unravelling our egos and start showing off how much they know about herbs and sauces like we were on TV. Ines is standing over the bratt pan. Her face is bright with goodness, currying broccoli with red peppers, tasting it and adding this, tasting it and adding that. Not me. Beth Marriot sticks strictly to recipe. I do music, not food. Though I do know a thing or two about the whims of the bratt pan, which is more than Ines does. I'll step in and explain, if she asks before it's too late. The first time we went out together Jonathan asked, 'Can you cook, Beth?' 'My mum's so good at it,' I told him, 'no one would dream of competing.' 'I love a girl who can't cook.' He laughed. 'Gives me a chance to show off the restaurants I know.'

With Jonathan you always wondered whether he had said the same thing to ten other women before you. Or fifty. Later I realized what he meant was, I love a girl who doesn't act like a wife, who isn't trying to possess me. Carl cooked. We had no money to eat out. 'You'll have to learn when we have a family, Beth,' he said. 'We'll have maids by then,' I told him. 'We'll be rich and live in hotels.' Carl hated it when I said that. He had no idea what he'd do with the loot if Pocus made it big. 'You spend so fast, Beth,' he said.

Is Vikram gay? I don't think so. Dasgupta men are beyond sex. They've taken vows. He's squat but trying to be tall. With a neat little beard. He makes you feel fantastically stupid if you ask a question. 'Anyone who experiments with the recipes is guilty of an act of vandalism,' Vikram says. His visits coincide with the arrival of the delivery van. We tramp out into the rain and pick up boxes of celeriac and carrots and lettuces. The van driver winks at me as he slaps down a sack of oats. He must be pushing sixty.

'The deliveries are carefully calibrated to fit the recipe schedule,' Vikram says. His accent is Indian, but upper class. 'If you swap ingredients, one day you'll find you haven't got something you need.' He stands in the cold room stacking the stuff on the shelves while we tramp back and forth. He knows where everything goes. Ralph was risking a hernia, carrying three boxes of spuds at once. 'You've left your apron on,' Vikram told him. Ralph looked blank. 'The apron is not to keep your clothes clean. It's to protect everybody's food from coming into contact with where those clothes have been. When you're going to get dirty you take the apron off.' Ralph cocked his head. His long hair dropped and showed an earring. He really is a cute boy.

What makes me think Vikram might be gay, or have been gay, is this prissiness he has, speaking so correctly, always very Indian and very posh. The Dasgupta must be great for gays who don't want to come out. You can forget the whole issue. Why bother telling the truth about your inclinations in a place where all physical contact is forbidden, even handshakes? I will never hug Mi Nu. Or touch her. Vikram wants each retreat's servers to make the kitchen tick like clockwork, to turn out the Dasgupta recipes time and again, always the same, the way the Dasgupta chanting turns on at six in the morning and the Dasgupta video at seven in the evening. He pins up printed sheets with cleaning rotas, days across the top and tasks down the side: 'Servers' Toilet—Male/Female—Kitchen Drainage Grids, Hats and Aprons (laundry)'. We're supposed to initial a box the day each job is done. Everything must happen so regularly it doesn't really happen at all. Does that make sense? I mean it would only be a happening if it didn't happen.

'Where's Paul?' he asks. 'Tea-towels should be laundered, not dried on the radiators. They're breeding bacteria.'

I like Vikram. Whatever problems he's had in the past, he's on top of them now. That's how I want to be. He goes round the kitchen checking things. The veg grinders haven't been cleaned properly. That's Rob. There's always someone who loves using the grinders but hates cleaning them. Why do I chuckle when Vikram shakes his dark head and wags his brown finger? I wonder why he doesn't tell me my hair has got loose from my hat. He scolds everyone but me. Perhaps I'm incorrigible. When I flash him a toothy smile he turns away. Never mind. I've forgotten my diarist for a few minutes, forgotten the envelope in my pocket.

The kitchen gets pretty wild after ten. People hardly know each other's names yet, never mind the equipment. There are still new servers arriving and old servers leaving. We're starting to panic. We must have lunch on the table at eleven. After three hours on their bums the meditators must find their food. They're suffering serious deprivation. Day one, adzuki bean stew. Day two, baked potatoes with grated cheese. Day Three, rice, kichada beans and curried tofu. People eat mountains. Plus the salads. Plus the special-needs menus: cheese and salad sandwich for Maureen Moss, glucose drink for Rita Howell. And the notices to write for vegan and non-vegan. And the covered portions to take to the teachers' bungalows. Meredith has sliced into a fingertip. I love the sharp knives here. I love choosing the right knife for whatever vegetable I'm chopping. There's blood on the broccoli. Kristin forgot to zero the scales and her soya mayonnaise is wrong. Everything's so frenetic, so completely un-Zen. Kristin is calm, though. She has that Baltic dourness. Big pale lips, wry smile. She knows soya mayonnaise is not important. Ines is in tears because the bratt pan keeps turning itself off. Her curry won't cook. Paul's fretting. Paul should never have been made kitchen manager. I pull out my steamed rice and kichada beans from the Rational Oven. There's a lovely fluffiness to the white and yellow. Like a cuddly toy. A million miles from the hard grains I washed.

'Ladle it into saucepans,' Tony proposes, 'and cook it on the stove.'

Tony only arrived yesterday. He's the oldest server this retreat. A professor, he says. Every job he's assigned he needs to be shown how to do it: how to scrub a turnip, how to peel a squash, how to mash potatoes. Some professor.

'It's too late!' Ines is wailing. 'It'll take for ever.' She's forgotten the rule about going to the hall to meditate if you can't stay calm. They've just started ladling the curry into saucepans when I go over and show them the trick with the thermostat.

41

'It sticks. See? You have to jiggle.'

The bratt pan sizzles. Ines holds tight to the big wooden stirring paddle while I twiddle the knob. She's afraid I'm trying to take over, I'll steal her glory. I'm still leaning over the pan—the curry does smell good—when I realize Tony is gawping down my cleavage. God! Ralph I'd have expected, but not the professor, balding with bushy eyebrows, bad breath, needing to be shown how to undo a bra, no doubt. What is it with me and older men?

But wrong. When I stand up, it's *Meredith*. She's planted right there beside me, holding out her bandaged finger, smiling, *looking.*

'Beth!' she shouts 'You cracked it!'

The red Ferrari syndrome, Jonathan called it. 'Or, rather, the *two* red Ferraris.' Even people who weren't remotely interested, he laughed, just couldn't help looking. 'Your tits are so *there*, Beth. Two spanking Ferraris double-parked on a zebra.'

Jonathan. Jonathan Jothanan Thanajon. I thought I'd got you out of my head weeks ago and now you're creeping right into the pre-lunch commotion. It's the diarist's fault. Damn you both. The curry has started to bubble. Ines is happy. Her tits went the way of all flesh years ago. Two old bangers. Bless them. Bless everyone. Accept everything.

'Too bad we dirtied the saucepans,' Tony says. He's realized I deliberately left it late before telling them about the pan. He's not stupid. A professor of psychology maybe? Meredith says since she can't chop or wash up she'll help me lay out the dining hall.

At the Dasgupta we move constantly back and forth between the same four or five spaces. The double doors of the kitchen open on to a short corridor. Ahead and left are the swinging double doors of the male dining hall. Ahead and right the female. We crash back and forth with our trolleys, pushing stacks of plates, cutlery, the salad, the rice and beans and, today, in the nick of time the curry. Done it. It's all in place. No, we've forgotten the dressing. 'Who was on salad dressing?' The recipe book says tahini. I rush to find the ingredients. Ralph starts to measure and mix. Paul comes over and says, 'Perhaps it would be better if you worked with Kristin, Elisabeth.' Meaning what exactly? Then I remember the gong. 'God, I'm on gong, Paul. Have to rush. *You* do the dressing.'

The gong hangs from a branch of the hawthorn tree a few yards from the Metta Hall. There's a fresh stillness here after the steamy excitement of the kitchen. The low hills are damp and silent. Nothing stirs in the hall. It's hard to believe there are a hundred and forty people in there. The gong is big and has a weird triangular hat shape with upturned corners. The hammer sits in a cleft between trunk and branch. It's heavy, all of old wood, probably oak or something, with a felt cover to protect the surface of the gong, which you have to hit at the corners, not in the middle.

Boing!

I'm playing an instrument again. I'm calling the meditators back from their trance.

Boy-oy-oyng!

What a great sound. So loud and long. The meditators will be feeling it on their skin. Your whole body rings when the gong's struck. The sound soaks through you. It's the opposite of a siren. Loud, but calming. No, it's the opposite of some small scratchy noise that irritates. The gnawing at night in our bedroom. Behind Kristin's bed. Or the drip from the hall roof when it rains.

Boy-oy-oy-oy-oyng!

I've released my diarist from his pains. Stand up and walk, old man. Come and get your Brazilian curry, courtesy of Ines. Then I'm sad that I didn't write those words in his diary. *Your pain is a door, go through it.* I mean, I *did* write them, but I tore the page out. I'm courageous, but not totally reckless. I hate that. Why can't I be *totally* reckless and the hell with it, or not self-destructive at all, sensible and serene? A good wifey for Carl. Why am I never one thing or the other?

I tore it carefully, picking out the little ears of paper that stick in the seams, then put the diary back where I'd found it, on the floor by his bed. To compensate for chickening out like that I rummaged in his suitcase, found an envelope and took it. It was in a side pocket in the lining, an open envelope with sheets of paper. I wonder why he is using a woman's suitcase, red with a pink lining. Why are the notebooks all red? 'Dearest Susie', it started. I felt pretty excited just having it in my pocket.

In the kitchen we're noisy individuals. We yell over the sound of the liquidizer. We argue. But the meditators are a silent herd. They stream out of the hall like cows driven from stall to pasture. I love the commotion of cooking and preparing food, the way I used to love the last minutes setting up stage before Zoë hit her bass and the drums began to beat. I grabbed the mike. The lights came up and the pink smoke. But now I wish I was one of the herd. I really do. Watching the meditators pour out of the hall, I feel such a yearning, to be dumb, to be silent. Around day three people begin to walk more slowly. They've accepted that they're really here, really in the Dasgupta, for the full ten days. There is nothing to hurry for. There is no more struggle. 'The achievement of meditation is to get out of a mentality of achievement.' Video day three. They find pleasure in moving slowly, opening and closing knees and ankles, shifting their weight from left to right and right to left. I wonder whether my diarist has begun to accept his pains, whether he has found the door he must go through if his time at the Dasgupta is not to be wasted. I wish I was opening that door now. I wish I was passing through pain to the other side, the *vipassana* side. Like Mi Nu Wai. Mi Nu is beyond pain. Even when she tosses her hair and flounces out of the hall, she's still on the other side. I'm sure she is. I'm sure it is possible to be there always.

Two servers must watch the meditators eat. Since they can't speak, can't ask for things, we have to check that they have everything they need. They stumble out of the hall, come down the path, past the bathrooms, past the dormitories, into the dining hall. They really do look like a herd, ambling to their trough. We watch them queue at the serving table, ladle curry into bowls, sit down to eat. When the kitchen roll runs out and they have nothing to wipe their hands on, Kristin hurries to get some more. Kristin's about a foot taller than me. Coming back, she brings a fresh stack of plates and bangs them down on the table. That's the second time. I'll have to talk to her about it. We must respect the meditators' quiet. All our noise in the kitchen is to make their silence here possible.

The women fill their plates, take their seats and stare into space. The favourite places are the stools at the counter under the windows and along the wall. You don't need to face people across the table. You can eat slowly, gazing out of the windows at the sheds and fields, or just staring at the white walls. A white wall is the perfect mirror for a calm mind.

I wish I could watch the men eating. That would be interesting. I'd like to know if they react the same way the women do. Maybe they don't like the places by the wall. Imagine Jonathan coming here to meditate one day, Jonathan hearing Harper ask for total surrender, Jonathan bowing his head and accepting, Jonathan joining the Dasgupta herd.

Or Carl.

The salad needs replenishing. Meredith comes with the news that the men's side is out of curry and can we spare some of ours. Even with total segregation the men are preying on us. Sorting her dirty plates on to the separate piles, a petite little girl lets out a loud belch. Brilliant. I wonder if she would have done that if there were men around. It's a big relief not to have to look okay for a man, not to have to think about clothes or makeup. On the other hand I always loved making up. I love seeing other women made up. What a riot with Zoë before a gig. With her black cowboy hat and huge eyes. 'Let me do your lipstick,' she asked. 'Please, Beth, let me.'

Not Strong Enough

Privacy is not a priority at the Dasgupta. If you don't have a self, why would you need to be alone? For eight months I've shared a bedroom with other servers, sometimes as many as four, women and girls, snorers, sneezers. I have meditated third from the end of a row of eight, six rows behind, two in front. I have cooked beside others, for others, cleaned up after others, eaten others' leftovers, cold. I have no problem with this. I had settled down to watch myself change. Perhaps I could become a kind of mystic, despite that itch to sing and dance. I've seen visions at the Dasgupta. I have passed through walls, felt eyes open behind my eyes, seen other eyes, deeper still, staring upward through the dark. I have been happy here. Then I walked into a man's room, opened a diary, picked up a pen.

Now I'm wired and zinging like I'd snorted a line. And anxious. After lunch duty I'd meant to go to the loo and read the letter. I even started whistling. Perhaps I was close to some big discovery. But what? And who *cares?* Who cares about this guy and his big dilemma? I'm ridiculous. I opened the loo door, stopped, closed it, walked away. At first I thought I was holding back till after we'd eaten. I'd been excited all morning thinking about this letter in my pocket, so I might as well stretch the feeling out and read it later when I had time to gloat. Then I realized I was thinking maybe I shouldn't read it at all. It would be too much. I'd remembered something: *Our minds are not strong enough to have the right relation to certain things.*

It was Harper said that, quite a while ago now, but the words come back. He'd been talking to the servers. 'I'm aware that you can't have proper male-female segregation in the kitchen,' he said, 'since obviously you have to cook together.' Harper always does this talk for the servers the first evening of every retreat. He sits on his cushion, on his platform stool, in his grey jumper, and grey slacks. We kneel in front of him, women to one side, men to the other, in the quiet of the hall, after the meditators have gone to bed, and he says: 'All the same, servers should try to adopt *an attitude of segregation.* For example, when you need two people, to cut veg, or to clean up at the end of the day, make sure it's always two men or two women. Don't mix. Never eat together. Don't chat.'

He paused and blinked. Harper has a bland uncle sort of face, friendly but distant. His eyes are set deep, so that you can never figure whether they're closed or open. 'Otherwise,' he sighed, 'well, you know what can happen.'

Sometimes someone sniggers when he says this and once a girl asked, 'I'm sorry, Teacher, but what is it that *might happen,* exactly?'

Harper sat still. He must have known this girl was pulling his leg. At last he said, 'The truth is, our minds are not strong enough to have the right relationship with certain things.'

I closed the loo door and went back to help with the dishes. We all share the washing-up. I grabbed the overhead hose in the first sink, spraying the crap off the dishes. Kristin stacked the trays over the second sink, slid them into the dishwasher and slammed down the hood to set it going. Two minutes later Meredith hoisted the hood, pulled out the trays through a cloud of steam and began to check and sort.

Ralph trundled back and forth from the dining halls with a trolley. Mr Professor was scraping the dirtiest plates into the bin. It's the only thing he doesn't need to be shown how to do. Stack after stack of dirty plates and bowls. The pans, the utensils, the cutlery. There's quite a din. All the knives, forks and spoons have to be separated and sprayed. The machine can't cope with too many solid bits.

'You should vare rubber gloves,' Ralph says.

When the sink blocks he reaches in to fish out the filth for me. I spray the sleeve of his sweater and he yells. I'm laughing all my teeth at him. *Our minds are not strong enough to have the right relation with certain things.* It's true what Harper said. But I've no problem at all with Ralph, I could tease this kid for ever and never feel anything. 'I love your teeth, Beth,' Jonathan said. 'I love how mad they are, how big.' Carl wanted me to wear a brace. I'd be in trouble when I was older. 'Why didn't your parents do something?' 'Because they only talked to me to moan about each other.'

Meredith asked Ralph what sign he was. I sprayed rice and beans off a bowl, the same rice I'd moved my fingers through a couple of hours ago, but changed again now, sticky and soiled. *Anicca. If the river keeps flowing, one day the rock will budge.* The nuttiest things come into my head when I'm working, like I'd swallowed the *Dhammapada*. 'As the bee collects nectar and departs without injuring the flower, so let a sage dwell in his village.'

But the spray-gun is fantastic. Squeeze the trigger and a jet of steaming water blasts away the filth. I love that. The big dishwasher is great too: fierce, hot and *fast*. Two minutes forty seconds and the plates come out scorching white and pure. I hate putting my hands in the yuck when the sink blocks. 'Please don't be spraying me again, Bess.' Ralph reaches in his arm. He has strong wrists with fine blond hair. His sign is Aquarius, he says. Carl's sign. 'I've never had an Aquarian boyfriend,' Meredith informs us. So much for an attitude of segregation.

Tony is scraping saucepans now. Perhaps he's a professor of waste disposal. Kristin has said nothing. She is stacking the dishes fast so we can finish and get our lunch. No one wants to eat before the dishes are done. IF YOU KNEW HOW HANDSOME THIS GUY TRYING TO CHAT ME UP IS! That's the kind of text I would have sent to Jonathan and Carl a year ago. Sometimes I sent the same text to both. BLOKE TRIED TO KISS ME AS I WAS COMING OUT OF THE TUBE. NOW HE'S FOLLOWING ME UP SHAFTESBURY AVE! Carl would drop whatever he was doing and come running. THERE'S A ROADIE BOTHERING ME. I'M AFRAID TO GO TO THE LOO IN CASE HE FOLLOWS. Actually, that was true. I was in the 12 Bar. Carl turned up spoiling for a fight. Carl was such a cavalier. TAKE CARE, BETH, Jonathan wrote. He was in a restaurant with his wife. Sorry, ex-wife.

When we take our food to the female servers' room to eat there's always someone wants to be silent, or observe the strictest rules of Right Speech, and someone who wants to talk, needs to talk, has to talk. Kristin is Latvian. She must have cut her own hair. It has that lank look. And her grey eyes are a bit out of true.

When she was assigned to our room the first thing she did was drag the mattress off her bed and lie down on the bare wooden slats. 'I know the Buddha said not to sleep on luxurious beds,' Meredith giggled, 'but isn't that overdoing it?' She does use a pillow, though. She plumps up the pillow, pulls a blanket over her and lies down straight on the slats. I like her. I like her big hands and clumsy, stooped walk. I like her energy. She does everything with too much energy. At lunch she sits on a chair in the corner with her couscous on her knee and eats fast in silence. She has big bones. Kiss-kiss, Zoë called it. We had to heat some from the freezer because the curry was all gone. Paul got the quantities wrong. Third day running.

At table, a new arrival was filling out the Dhamma Service Form, a hefty type in her forties. 'What do I write,' she asked, 'if I haven't exactly kept the five precepts since the last retreat?' She had an Aussie accent and a double chin.

Kristin went on eating.

'Everyone gets thrown by that question,' Meredith said. 'Tell the truth.' Ines beamed. 'You can never be wrong when you tell the truth.'

'The exact question,' the Aussie said, 'is: "Have you scrupulously kept the five precepts since your last Dasgupta Retreat?" I suppose they'll still accept me if I haven't.'

'Listen,' I interrupted 'they're not asking for details, are they? You don't need to tell 'em you got razzled *every* night.'

The Aussie didn't smile, but Kristin burst out laughing. She roared. Out of nothing.

Mrs Harper came in with Livia, the female course manager, and a French girl called Stephanie. Livia was saying she kept meeting people she must have known in other lives. She'd be

51

checking off the list of meditators in the hall when suddenly she'd see a face she just knew she knew. *More* than knew, somebody she must have been close to once. Mrs Harper said this happened a lot at meditation centres because these places drew together people who had been on the Dhamma path for a number of lifetimes, people who were close to becoming *arahants*. Meredith began to say how her mum knew her dad's name *and* star sign and even ascendant the very moment she set eyes on him. 'She always says it's a marriage that's lasted a thousand lives.'

I laughed. 'My mum and dad always said the only difference between their marriage and the Thirty Years' War was that the war was over.'

Mrs Harper turned from the table to smile, and I could see her smile meant, That is exactly the kind of thing Beth would say, bless her.

'So when do I get started?' the Australian asked.

'First you must meditate for an hour, then someone will take you to hear the Dhamma Service Discourse.'

Nobody volunteered. We were scraping our plates.

'Beth,' Mrs Harper asked, 'when was the last time you heard the Service Discourse?'

The Letter

Dearest Susie,
I wonder if there is any point in my writing to you.

In my room I unfolded the letter. I knew I would. Aside from Vikram's recipes and the *Dhammapada*, I hadn't read anything since the last text messages with Jonathan and Carl. I'd been happy for my head to be empty. Now it is going to be filled again.

Dearest Susie,
I wonder if there is any point in my writing to you. It's axiomatic, I suppose, that a twenty-two-year-old in love is blind to reason.

Axiomatic?

Nothing I can say is going to change your mind. Anything negative I try to tell you about Sean will only increase your determination to be with him and your distrust of me.
So what can I say?

I want you to know that if your mother and I are anxious for you, it is because we love you. We really do. It's not true that we are obsessed by money and security. We just fear that one day you will regret throwing away such a huge opportunity. Then you'll find yourself hating Sean for having taken you away from your vocation. You've worked all your life for this. In fact, I can't understand why he isn't telling you to accept and wait until life together doesn't have to come at the expense of your career.

It's not true that we were against Sean from the start. Not many parents would jump for joy to see their daughter in love with a man with such a serious problem. But we did recognize that you were in love, and I must say it's been very beautiful to see you that way, rather as if all the spotlights had been turned up full on your shining face. You're a marvellous girl, Susie, a fantastic daughter. We made Sean welcome. He's eaten with us, slept over many times. But from the moment you announced that you were giving up everything to be near a man who has only himself to blame for what's happened, we could no longer see this relationship favourably.

It is damaging you and it could destroy you.

You say that age doesn't matter and that there's a hell of a gap between myself and your mother too. All I can say is, that gap <u>has</u> mattered. There have been times when both of us have wished

The letter stopped. Damn. Just when it was getting interesting. Or, rather, it changed, it stopped being a letter. The neat, I'm-a-reasonable-guy handwriting broke off. Two lines had been crossed out, pretty violently, then it was all scrawl.

Tell the little idiot you won't have the cash to bail her out this time.

Tell her it's making her mother ill.

Tell her Sean doesn't give a shit for anyone but himself. Otherwise he would never have been driving drunk.

Tell her if she drops him I'll

No. The opposite. Tell her I'd give my right arm to be in love the way she is. My right arm. I envy her. I'd give anything to be as <u>mad</u> as she is now. She's mad. She's lucky. To be able to give up everything.

The truth is you hate yourself even more than you hate L.

Tell her bankruptcy will be comic relief compared with the rest.

Exhausted exhausted exhausted exhausted exhausted exhausted

EXHAUSTED.

If you'd asked me a year ago, Can things get worse? I'd have said no.

L keeps me to punish me.

Or for supposed financial security?

OH PLEASE DO GO OVER THE WHOLE FUCKING NIGHTMARE FOR THE TEN MILLIONTH TIME.

The age gap with the older man is not the same as the age gap with the older woman.

You and T.

Married now. You <u>wanted</u> T married. Can you believe that? You <u>made her</u> marry. Idiot.

What have you become? A worm? A snake? How did it happen?

You came here to avoid killing yourself.

Melodrama. Yawn.

Or killing <u>her</u>.

Alas impossible. Despite all the murder stories.

Kristin had come in. When I looked up she turned away.

'I'm reading a letter.' I waved it.

No one reads letters at the Dasgupta. Not during retreats. In the remote event of a letter arriving, it's held back till the ten days are up.

Kristin lay on the slats of her bed, put her head on the pillow and closed her eyes. I stopped reading and turned on an elbow. She's taller than me and broader, makes you think of words like 'sturdy', 'staunch', 'stalwart'. Why do I like her? We haven't even spoken.

'Stttart-tagain!' I said, imitating Dasgupta's guided meditations. 'With a caaalm and quiet mind.'

She stayed blank.

Stolid.

'Does your boyfriend know you're here, Kristin?'

She didn't reply.

Steadfast.

'What was so funny when I said that about getting razzled?'

Her skin is pale and solemn.

'What's your position on age gaps in relationships? I mean, could you ever see yourself with someone as old as Harper? Do you get a lot of that in Latvia? An older man can be fun. They have more cash.'

Nothing.

'This letter's from my dad. He reckons I'm screwing up completely staying here. Throwing my life away. He wants me to come home. Says he loves me.' I laughed. 'Can you imagine?'

Nothing. Noble Silence.

'Speaking of which, I'd love a foot massage. Want to try? Me on you, you on me?'

She knew I was provoking her. Touching is forbidden at the Dasgupta. I wondered if she'd report me. No. Meredith might, but Kristin is different. She lay very still, on her back, her hands along her sides, palms upward.

'Be *vvery* vvvigilant.' I mimicked Dasgupta again, sighing deeply. '*Vvery* aware. *Vvery* aware.'

The corner of her mouth curled slightly

'Alllert and att-ttentive. With a balllanced, eqquanimous mind,' I tried to do his deep Indian voice. 'Eqquanimous mind, eqquanimous mind, eqqqqquanimous mind.'

Her eyelids quivered. She was smiling.

'If you are experiencing a free flow of subtle sensations, let your mind sweep freely across your whole body. If you find an area of pain, make an objective note. Pain. Pain. Not *my* pain. If you feel the little mouse that's crawling over your blanket towards your chin, make an objective note. Mouse. Mouse. Not my—'

'No!' Kristin sat bolt upright. The slats creaked. 'Where?'

Laughing, I gathered my dirty laundry, blessed her and went out.

Strong Determination

I love the way wet cotton clings to your fingers. I was next to one of the meditators. A Chinese woman. We scrubbed our clothes in adjacent sinks. Five pairs of pants. I like watching them change colour when you plunge them into the water. Wetness makes them dark, but see-through too. I can see the pinkness of my fingers through the fabric. The Chinese woman sighs wringing out her jeans. Sometimes the meditators get on my nerves. They're so proud of their big Dasgupta experience, their vows and visions. Sometimes I love being around them. Their heavy silence pulls you in. There's a clinginess to it, like cottony wetness. The more you don't talk to the stranger beside you, the closer you feel to her.

I would never disturb a meditator like I bothered Kristin.

I scrub at crotches. Blue, red, green, white, black. Five pairs plus what I've got on. The cotton stretches and wrinkles. The stains fade but won't go. Stuff from my body. Me. I never hand-washed clothes till I came to the Dasgupta. At home anything dirty disappeared the moment you chucked it on the carpet.

58

Mum loved to slave, then whined about our being spoiled. I never chopped a carrot either. On tour I wore the same clothes for days. Zoë was always happy to swap. I liked her black smell. 'You mucky little beast.' Jonathan laughed. He'd paint me so people could *smell* it, he said. They'd look at the painting and smell I was wet. Carl wanted me to shower with him. Carl loved long hot showers. The quality of a hotel was the quality of the shower, for Carl: how long you could stay there rubbing soap over each other. Carl was always clean. Now I'm scrubbing hard. I'm scrubbing the sweat out of the cotton. Don't even try to scrub out the letter. *Because we love you. Blind to reason.*

What did he mean, *all the murder stories?*

The kitchen servers ring the gong for meals and the course managers ring it for meditations. They carry their registers and their notebooks. They have biros. They are available if someone has an urgent question. They won't offer an answer. They refer you to the course leader, to Harper or Mi Nu Wai. If people are skipping meditation, the course managers check their rooms. They catch them talking. They look for footprints in the mud along the fence at the bottom of the recreation field.

I've never been asked to be a course manager. Some people are invited the first time they serve. They must know I'm not the right person. I'd find it funny when people sneaked off for a pint. Sometimes it is hard to square the idea of having no self with the fact that they always know which person is right for which job. You are who you are even when you're no one. That's *Anatta.*

Another thing I wonder is how they decide which meditator will sit where. They have a plan of all the cushions. Rows A B C D, then the numbers along each row. Like stewards at a smart venue, they assign meditators to their places. That happens the first evening. It's not alphabetical, but they keep a record, so when a cushion is empty they know whose bum isn't on it, and they know what room that person sleeps in, they know where to find her. I had almost reached my place, late as usual, when I realized I was beside Marcia, the big Australian. They'd moved Meredith to the empty cushion on the right and put Marcia between us. When I sat down there was a smell of fart.

Equanimous mind. Tranquil mind.

Two thirty to three thirty is Strong Determination. 'We are not masochists,' Dasgupta says, 'but there are great benefits to be gained from remaining absolutely still for a whole hour. This resolution is known in Pali as *adhitthana*, or strong determination.'

Marcia couldn't decide if she was going to cross her right leg over her left or her left over her right. Her thighs are thick. She was wearing nylon trousers that swished and hissed. She lifted her backside and removed one of three foam cushions. Then she put it back. The fart is a rice-and-beans fart. I mustn't attach my mind to an irritant. I mustn't criticize. Will Kristin laugh about this in bed or will she lie silent on her slats? That's how I should be: silent, concentrated, uncritical. Meredith will giggle. But I want Kristin to laugh. When she laughs I will bless her. Without any effort. She laughs and the blessing will rise from my gut, from my heart.

'Sttart-tagain,' Dasgupta intones. It's the CD for day three, two thirty. The last day of *anapana*. 'Concentrate on your breath as it passes through the nostrils and across the upper lip. Don't try to change it or control it. Concentrate on the breath, *as it is*. *As it is*. If it is soft, it is soft. If it is hard, it is hard. The in-breath crossing the lip. The out-breath crossing the lip.'

Marcia huffs and puffs. She puts her hands on her knees, then moves them back to her lap, then back to her knees again. She can't decide whether to have her blanket over her shoulders, or round her waist. Why is she so useless?

'Eyes always closed, remain vvery vigilant, vvery aware, vvery vigilant, vvery aware.'

I open my eyes and look to Mi Nu Wai. She's statuesque. No, a statue doesn't vibrate. It's a breathing stillness. I watch her. Words are popping and crackling in my mind: *We recognized that you were in love. So beautiful to see you that way.* A father was writing this stuff to his daughter. Not *my* father for sure. My father didn't see anything. Maybe he saw the first daughter, maybe the second, but not the third, not Beth. Dad just did not notice when I was in love, or when I was out of love. 'Carl tells me he loves me every day,' I told Jonathan. 'So do a couple of other guys, actually.' It was true. There was an old guitar teacher in Swiss Cottage. Jonathan smiled. 'But I don't believe in love,' I told him. That was what he wanted to hear. 'What is love? A word? A sound? How can a girl in a band, with a solo career too, plus loads of session work, how can a girl like that not have other men? I love men. That's what I love.'

Mi Nu is so still on the dais. There's definitely a light from her cheeks and forehead. She's lit up by her stillness. *As if all the spotlights had been turned up on your shining face.* The fact that that letter hurts should be a warning. I can feel the words in my ankles. Stay away from this man. Stay at the Dasgupta. Wrap yourself in the spirit of the Dasgupta. *You came here so as not to kill yourself.* So *be* here, Mr Diarist, damn it. Be here in this stillness and leave be. Stop writing your sad stories. Leave Susie be. Leave your wife be. Concentrate on your bloody meditation. I'm

61

sure Mi Nu has a story behind her, but it's long since dissolved into quietness. It's an old magazine, read and forgotten. What's forgotten can't harm, has no power. Still, I'm hungry to know. I want to know. Why? *The age gap with the older man is not the same as with the older woman.* What is that supposed to mean? 'I'm old enough to be your father,' Jonathan said. 'Hmmm, incest.' I laughed.

My father *was* obsessed by money and security, no doubt about that, and he would never have denied it. Janet must study accountancy, Helen marketing, Elisabeth design. Each Marriot must take his place in Marriot's Ltd. Or, rather, her place, defending Marriot against the taxman, promoting the Marriot brand, designing Marriot's fabrics. Your life a project in Dad's head. Mum's role to shop, cook, clean and spend. The house must look good enough for all this work to have been worthwhile. Without spending too much. 'It's true your father's a tyrant, Beth. But he came from nothing, remember.'

We all came from nothing, Mum.

Truth was Dad wanted a son. He would have left us alone if he'd had a son.

Marcia uncrosses and re-crosses her legs. She sighs and sniffs. It has begun to rain. Drops clatter on the roof of the Metta Hall. In a few minutes it will start to leak. The drip will begin.

Sit still. Right effort.

A still body *is* a still mind. Right concentration.

Stillness *is* awareness *is* equanimity. Right understanding.

What was Susie's huge opportunity? Has she been signed up by a major recording studio? Have they invited her to play at the Coliseum? Do it, Susie! Your dad's right. Blow 'em away! Or did they just give her a good place in college? A chance to go to

Cambridge with Meredith? Then the hell with it. Go for your man, girl. You are in love with a man who is in love with you. How often does that happen? Do it. Go for it. Carl loved me, really loved me. Telling Jonathan love didn't exist, I discovered what it was. *I'd give anything*, my diarist said. Who hasn't got behind the wheel drunk some time? Who hasn't risked killing and being killed? Damn.

'Never try to regulate your breathing. If the breath passes through the left nostril, then let it be the left nostril. If it passes through the right nostril, let it be the right nostril. Just observe. Just observe.'

Between long pauses Dasgupta's voice breaks the silence.

'Things as they are, *as they are*, not as you would like them to be. The breath, as it is. *As it is.*'

I can't sit still if I'm thinking. I tense up. The more I don't want to think, the more I tense up. I think about tensing up. Everything aches and cramps, because I'm thinking. The thoughts are in my ankles now, they've crept up to my thighs, bad thoughts, gripping my shoulders, pressing their thumbs in my neck. Thoughts are pain, pain, pain. I'm thinking about thinking about tensing up. I start to *hear* everything. Every sniff and shuffle and cough. Marcia shifting from ham to fat ham in those nylon trousers. Huff puff, huff puff. The rain drumming. A man yawns on the far side of the hall. Pretty loudly. And again. So loud it's even funny. And *again*! He's doing it on purpose. I let my eye slide to the left. Yep, the course manager on the male side is hurrying along the aisle. He's going to warn him.

I can't go on. The pain in my ankles is worse. The thoughts in my ankles. Bad thoughts. Jonathan. Pain is a door. Locked today. Pain is a locked door, a bolted door. You can't go through.

Out of bounds. And there's the drip. It falls from the roof and ploofs into the carpet, behind me, to my right. A couple of yards back. I *never* change my posture in Strong Determination. Never. Servers should set an example. Old students should be capable of sitting an hour in stillness.

Ploof.

Pain is welding my calves together. Painful thoughts. I can't relax. I'm one with my diarist now. Back to day one, that is. *Sankhara. Sankhara.* The unskilled actions of the past resurface as pain when we meditate. How can anyone believe such crap? But they do. It's true. I feel it's true. Ghost words coming back. Pain is pus pushed from old infections, old betrayals. I was so skilled in unskilled actions, so good at playing off boyfriends, parents, producers. Now their words come back. Cruel words. Kind words. The kind words are the cruellest. Be happy, Beth, be peaceful, be liberated, li-ber-a-ted, liberated. You are in the present now, Beth. Not the past. The present where there is no conflict. Here in the Metta Hall there are no decisions. All memories, all plans, are insubstantial. Your diarist is insubstantial. His daughter insubstantial. Jonathan insubstantial. Carl insubstantial. Dad insubstantial. Beth insubstantial. Insubstantial the night on the beach, the night on the beach. Philippe. Hervé. The shouts. The breakers.

Despite all the murder stories? God.

On my left Kristin is silent as the grave. She is not happy or calm, but she is silent. How do I know that? How do I know that she has issues too? I know. She has issues but she is dealing with them, she is sitting her way through them. Her back is bowed. Her head falls a little to one side. Meredith is upright and composed. Meredith is a girl doing well at finishing school. Her back is so straight. She balances a book on her head. With no effort. She knows her *ps* and *qs,* pronounces her *ts* and *ds* correctly. Meredith is learning a lesson because her parents have paid for it, even if you pay nothing to come to the Dasgupta. The Dasgupta costs nothing but total surrender. Mrs Harper is in front of me, her big square back quietly breathing. Livia is to her right, then Stephanie, then Ines. They are all bathed in Mi Nu's glow. Only Marcia and I are out of it. I hate Marcia. I've barely met her. Marcia's a bag of shit.

Bless her. Blessings on odd days. Resist aversions on even.

The moon is impossibly distant. Was there a moon that night on the beach? Take all his diaries away and chuck them. Do him that favour. Take his life and trash it. Do it! Go to his room, gather his books, chuck 'em in the trash. Best forgotten. Concentrate on your breathing, Beth. The breath playing round the nostrils. You imagine your thoughts are so interesting, don't you, Mr Diarist? That's the truth. It doesn't matter if they're painful. Your thoughts make you interesting. Oh, I have such complex thoughts. Oh, I'm such an *interesting* person. He loves himself writing that letter, writing his diary. Oh, the poor tortured soul. I'm such a fascinating man. The way I suffer. I'm so tender to my daughter. Oh, bollocks! Spray the crap away. Excuse me, Professor Tony, could you scrape off these diaries? This wordshit. So I can stick them in the dishwasher. A professor of linguistics maybe? This storyshit. Or literature. Concentrate on your breathing, Beth. Your breathing is more interesting than this diary. The nature of your breath at the present moment is a matter of the utmost importance to you. The utmost importance.

I'd give my right arm to be in love the way—
No!

I uncrossed my legs and struggled to my feet. My ankles were numb. They weren't there. I stumbled between the cushions and out into the porch.

Mrs Harper was on her feet, following.

I dragged on my shoes and out into the rain.

'Elisabeth! You're not supposed to leave the hall during Strong Determination. You know that. You're a server.'

I made a face. 'I've got wind, Mrs Harper. I didn't want to disturb.'

Vegetables

There is no killing at the Dasgupta, but endless cutting up, endless topping and tailing, chopping and dicing and slicing and grating. We're doing the veg again. This is a kind of punishment, as Paul sees it. Paul's another blandly sexless Dhamma bloke, the kind who always obeys the rules. Without thinking. He doesn't think. He has a barber's haircut with a parting and wears pale blue shirts and grey pullovers. Harper wears a grey pullover too. They've surrendered totally. Kristin obeys the rules, but Kristin is thinking and suffering. Kristin is trying to grow. Oh, but it's crazy liking and hating people you're only going to see for ten days, especially when the whole point of the Dasgupta is how mad it is to get attached to anything since everything in all existence arises only to pass away.

At the three o'clock meeting, Kristin was the only one not to volunteer, for anything. We pull in chairs from the male and female servers' rooms and sit in a semicircle round the Tasks Board by the small fridge. Tomorrow is black bean stew and fig roll. Day four. *Vipassana* day. Ines volunteered to be main chef. Again. Ines volunteers for everything. She has nominated herself for Miss Dhamma Server 2010. Bathing suit not required. Paul assigned Marcia to work alongside her. 'The bean stew's a bomb,' I told Marcia. Meredith began to grin. Yesterday I found out that Meredith's been coming to the Dasgupta since she was thirteen. Her mum brought her to the children's courses. Now it's a home from home. 'I've always meditated,' she says, and starts to giggle.

Kristin never speaks to Meredith.

I volunteered to do Special Requests. Paul read them out. A cheese salad sandwich. A bowl of stewed fruit and yoghurt. A plate of toast and margarine.

'Chicken salad it is,' I said.

Rob grinned. And Tony. But Paul didn't get it. Then he saw Meredith heaving.

'*Cheese* salad, Elisabeth, I said *cheese*.'

'We're out of chicken, Beth,' Rob said.

'Slip of the tongue, Paul, sorry.'

'Fowl slip.' Tony laughed.

Paul hates this jokey stuff. He assigned me to veg and salad as a punishment. He doesn't know I love chopping. I love getting inside things, right into a squeaky lettuce heart, or the bloody pulp of a big salad tomato. I love that odd rubberiness broccoli has when you pull the twigs apart. I adore putting the big saucepan on the floor between my ankles and using all my weight to ram down the masher into boiled spuds and milk. Mum would be amazed. 'You never did a stroke at home, Elisabeth.' But really she liked to do everything herself. Otherwise how could she have felt exploited? At the Dasgupta I've learned to love the way a carrot bends a bit then snaps clean. I love using the big chopper to slam right through a head of crisp cabbage. The green halves fall apart and you see the crinkly layers whitening to the core. It's so simple *and* mysterious. I never have any problem blessing a cabbage.

Today we've got celeriac, swede, turnip, potatoes, carrots, cauliflower, onions. There are peeling knives and chopping knives and sinks and boards and basins. The swedes are really small with shiny dark- and yellow-green stripes. Maybe they're squashes, or pumpkins. I'm not sure. They glow on the work surface under fluorescent light. But it's frustrating peeling them. There's more peel than pulp. When you gouge out the seeds and slime they cling on by sticky threads. You scrape and scrape and they're still there.

'Place the cubing disc in processor R302.'

Reading the recipe book I can hear Vikram's voice. He's explaining to an idiot in idiot-proof formulas.

'But which is the cubing disc?' Meredith asks, pulling them all off the wall and checking blades and perforations.

'There are labels under the hooks, sweetheart.'

Now she doesn't know which disc she took from where.

We go at it for an hour on the long surface with the three sinks. The stuff mounts up under the grinder. Celeriac is filthy when you plunge it in the water, the rind is gnarled and grizzled. I use the biggest knife to slice it off. Inside it's like white marble with twisty brown imperfections, then creamy and sticky when it's cubed. The orange of the carrots clashes with the orange of the swedes. The grinder clatters. Sometimes it jams.

'Parsneep, turneep, pumkeen.'

Stephanie's practising her vegetables.

There are always foreigners serving at the Dasgupta. They treat it as a kind of language school, which is funny for a place that sets such store on silence.

Meredith's giggling again. She's discovered her parents' flat in Paris is only a block away from Stephanie's home.

'With a swede'—I pull one from the sack—'you can breed.'

Stephanie did her puzzled look. Like Ralph's, but with freckles. She's studying acupuncture somewhere.

'What sort of vegetable is Paul?' I ask Meredith. Her hair is escaping her hat. She won't use anything but a small peeler, for fear of cutting her fingers again.

'Well, not a carrot.'

The carrots we've got look like they've been in the ground a thousand years. They're gnarled and knobbly.

'Not a cucumber,' says Stephanie.

Meredith's voice is squeaky and Stephanie's deep. The opposite of what you'd think looking at them.

'Or a leek,' I agreed

'Ralph is a carrot,' Meredith announces.

'Maybe. The neat garden-salady kind. Perky and pink. And Tony is an old turnip.'

I've played this game before. The grinder roars. The peelings are heaping up. Thoughts are peelings maybe. Scraped from the mind's surface and chucked. Think of all the thoughts in all your life. You are the fruit beneath. You peel and peel, every moment a thought scraped away, and never get there. No self, only thoughts peeling off.

Is that what *anatta* means?

'Let's make it easier: between a leek and a cabbage, Paul is?'

'A cabbage!' says Stephanie.

'My turn,' Meredith shouts. 'Between a broccoli and an onion, Mrs Harper is?'

'Mrs Harper is an aubergine. That's obvious. Sorry, *two* aubergines.'

I pretended I was holding them just above the stomach. Meredith cracked up.

'And Mi Nu is an asparagus. The kind so white you can almost see through it.'

'That make your pee stink.'

We're all giggling when Mrs Harper says, 'Is this Right Speech, girls?'

She's standing behind us, smiling sadly. I hope she didn't hear the stuff about the aubergines. Meredith apologizes in a posh voice. 'Sorree,' Stephanie says.

On second thoughts, I hope she did hear.

Mrs Harper says: 'The wise man does not speak unless his words bring benefit. His speech is full of mindfulness.'

She's saying this for me, not the others. She doesn't give a damn about the others.

I stay bent over the celeriac. 'We're not men, though, are we, Mrs Harper? We're girls.'

She studies me. 'But you do want to be wise, Elisabeth.'

'Is that something a person can choose?'

'You have already chosen, Elisabeth. You know that.' She smiles. 'Actually, I came to suggest you take Marcia to hear the Server's Discourse at six. Always assuming you've got over your little problem.'

What's she talking about?

'The problem that obliged you to leave Strong Determination in such a hurry.'

She always has that generous smile.

'Oh, right.'

I start on the onions. Ten big onions. Sliding off the crackly brown skin, I wait for my eyes to water. There's no question of an onion being just a product you move from plastic pack to pot. An onion goes on the attack. You chop it up, but at a price. Jonathan was an onion. Slithery inside, with so many layers. I never got to the heart. Carl was a baked potato. With melted butter. Now I'm smiling through onion tears. Whatever Mum and Dad were, it's long past its sell-by date.

When Mrs Harper is well gone, Stephanie whispers, 'And you, Beth?'

'Me what?'

'What vegetable are you?'

I laughed. 'I'm a beetroot, of course.'

You stain everything red, Beth, Jonathan said. You really do. You stain the whole world red.

Noble Truths

Things are coming to a head. Why? Are they? I'm so excited. So frantic. *I'm trapped in something. Not a cage. A process.* My diarist's words. Midnight, one, two o'clock, three. Day four now. In the female servers' room, the kitchen, the dining hall. In the male servers' room. Why not? Hunting for paper. The men have a tin of chocolate biscuits. How did that get there? Writing on the back of server admission forms. Rota sheets. The kitchen hygiene protocol. *leftovers can be heated once and once only.* Couldn't agree more. And drinking Rooibos. I hate Rooibos. I love chocolate biscuits. Yum. They'll never suspect one of the girls. I remember Zoë saying that. 'Nobody'll suspect it's a girl, Beth.' Jonathan had bitten my neck. I told Carl it was Zoë. 'You know how *nutty* she is. She just grabbed me, kissed and bit.' Jonathan couldn't believe it. 'You're a genius, Beth.' I mean, he couldn't believe *Carl* believed it. 'You don't know Zoë,' I told him. 'I wish I did,' he said. And I wish I could be free from this, free from this, free from this. This crap clinging, these seeds and slime that won't scrape out.

The Buddha meditated and meditated and meditated until he found the First Noble Truth: suffering is universal. Is it? Really? What's so noble about that? Mum suffered, no doubt. She was treated like shit. Imagined she was. Dad suffered, in his way. I think he did. The world was never as he wanted. I made sure of that. Carl definitely suffered. Carl suffered with Dad. With Mum. *I just could not be what he wanted me to be.* Love Dylan. It's funny Carl was such friends with Mum *and* Dad. He was the only friend they had in common, maybe the only thing they agreed about at all. Carl would save me. 'Help yourself to the Scotch, lad. Have yourself a chocolate, son.' They knew Carl would chuck the music soon enough, and that would be the day he married me and we had a kid, pets, a house. 'Our Elisabeth's a kamikaze, lad. Slow her down before she does for all of us.' Marry Beth, have a kid, get out of the music, make some sensible money. Marry Marriot's! There's work for everyone. If only mad Beth would say yes. Why doesn't she? He's such a nice boy, *so* handsome. The son we should have had. Carl. It drove them crazy that they couldn't force me. Marry Carl, make us happy. Give us a son. Then a grandson. How they suffered! *Dukkha.* The more blindingly obvious the solution, the more it drove them mad I wouldn't go for it. Did Jonathan suffer? I don't think so. I did my best but I couldn't hurt Jonathan. I didn't even draw blood. What do you expect from an onion?

The Buddha meditated and meditated and meditated until he found the Second Noble Truth: the origin of suffering. Video day two again. Near the end. 'The origin of suffering, my friends, is our craving. We are always craving this and craving that. Are we not? Our hunger, our thirst. Our materialism. Or the opposite:

we are craving to be free from this, to be free from that. Aversion. We hate this task. We hate this headache.'

Is it true?

My diarist was furious after the video: 'I crave nothing but to be left alone.' Words to that effect. 'Nothing but not to be myself, nothing but to have L vanish into thin air.'

Already a long list, if you ask me.

I craved a man who didn't crave me. Craving success I could handle. Pocus would have made it, with time. We would, we really would. And I could handle being craved without craving. That was flattering. It was fun. Friends were so impressed by Carl. He was so good-looking, so *in love*. With me!

'You're so *lucky,*' Zoë sighed. 'Why in God's name do you screw around, when you have a guy like that?'

Because I was craving Jonathan. Who didn't crave me, didn't crave anyone, didn't crave at all.

'So you would let me go, Jonnie, if I told you I'd found someone else?'

'Yes, Beth.'

'Just like that?'

'Is there any other way?'

'Carl would never let me go, never. Carl loves me.'

'I know, Beth. Carl's young.'

He was smoking. He didn't crave cigarettes. It was one of my roll-ups. Jonathan could take them or leave them. Take chocolate biscuits or leave chocolate biscuits. Beer, dope. He could take love or leave love.

'What if I said I'd kill myself, Jonnie? What then?'

I loved to say his name. I'd been drinking, from the flask in his coat pocket.

'My mum tried to kill herself, you know.'

He shook his head.

'You wouldn't fight to stop me?'

'I'd do everything to *dissuade* you, Beth.'

'You'll never find anybody like me.'

'I know that.'

'Never. You can never replace me.'

'I don't want to replace you, Beth.'

He was smiling. A bit sadly. Did he suffer? I think he enjoyed smiling sadly. Did he realize how much he was making me suffer? Yes. He did. He really did. What kind of craving is it sends me back to this stranger's diary? *I acquiesce to my punishment,* he writes. Acquiesce?

I liked it that Jonathan knew he was making me suffer. That's weird but true. Why wouldn't he fight for me? Why? He did care for me. *I'm trapped in a process.* This is stuff the diarist wrote. What process? I'm writing down another person's thoughts. But they feel like mine. Thoughts are peelings. You're turning over someone else's peelings, Beth. Waste. Leavings. You live in a bin full of crap. Yours or someone else's. Who cares? Meditation equals sifting through crap. Old thoughts, old peelings. When will they decompose? Six months? Six years? Six lifetimes? One day Jonathan did this—OK, but now, peel it off. Another day Carl said that—fine, now peel it, chuck it. Mum screamed, 'I'll kill the bastard!'—into the bin. Dad says: 'Your mother's impossible, Elisabeth.' Hoover it up. What about waste separation? Sort the shit into separate boxes? No need. It recycles itself anyway. I must have chucked that thought a thousand times already. The peel grows back. Like a scab on a scratch. So peel it off again. Chuck it *again.* If only we'd never met—feed it to the dogs. If only I hadn't got drunk that night—kill it, bury it. If we hadn't met the French boys, if we hadn't camped on the dunes—stop, Beth, *stop*! In January—get rid of it! Born in January, an Aquarian—I said, Get rid of it!

But I did. I did get rid, I did I did I did get rid.

Jesus.

Peel till there's nothing. Think till it's all thought and gone. But there *is* nothing. *Nibbana's* what's left after the peeling, after you find there's no self under all that thought? *Nibbana* is *anatta*, then? No self. Nothingness.

Where did you put the veg, Beth?

I peeled it all, Ines.

But I can't find it, Beth, I need to get the stew on. I'm head cook today, you know. I have my responsibilities.

I'm afraid there was nothing there, Ines. It was all peel.

Heaps of peelings, years of sticky fingers and now all this crap I've been writing through the night, all this dirty paper to be thrown away too. Paper peel. Scribbles. Why does it cling to my fingers, why won't it go? Oh, just *go*. Fuck off!

What craving is it makes you go back and back and back to the diary of a bloke *you don't even know*, a bloke who hates himself, hates his wife. Nothing special there. Doesn't even seem to love his girlfriend. The craving to suffer, to suffer again, to suffer the same things through someone else. I was so alive when I was dying. Fantastic. And now I'm dead I wish I was dying again. I'm dead I did get rid of it, I did get rid I'm dead.

Oh, do go on, Beth. On and on. Keep repeating so the moments pass. As if they wouldn't anyway. Keep writing. Fill the pages. The pen is a peeling knife, peeling the thoughts from my head. Throw the pages straight in the bin, recycle the paper. Why not? Then write it again. And again. It would be *exactly the same*.

What else could come out? My songs were all the same in the end. They all sounded the same said the same meant the same. An Aquarian. Forgive me forgive me forgive me.

If I have offended anyone in today's Dhamma Service, I seek pardon of him or her, I seek pardon of him or her. If anyone has offended me in today's Dhamma Service, with all my heart I pardon him or her, I pardon him or her.

Loving kindness.

Marcia farted right through the servers' evening *metta*. You have to laugh.

So laugh!

Why aren't you laughing, Beth?

May all beings visible and invisible on this Dhamma campus be free from all suffering, all attachments. May all beings be liberated, liberated, libbberated.

I love those words: I seek pardon, seek pardon. With all my heart, I *pardon* him or her, I *pardon* him or her.

Kneeling in the silence with the others, sinking into the ache of knees and thighs. I love the *metta*. What's with the invisible beings, though? What do *they* need to be liberated from? Imagine if the thoughts go on after you die. In invisibleness. Fruit all gone and the thoughts *still* peeling off. Nobody, but still thinking. Or in the unborn, the miscarried. Unborn but churning thoughts.

Whose are the faces I see? And the eyes that gaze when my eyes are closed? A face turns to me. A little girl. A young man. The eyes, peeled eyes. Incinerate. The mind burns and burns but never burns out.

The Buddha meditated and meditated and meditated until he found the Third Noble Truth: the cessation of suffering. That's good news. Video day four. 'Buddhism is not a pessimistic doctrine, my friends. Not a shred of pessimism in it. What does the Buddha say? He says your suffering can cease. Your suffering can cease. Is that pessimism?'

Dasgupta on his armchair in his white suit. He has a folded handkerchief to dab at the sweat. Narrow shoulders, big bulk. Bombay Rotary in the sixties. My diarist's words. The cessation of all suffering. Dad asks if Pocus will play at the Ealing Rotary. They'll pay five hundred pounds. Better than a kick in the crotch. Me blind drunk. Blind as a Beth. A batty Beth.

'Beth, this is Jonathan.' Dad introduces the famous painter. Supposedly. He was painting someone's portrait. A founding member.

'Beth, Jonathan. Jonathan, Beth.'

Jonathan Beth Jonathan Beth Jonathan Beth Jonathan Beth. Say it a million times. Say it for years and years while the world turns and the stars fall.

Romance. I sang, *Better off on my own.* The acoustics were awful. Mum shocked. 'Your skirt, Elisabeth!' Carl played brilliantly. What a brilliant guitarist Carl is!

'There's some famous painter here,' I told him, 'said he'd like to paint my picture.'

Peel it, bin it. *Nibbana.* Cessation of all mental formations. All your old *sankhara*s burned away. Peel peeled and gone. Fruit of nothingness at last. Passion fruit. Nothing fruit. 'I can't believe this numbers crap,' my diarist wrote. 'Three refuges, four noble truths, five precepts, seven stages of purification, eightfold path to enlightenment, ten perfections, and counting counting counting, all to get to zero, to nothing.'

Bliss.

Dana

At five o'clock I took Marcia to the cells to listen to the Dhamma Service CD. There were no cells free. What a relief. I had no desire to sit with Marcia for an hour and more. She was a lawyer, she said. I hadn't asked. She specialized in cases of child abuse, which required 'experience and sensitivity'. People are so proud of their lives, their jobs, the words they use. 'We mustn't talk when we are in areas where we might meet meditators,' I told her. 'They mustn't even see us talking.' In silence we headed to the female leader's bungalow to hand back the CD.

This was only the second or third time I had been to the bungalow. I never volunteer to bring the teacher's lunch tray. Why not? I would rather clean the loos or mop the floors. Mi Nu lives in the bungalow. Her whole life is lived between the bungalow and the Metta Hall. That's thirty yards. Maybe fifty. Does she ever leave the campus? Every day I plan to go to Mi Nu and ask a question, at interview time after lunch, or in the evening kneeling before the others. I have never spoken to her. Has she noticed I never volunteer to bring or fetch her tray? I hope so. I'm waiting for the day when I'm ready to ask her my question. What question? I don't know. It's the question Mrs Harper would like me to ask *her*, but that will only make sense because I am asking Mi Nu Wai. Mi Nu Wai. I don't know what the question is, but it will come. It will come quite soon now. Oh, but why am I so mysterious? Isn't it silly?

'Many abused children are particularly attracted to the parent who was most dangerous to them,' Marcia was saying. After I had told her not to talk. Perhaps I could ask Mi Nu why I dislike Marcia so much. Mi Nu Why! The Australian still had her shiny nylon tracksuit on her fat bum. I hate fat people. I hate people with poor posture. I'm so critical. At least the finishing school has taught Meredith to stand up straight.

There was a trellis of roses round the bungalow door with a few ragged flowers in the wet leaves. Very picturesque. We were knocking on a picture. Let me in. I was expecting Livia maybe, but Mi Nu came to the door. She had loose off-white trousers and top, her black ponytail hanging round her neck over one breast. Only she doesn't have breasts. Her bare feet are tiny.

'Mrs Harper told us to bring back the Dhamma Service CD.'

She looked at me, then at Marcia. I hid my teeth.

'The cells are all taken with students following the guided session,' Marcia said. 'In different translations.' Her Aussie accent was a sort of smell.

'You haven't been able to listen?'

'No. I guess we'll just go and sit in the session.'

A flicker lifted the corners of Mi Nu's mouth. 'No, please come in.'

81

If Mi Nu had asked whether we wanted to come in, I would have found an excuse. It was too soon. We took off our shoes. At the end of the passage ahead of us I could see a large room opening out with dim, tropical colours and a strange, scented coolness. It seemed a special place. Perhaps the bungalow was bigger than I'd thought. Had I ever walked round it? But Mi Nu pushed a door to the right.

'Sit down, you can listen here.'

She left.

It was a small room. There were half a dozen cushions and a CD player on a low table.

'Is she Thai or Burmese?' Marcia asked. 'Don't you envy their figures?'

I put in the CD, crossed my legs, closed my eyes, shut down my senses. If anyone has a figure to envy, it's Beth. 'You are sunshine made flesh, Beth.' Mi Nu is a sort of lunar eclipse.

'Blessed is the man who gives.'

Dasgupta began his spiel on *dana*. However little you possess, you can always make *dana* in some way or other and you will always reap the rewards. Giving is always better than taking. You always get greater benefits from generosity than from caution.

It's not a stupid talk. Dasgupta is never stupid. All the pleasure in sex is giving, Jonathan used to say. Even learning how to take, in sex, was a form of giving. Funny how Dasgupta talks about *dana* and I'm thinking of sex. No, I'm thinking of Jonathan talking about sex. We talked so much. I never think about sex itself. I'm cured of that.

It was harder to give time than to give money, Dasgupta was saying. It brought you more merits, it helped fill the jars of your perfections. When you have money to spare, what's extra costs you nothing. You don't have any less for yourself because you've given some away. Try telling my dad that. But time is all we have. Now and now and now. You say it and already it's gone. Time is the supreme gift. And the same for rich man and poor. Giving time is giving *life*.

'So your Dhamma Service, in the kitchen, my friends, or in housekeeping, or gardening, or offering your assistance to the teacher, is a chance to accumulate many merits, many *parmi*, or perfections, which will be of service to you in this life and the next. It is an important step on the Dhamma path.'

I kept my eyes closed. I didn't want any exchange with Marcia. I didn't want to breathe the air she polluted. At the same time I knew exactly what Dasgupta was about to say: that just as this Service was a great opportunity to grow in Dhamma there was also the risk of slipping back, the risk of generating mountains of new *sankharas,* oceans of new unhappiness, while actually serving at the Dasgupta Institute.

'"How can that be, Mr Dasgupta?" you ask me. How can that be? We come to the institute to serve, you say, and yet we make bad karma, we generate new *sankharas*, deep negative *sankharas*. Then we are worse off than if we hadn't made *dana*. '"What is Dasgupta talking about?" you ask.'

I could hear Marcia shifting her hams in their nylon. I had known her only a few hours and she had poisoned my mind. Tell yourself she will soon be gone. Seven days. Her and the diarist. And Kristin. And Meredith. Cravings, aversions.

'Dear friends, if you knew how many letters I receive from people who have come to a Dasgupta retreat, in this or that campus—California, Germany, Spain, India, Australia, doesn't matter—and their experience has been spoiled by the servers.

Maybe a server was rude to them. They asked this server a question and the server, he or she, didn't even reply, didn't give them the time of day, as they say. That is a very interesting expression, to give someone the time of day, to give someone your presence, your nowness.

'Well, this server thought himself superior. He thought himself too important to waste his time responding to a silly student who knew nothing about *vipassana*. He didn't listen. Or worse still, he answered with a harsh word, or in a harsh manner.

'"You can talk about serenity and happiness till the cows come home, Mr Dasgupta, and *vipassana* this and *vipassana* that, it is all very well and very interesting, yes, but if your own servers who follow your doctrine won't listen to me when I say I have a bad headache or I am not understanding why we mustn't change our posture in the hour of Strong Determination, well, I am sorry but all your teaching is so much hot air."

'And, my friends, my friends, this is a sensible deduction. We know a tree by its fruits. We know a doctrine by how its disciples behave. A server is rude to a student and the student deduces that *the whole doctrine is false,* it doesn't work. This is understandable. And you who came here to help and to grow in the Dhamma have only hindered. You haven't grown. You have *shrunk,* my friends, you have withered. And I ask, for heaven's sake, what are you thinking of? What *are* you thinking, my friend? This is madness. You came here to *serve* and instead you have chased someone away. It was better if you had never come. Better for the student, but most of all better for you.

'Or I hear of backbiting between servers. "I am a better server than she is, I have more experience, I can sit stiller than he can, why wasn't I given the more important job? I have been insulted."

84

'What? What are you thinking of, comparing yourself with others, worrying about your prestige, your sensitive ego? Oh dear, are we mad? Are we mad?

'Dear friends in Dhamma, it is much easier to come to a retreat as a student than as a server. Of course it is. True, the students must sit for many hours, true, they get pains in their legs, pains in the back, pains in the shoulders, but what *wrong* can a student do here at the Institute, what *sankharas* can he or she cause? He has taken refuge in the Triple Gem. He has sworn to keep the Five Precepts. He is protected by the Noble Silence. It is much easier to keep the Noble Silence than to practise Right Speech. A silent man is a safe man, my friends. He is not tempted to gossip, to tell tales, to slander and disparage. In silence it is soon clear that the self is an illusion. What self can there be when I am silent, when I come to my meals with my begging bowl in my hand? But when we serve and there are jobs to do, ah, my friends, then we start imagining we are important. It's true, isn't it? We start to *compete*. We want to be first. "I'm the best server, I deserve the most important jobs."'

Marcia sighed heavily. Opening my eyes I saw she had stuck the little finger of her right hand way up her left nostril. She was absorbed, listening to Dasgupta and exploring her nose. Without thinking, I jumped to my feet, dragged the door across the carpet, slipped out and shut it behind me.

Damn!

I stood in the porch. I was trembling. Why? To my right was the corridor and Mi Nu's sitting room. I suppose it's her sitting room. A small Buddha sat by the open door. It was faint, but there was definitely a smell. Of jasmine? Definitely an aura, a dim green light, like under leaves in a wood. A special stillness.

It was drawing me in, the way, when you finally get close, your mind is drawn towards *jhāna*, you can feel the stillness pulling, the emptiness pulling. So I could walk down there right now and ask Mi Nu that question. Why can't I be good, Mi Nu? Was that the question? Why can't I be happy? Or, Why do I want to be good, when I'm obviously not? What was I thinking of when I ran into the sea? Why didn't I die, Mi Nu? Why didn't I die? Why can't I die? Now.

I stood in the porch. There was no need for me to sit with Marcia. Why had Mrs Harper asked me to do that? As if a practising lawyer couldn't listen to the Dhamma Service talk on her own. Teach me to be like you, Mi Nu. How can I be like you, how can I live in your world? Maybe that is the question.

Is it?

Then I heard a strange sound. Someone was wailing. Or whimpering. Very softly. What was it? I advanced a step. A seagull? A kettle? Now there was a chuckle. Weird. Definitely a low chuckle. A growl!

I turned and walked out.

I walked out of the bungalow, past the Metta Hall, along the ivied fence that divides the sexes, down to the dining hall, through the female side to the kitchen, then back through the male side, out into the male compound and straight to Dormitory A and the diarist's room.

I didn't plan to go. I went.

Beth on the Bed

I acquiesce to my punishment. I can't help it. I'm trapped.

The guided session was about halfway through when I arrived. I had time. Mrs Harper thinks I am with Marcia. I settled on the bed.

I never realized how futile my mental life was. An endless loop, disconnected from reality.

One moment I had been planning to ask Mi Nu how I could become like her—there was that inviting light, that whiff of incense where the passageway opened into the stillness of the bungalow's main room—and now I was stretched out on a man's bed in a room that definitely had *that* smell: the socks, the smoker's overcoat, the slept-in sheets.

I took off my shoes and lay down. God. It was so like old times. 'I'm modelling for a painting,' I told his wife, when she found me there. I heard the key turning and saw a boyish haircut on an ageing head. 'And he lets you stay in his studio and sleep in his bed?' She seemed tired, not angry. 'I was feeling cold,' I said. Jonathan was shocked that his wife had come round without warning. 'We haven't lived together for years,' he protested. 'She only has the key for emergencies.'

I turned a page.

Just a disturbance, milling round and round, an eddy in a backwater, the same water turning round and round with the same dead leaves. My thoughts.

Why am I reading this old guy's guff? I flicked here and there through the notebook. What was the cry I had heard from Mi Nu's room? The growl? Does she keep a dog?

What if Dasgupta were dead and we were listening to the voice of a dead man?

That was a funny idea.

Every night, every session, he speaks to us on the video. When in fact he's dead. Decades ago. Would it matter? Is the message any different because the person isn't physically there? Because the person isn't <u>alive</u>? What if they had recorded Christ, Muhammad, the Buddha? The Sermon on the Mount. On DVD. Listen to your Saviour's voice in the original Hebrew with English subtitles (choice of King James Version or the Revised Standard).

Imagine Dasgupta's recorded voice going on for centuries. It's possible. Maybe he is dead.

The Fire Sermon, on CD. Ideal when driving in heavy traffic.

St Paul Preaches to the Athenians, available as an MP3 download. Take it on your trip to Greece.

Would everyone be Christian?
Would everyone be cured of their Christianity?

Some of the handwriting was tricky. The man was scribbling fast. It was getting more and more slanted, more and more windblown. For a moment I thought I could hear him. It was Jonathan's voice when he got on a roll. Gravelly. Jonathan hated religion. How we made fun of my mum for doing the flower arrangements in church. Of his wife for teaching in Sunday School. 'For Christ's sake, Jonnie, how did you marry someone who teaches Sunday School?'

I turned a page. It was strange being here on this man's bed, like I wasn't in the Dasgupta Institute at all. I'd hopped over the fence and walked two miles to the Barley Mow and now I was sinking gin and tonics, listening to Jonathan. It was a different world.

Mi Nu's room was a different world too. But that would be like when faces appear in the darkness, eyes calmly finding yours, drawing you down the tunnel to bliss. Instead I came to the pub. This diary is at least a fifty-fifty gin and tonic. I should check to see if he keeps a flask in his overcoat.

Perhaps that's how I could have saved the company. A box-set of the great religious speeches of all time.

If we had the Buddha in person pronouncing his Fire Sermon, what room would there be for Dasgupta and his unctuous smile? Imagine a man with huge charisma, a huge ego—Christ, Buddha, Muhammad—he fears that ego, he knows it's trouble. He preaches against egotism, he erects a religious system against egotism, satisfying his ego as he pulls in the disciples and demands total surrender.

The ringed fingers, the white cushions, the big belly wrapped in clean cotton. My friends this. My friends that. I CAN'T BELIEVE WE ALL SIT THERE EVERY EVENING LISTENING TO THIS JERK.

If we had Jesus videoed on the cross (adults only), the Resurrection on streaming, the Ascension captured on St Peter's mobile, where would that leave the popes, the heresies?

Revelation on record. Where would that leave history? Or science?

How can the idiot preach anicca anicca anicca all is flux, feel the flux in your fingers, in your toes, and then fix his words for ever on a DVD, _for ever_ the same, every Dasgupta Institute all over the world, retreat after retreat, the same recordings and video discourses day one day two day three day four five six seven, with translations in this language, translations in that, and the course leader actually present reduced to slotting a disk into a machine. How humiliating.

Dasgupta arises but he won't pass away.

I should go forward tonight at question time and ask the bloke, Harper, How do you feel about all the preaching being done on DVD? Wouldn't you like to preach a bit yourself? Since you're here.

Plot. A secret society of frustrated priests schemes to destroy the videos of their deceased religious leader so as to make space to preach themselves. But the religion's followers believe the dead man is God and tear the priests to pieces.

The blockbuster that could have saved Wordsmith.

Why oh why did my writers never write a blockbuster?

Just one Harry Potter. One!

90

Because you chose crap writers.

L.

Because you were scared of success.

L.

You published books because you didn't have the courage to write them yourself.

L.

Writers write because they don't have the courage to live. Everybody knows that.

L.

And you didn't even have the courage to write.

L.

The publishing company goes bankrupt and the publisher runs off with his tail between his legs. To get religion. Pathetic. Right when his family needs him most. His daughter needs him desperately.

L.

If you knew how much you've disappointed me.

L.

Why not stick naked babes on the covers, since you never think of anything else?

L.

You don't even have the courage to sell the filth you're always thinking.

L.

Turn Muslim and marry a child bride.

L.

You won't even have to divorce me.

L.

The next Mrs H has her first period.

L.

The next Mrs H has her first driving lesson.

L.

The next Mrs H enjoys her first drink in the Crown.

L.

Sorry, I forgot, you're Muslim now. No booze.

L.

Is everybody here plagued like this? Does everyone come here because their mind has become <u>unbearable</u>? A litany of self-accusation.

Plausible.

The reason you're listening to a nerd like Dasgupta, of course, is because <u>you need to.</u> Because <u>he is not half as much a nerd as you are.</u>

Be humble at least. Even if his ego is absurd, his system may be helpful.

Idea: so as to suffer it no longer, summarize everything in one hundred words. Your life in a blurb. THEN FORGET IT FOR EVER.

Exorcize your life in a blurb and spare yourself the book.

It's weird. Sometimes this guy sounds like Jonathan, mostly when he's being witty, sarky. But when he's really unhappy he sounds like me.

Question: If there is no self, why do we fall in love with one person rather than another, and why always the wrong person?

Stop reading, Beth, get out of this bed and go to Mi Nu. Now. Ask her: how can I become like you, Mi Nu? How can I finally change, really change?

From 4.30 to 6.30 this a.m. sitting, eyes closed, on burning ankles writing and rewriting the hundred-word summary in my head. Exorcism turned obsession. The exorcist is the ghost. The blurb the book.

Talented mother's boy, GH, youngest of four, unwisely marries at twenty-three a woman fifteen years older than himself.

Cut 'unwisely'. Redundant.

Cut 'than himself'. Redundant.

Cut 'talented'. Please.

Mother's boy GH marries at twenty-three accomplished lawyer, thirty-eight. Her money funds his ambition to run independent publishing house.

She flattered me, what a bright little boy you are, what a clever young man, what a promising future. She made me dependent on her. She stopped me growing up. I never grew up. I need to grow up.

But I told you I was too old for you. I said it a million times. Only you were so stubborn I began to believe you loved me.

L.

Life, life, not my life.

Summarize and dismiss. Go to this evening's meditation with a free mind, a clear mind, an empty mind. Everything described and dismissed.

So.

Mother's boy GH marries accomplished lawyer whose wealth funds his independent publishing venture.

Cut 'independent'.

Why publishing? Why would anyone be ambitious to be a publisher, of all things?

Unable to write yourself, you hide behind other people's books.

L.

Behind the arrogance of a cultural project.

L.

Three years later, the marriage is already on the rocks when a daughter is born.

I notice all the novels you are publishing are about adultery.

L.

Actually, darling, the majority are murder stories.

Combine the formulas, sweetheart. Uxoricide. Don't let me get in your way.

L.

Four years later his marriage is already on the rocks when a daughter is born, more or less simultaneous with the beginning of his love affair with T, eight years his junior.

Cut 'more or less'.

Cut 'love'.

Reinstate 'love'.

Too much chronology?

Because wife becomes increasingly hostile and unstable he feels more and more attached to T. To leave, however, would be to expose his daughter to a woman who has left her job and is drinking heavily.

Break for word count.

I always enjoyed writing blurbs.

It's your blurbs sink the books, sweetheart.

L.

You say too clearly what kind of rubbish they are.

L.

Querulous mother's boy, GH, marries accomplished law-
yer who generously invests in his publishing venture. Just
when his passion for his secretary seems bound to sink the
marriage a daughter is born, giving GH the excuse for stay-
ing with his surrogate mother/wife who never recovers from
postnatal . . .

48 words.

52 to go.

Not a syllable over a hundred.

I cuddled myself in the sheets. How intelligent this man makes me feel. How awake. As if any of this mattered. The bloke is awesomely attached to being who he is. I could see that. To his own shit. I hadn't hung around failing rock musicians for years without seeing how they all adored the drama of their frustrations. Jonathan's studio was full of paintings he hadn't managed to sell. 'Famous in a manner of speaking,' he used to say. 'Famous at the Ealing Rotary.' Most of them were old girlfriends. He didn't hide them from me. But from his ex-wife, yes. They weren't legally divorced, he said. As if there was some other kind. 'Just that we don't live together.' I didn't mind because I was a million miles prettier than any of them. The wife in particular. She was boss-eyed. 'I don't need an exclusive deal,' I told him. I felt pretty confident. After our afternoons at the studio, I'd text JUST TOPPED UP THE CHERRY WITH CARL IN THE SHOWER. It wasn't true. I LOVE YOU FOR ADMITTING THAT, he texted. I thought: I'll get a couple of good songs out of this fling.

'To be like me, Elisabeth, you must first take refuge in the Triple Gem. But really take refuge. You must first keep the Five Precepts. But really keep them. For a long time.'

Is that what Mi Nu will say?

Read to the end of his life, then get out of here. Quick.

Feeling he would fail in his duty to his daughter if he leaves home, GH abandons love and eventually persuades T to marry her old boyfriend.

How could I do something so stupid?

Years later, the folly, the beauty of his daughter's reckless, sacrificial love for a man who shares her mother's drink problem opens GH's eyes to the squalid compromises he has always sunk to. In a blaze of romance . . .

What?

Blurb talk.

At which point the bank pulls the plug on . . .

Cut 'eventually'.

Cut 'old'.

Cut 'reckless'.

His wife seems to live only through him. By now he is her only contact with the world. She punishes him for that. He acquiesces. Hating her, he can't deal the death blow. She is so fragile. This remarkable psychological thriller puts one man with his back to the wall of a tremendous dilemma that will ultimately . . .

Way over a hundred.

Cut 'remarkable'.

And 'tremendous'.

And 'ultimately'.

'Ultimately' what?

The gong sounded. The gong. They'll be coming out. My eye rushed over the page, and the next, and the next. There must have been a dozen completely different versions.

Adventurous crime publisher seeks to save his marriage by showing his wife how much he cares about their daughter who is dangerously besotted with a middle-aged manic depressive. Meantime his beloved mistress is concerned that the child she is carrying

There were footsteps. I jumped out of the bed and moved the curtain. The blokes were streaming out of the Metta Hall. Ten minutes' break before the evening video discourse. People would take a pee, stretch legs, grab a glass of water. Down the corridor, the outside door banged. Men kicking off their shoes, padding along the wooden floor to their rooms.

Beth paralysed. Too late to make it to the kitchen. Could I slip off in the other direction, towards the Dormitory A loos, hide in a cubicle? Go now!

I didn't move.

Breathe. Control your breathing. Control this excitement. Focus on the physical turbulence and the mental will subside, Dasgupta says.

I breathed. I felt the breath on my lips, my chest rose and fell.

Footsteps along the corridor. Hurrying. Doors opened and closed. There are no locks at the Dasgupta. Someone sat on a bed in the next room, sighed. Someone was opening a window.

Men all around.

They only have a few minutes between sessions. Most will have gone for a cup of tea in the dining hall. Or for a stroll round the field.

I sat on the bed, picked up his pen from the floor. He uses a fountain pen.

'You love your pain too much.'

The nib scratched.

Footsteps slowed at the door, then started off again. Others coming back from the bathroom end. Someone dropped something.

I sat waiting.

GH.

Gary, Graham, Greg, Gerald. Gerald is horrible.

Then I was overwhelmed by the question, what am I doing here? Why why why? Trapped here, in a man's room, in a community that does everything to keep men and women apart. I'd known perfectly well that when the gong rang my diarist could come back.

He's not *your* diarist.

Why didn't I leave earlier? Why do I always end up asking questions about the way I behave? Misbehave. You came to the Dasgupta when you were desperate. You had hit bottom. Remember how bad it was. You couldn't face anyone, you couldn't look at people, let alone yourself. You were sick sick sick. Dasgupta saved you. He did. He showed you a way. Alive or dead, his talks are fantastic, fantastically useful. Except I'm not quite there yet. I'm walking the Dhamma path. Trying to. Everybody at the Dasgupta has an old story. Why come otherwise? We're here to dump our stories, not to write them down, not to read people's diaries. It's because I miss my suffering that I'm reading about his. Which is stupid stupid stupid. Is that why people read books? They want to suffer. Jonathan loved sad movies. All the Swedish and French videos he made me watch. Tarsky, Tartosky? I hated it.

'Why do you want me to share your gloomy view of the world, Jonnie?'

'It's safer, Beth. It's safer.'

'I don't want to be safe, Jonnie, thanks very much.'

'I know, Beth. That's why I love you.'

'No, you don't.'

'I do, Beth.'

'If you loved me you'd fight for me. You'd be jealous of Carl.'

'I love you, Beth.'

'Not enough.'

I was on the edge. I'm back there. I'm sliding back. Resist. Breathe. The footsteps were gone now. He's not coming. I can wait it out. Someone was hurrying at the end of the corridor. I felt very *there,* in the room, on his bed. Nowhere to hide. Vulnerable. Wired. And really far away too. Calm. Dead. Really *not* there. Like, if he came, who cared? Every time I feel something I feel the opposite. Maybe that's what makes it real.

I looked down at the diary on my knees. Its slanted handwriting. Almost horizontal. In a hurry to eat up the page. He was attacking the page. What a stupid idea that you could get a story out of your mind by writing it down. Instead of a hundred words he'd written a thousand. He'd write thousands more with the stupid excuse of trying to forget it. Really, he wants to fill every white page with himself and his shit. I've painted you red, Beth, because that's your colour. You stain the whole world red.

And I was proud!

Stop writing, Mr Wordy Diarist. Stop writing about yourself. Stop tempting me to read you, to write like you and think like you. If you were really suffering you'd prefer these pages to stay white. You'd prefer to be looking at white . . .

The door banged open and he came in.

He was a big man, taller than I'd imagined. I'm not good at age. Early fifties? Must be. Tall but a bit stooped and he hasn't shaved since he arrived I don't think. His face was dirty with beard.

Actually, he was pulling off his sweater as he came in. He was in a hurry. He must have decided at the last minute he needed something warmer for the evening session. The gong for evening discourse had already rung. The last footsteps were gone. He came in pulling up the sweater over his face. Something green. His shirt lifted with it. His stomach was pale and solid and hairy. Then as the sweater came over his head he saw me.

Beth on the bed.

I put a finger over my lips. He was astonished. If he'd seen me before it would have been across the hall on the female side in a sea of other faces. Female faces. Now he was really alert, really fired up. You could see. His face is thin with a beaky nose, high cheeks. Nothing like Jonathan. His eyes looked pleased, curious. He opened his mouth, saw me shake my head, my finger to my lips, and closed it again.

I stood up, still holding the diary, and we were staring at each other. He had his hands in the sleeves of his pullover where he'd pulled it over his head, handcuffed. His skin was pale under the dirty beard, a red beard. He looked tired. But his mouth seemed ironic and kind.

I liked him. More than the voice in the diary. Not speaking, we just looked.

I've got big eyes, big tits, big teeth, a ton of frizzy hair. There was a weird knowing in the way we looked at each other. He knew at once I had been reading his diary. I knew about his shit,

100

that he was a married guy who'd maybe got a married girl pregnant and had a daughter who was screwing up big-time. But as we looked—it must have lasted thirty seconds at least—I realized that the most shaming thing was that he wrote about himself in *that way*, all vanity and drama. And what was shaming for me was that I was reading that stuff. I kept on reading it. I was a Dasgupta server supposed to be setting an example. We should both be ashamed of ourselves. Instead, as the seconds passed—and I kept my finger over my lips, still shaking my head very slightly to stop him talking—instead, I could see he was pleased he had run into me. He wasn't upset. He was glad of anything that took him out of himself. He knew I was embarrassed and his expression was telling me he wouldn't cause trouble. His thick eyebrows gave him a severe look, headmasterish, but the way he lifted them, one higher than the other, just meant, OK, sweetheart, so what do we do next? What's your plan?

Dasgupta rooms are not generous with space. This single was maybe nine feet long by six wide. Door on one narrow wall, window opposite, one long wall empty, the other with wardrobe and bed. Nothing else. I would have to push past him.

We were looking into each other's eyes. Not speaking had drawn us close. I took a step and handed him his diary. He had to free a hand from his pullover to take it. He could see I'd written something there. My handwriting was big and square. A puzzled look crossed his face, but he saw I wanted to get out and stepped back against the wardrobe.

I squeezed by. His smell was strong. The room changed colour. I opened the door. There was no one in the corridor now. Why did I look back? He had half opened his mouth. Something had occurred to him and he needed to say it. I put my finger to

101

my lips again. No! Then he raised a hand in an offer to shake. Now that he had the window behind him and was free of his pullover, I got a different impression of him. He was an animal, but on a chain. He was pretending to be tame in the hope he'd be released. And though he hadn't spoken I knew he was lying. I knew he was dangerous. His hand reached out and stayed there. I shook my head and hurried down the corridor and back to the kitchen for evening clean-up.

Krsa Gautami

'Sttart-tagain.'

Those words drove me nuts the first days. The hum of the recording, then his voice: 'Sttart-tagain. Sttart-tagain.'

The one-thirty session is the hardest. I've had too much lunch. The day is mild. The field is full of grassy smells. The leaves are alive in the breeze. The trees are all very alive, very there. 'I'm in trouble,' I said, after the servers' evening *metta*, day four, *vipassana* day. 'I'm in such big trouble.'

As soon as I'd spoken, I looked away. I didn't want to catch Mrs Harper's eye. The students were gone and the light was dimmed. I turned my head and looked behind at the muddled rows of dark blue cushions, the grey blankets and the white and the empty hall, and suddenly I saw they were the sea. They really were the rumpled waters of the sea. I was on the beach again.

'My friends, let me give you another example of the Buddha's wisdom and compassion. One day, in the town of Kapilavastu,

Krsa Gautami, the wife of a very rich man, was plunged into deep grief by the loss of her baby son.'

Take a deep breath, Beth.

At one twenty-five after a stupidly heavy lunch I go to my place and sort out my cushion. Two foam slabs. Kristin and Marcia must be in the kitchen. There is space around me. I tuck in my ankles, I let my back sink and settle. The thigh muscles stretch. I can feel their heat expanding. My knees press into the mat, they're one with the mat. Today I'm going to sit still, very very still. My still body will still my mind. I'm going to be vigilant. So vigilant. I won't be distracted. I will not think of Krsa Gautami.

Really Dasgupta should say Stop again not Start again. Sttop-pagain, my friends. Return to the still point, to the breath on the lip, where everything is suspended, everything is transparent, where there is no conflict. To start again I think would be to leave here, to leave the Dasgupta Institute, to go off with GH, for example, my diarist. Yes. Or with any man. I know if I went back to his room, if I let him find me there again, on his bed, if I said to him, Graham, or Garry, or Gordon, whatever, let's get out of here, let's run away together, he would say yes. I know he would. I saw it in his eyes, greedy men's eyes. He would say yes yes *YES!* He's better-looking than I thought, thinner, fitter, more *real* than the words in his diary. A real man. Let's get out of here, Graham. Come on. This place is death. We won't achieve anything at the Dasgupta. In the dead of night I smuggle him through the dining hall to the locker room. He grabs his mobile and we walk out on to the moonlit lane, striding towards freedom, towards a fresh start. Of course after we've been walking a while he puts his arm round my shoulders and we begin to talk and talk and talk. In a hotel somewhere we talk ourselves deep into each other's minds, deep under each other's skin. We talk ourselves between the sheets. We make love. He's better-looking than Jonathan, lean and pale, sad and funny. I'm sure he can be very funny. I know it. He's excited that I'm so young. He's adoring. *All the spotlights turned up on your shining face.* Jonathan adored me. He did. He wouldn't fight for me, but he did adore me. Your eyes, Beth, he said. He adored my eyes. I don't think it made him suffer. We hug ourselves into one. His pleasure sinks into mine. *Even learning how to take is a way of giving, in love.* You're with a man again, Beth, you're laughing and smoking at a hotel window. 'Start-tagain.' His hands are on my hips. Sighing, smiling.

'I'm in such deep trouble,' I said.

We were kneeling after the servers' *metta.* Mr Harper and Mi Nu on their raised platforms at the front, the male servers to one side, the female to the other, on our knees in a line in the dim light of the hall after the students had gone to their beds to mull over the story of Krsa Gautami and the three sesame seeds, to reflect on the Buddha's wisdom, to remember their first day of *vipassana.* The field of *paññā.* The world of sensation and suffering.

Harper smiles. He says, 'Well, *vipassana* day is always tough. I thought it went quite well.'

The servers listened.

'Hard to know what to do when someone starts crying like that,' he added.

As Harper talks to us, he scans our faces, smiling in a restrained sort of way.

'In the end, I thought it best to ask her to leave the hall.'

Mi Nu nodded.

105

One of the male course managers said: 'I thought it was rather wonderful how people's faces were glowing afterwards. Really glowing.'

Harper nodded.

Tony the professor said: 'I thought they looked shellshocked.'

'That too.' Harper smiled again. 'That too.' He sighed. 'But how did it go in the kitchen today?'

He asks the same question every evening. His voice is gentle, and distant.

'Hectic,' Paul said. 'The problem is that no one's familiar with the appliances. And there aren't enough of us.'

'Beth is,' Meredith said.

'Oh, I'm sure we can manage.' Ines beamed. 'Each day gets a bit easier.'

'Now you have Marcia as well,' Mrs Harper said.

Rob said he thought it was a question of being better organized, dividing up the tasks better.

I looked across to the men and found Ralph gazing at me from his soft, doggy eyes. Ralph's been sniffing around me all day. He knows something's up.

'Well, don't let it stress you,' Harper said cheerfully. 'The fig cake was wonderful, by the way.'

'Thank you.' Ines was still beaming.

'And the dripping roof?' Livia asked. Two students had wanted to be moved away from the puddle, she said, and others were grumbling about the distraction. Wasn't there any way of fixing it?

One of the maintenance servers explained that since the roof was curved, the water didn't fall to the floor inside at the point where it actually came in from outside. They couldn't locate the leak.

'No harm done.' Harper smiled. 'It's only a drip. No one's getting wet. A good test for the students' equanimity.' He sighed. 'Let's call it a day and get to bed.'

He settled himself for the final few minutes' meditation. He had closed his eyes.

'I'm in trouble,' I said then. My voice squeaked in the silence. I hadn't planned to speak. It came out. People turned. 'I'm sorry, folks. I know I shouldn't.' I was shaking my head. Then I said I couldn't serve the following day. 'I can't. I'm sorry. I'm in such deep trouble.'

The words just came. I was going to cry. You're not supposed to cry in the Metta Hall. There must be no passions here. Only compassion. Compassionate love. Sympathetic joy. Mrs Harper caught my eye. I turned and looked across the empty hall at the grey blankets and the white surf.

'What's the problem, Elisabeth?' Mrs Harper asked. 'Is it the kitchen?'

The tears were rolling.

'Drama queen,' Zoë would say. 'Queen Beth.'

'I can't serve, I'm sorry, everybody. I need to sit. I need to be still.'

'That's going to be difficult,' Paul began, 'since Elisabeth really is the only one . . .'

I turned to Mi Nu. Mi Nu could help. She had wrapped her shawl round her hair. Her hands lay joined in her lap. Her head was bowed. Her eyes were closed.

For the evening discourse the meditators hurry to get a place by the wall. It is hard to sit still when you're not meditating. It is hard to keep your back straight. There's a rush for the side wall, the back wall. I remember when I first saw this, at the beginning of my time here, I was struck by the power of what we do when we meditate. Focused on your breathing, behind closed eyes, you can sit cross-legged, straight-backed without fidgeting. You can slip outside time. But listening to Dasgupta bang on about the Triple Gem, the Four Noble Truths, the Eightfold Path, the Ten Perfections, you itch and twist and turn and scratch. You can't help it. That fourth evening, *vipassana* day, I went to hear the discourse, even though I knew that day four meant Krsa Gautami.

Of course, the walls aren't long enough for all one hundred and forty students to find a space. People rush to stake their claim, the same way they rush for bananas at breakfast. They throw their cushions against the wall, knowing that they are taking a place from someone else, maybe someone who needs it more than they do. Along the back wall a couple of yards have to be kept free between the women and the men. You can't have a man and woman shoulder to shoulder, resting their backs against the wall while they watch Dasgupta on video. Something might stir. Something impure.

The course manager goes over to whisper in someone's ear. A petite, white-haired woman brings her cushion back to her mat and sits with her arms clasped round her knees. The videos go on an hour and more. She rocks slowly forward and back. It is disrespectful to lie down or to prop yourself on an elbow. The course managers cruise around, they crouch beside the culprits and whisper. It is also disrespectful to stretch your legs in the direction of the teacher, in the direction of Mr Harper and Mi Nu Wai. The course managers seem to like their jobs. The students who haven't found a place by the wall sit on their mats crossing and uncrossing their legs. They grab their ankles. They organize and reorganize their cushions.

I had been assigned to clean-up. I hadn't meant to come. Evening discourse is not obligatory for servers. *Vipassana* day means nothing to us. Walking between the rows of cushions, I was looking for *him*. I know where he sits now. Middle of the row towards the back. No doubt he was looking for me. Soon I would feel the pressure of his eyes and he of mine. My weak eyes. There. I can just make him out, in the blur and shuffle. All day his eyes have been asking me why I was in his room, what exactly I read in his diary. And I have a hundred questions to ask. What is Susie giving up that is so important? Why doesn't he leave his wife, if he hates her so much? So everything has changed. There is a disturbance in the Metta Hall. It isn't a refuge any more.

'It's pretty odd you staying so long at the Dasgupta,' Rob said, during clean-up. He was sweeping the kitchen. I was wiping the work surfaces. I hadn't talked to Rob before. He's burly, jowly, with small, bright, protruding eyes. In his thirties. No chin. We were working silently. Perhaps he was observing an attitude of segregation. Then he came and started sweeping round my feet, so I asked him what he did, 'in the real world. For a living?'

He stopped sweeping. 'Clown,' he said. He laughed. 'No, really.' He clowned for sick children in hospitals. He put on red noses and giant shoes, one green one yellow. 'Cancer wards mainly,' he said, 'and leukaemia.'

'God, how sad!'

'Not as sad as you'd think. They're always glad you've come. They always have a giggle.'

'But I mean . . .' I wished now I had kept the Noble Silence. 'It's very brave of you.'

'Not at all.' His smile seemed to be challenging me. There's a quiet meatiness about him, completely different from Paul or Vikram. 'Kids find it easier than adults,' he said. 'They're more in tune with life, with their bodies.'

'Find what easier?'

He hesitated. 'Dying, I suppose.'

I bent down and started to drag out the saucepans and colanders from one of the lower shelves. There was quite a clatter. He leaned on his broom.

'So what do *you* do, Beth?'

It was filthy at the back behind the pans. But on even days we go to meet aversions. On odd days we bless the things we like, bless them, not crave them, bless them and let them go. On even days we embrace the things that bother us, we accept them completely, even if we can't bless them. I've always hated everything dirty and sticky and old, places where old shit has stuck. Places that smell.

'You must do something,' he said.

'I clean shelves, *n'est-ce pas?*'

'I said, "What do you do?" not "What are you doing now?"'

When I went on wiping, he told me, 'Actually, I don't think that shelf's part of the regular clean-up. We never use those things.'

He went back to his sweeping, between the sinks and the bratt pan. There were peelings, rice grains. Rob is conscientious, but without the zeal Ines has. He's a sprout, I thought. Rob's a stout Brussels sprout.

He stopped again and said: 'You know, it's odd your being so long at the Dasgupta, Beth.'

I said nothing. My damp cloth went to meet the filth.

'You've been here quite a while, haven't you?'

I don't answer this question.

'But you're not really a Dasgupta person. You know what I mean? Like Livia. Or Paul.'

He swept the mess into a pile.

'You don't have that look on your face.'

Now he began with the hand brush and dustpan.

'Ever thought of clowning?' he asked. 'I reckon you'd be good. It was pretty funny how you came out with the chicken-sandwich line.'

I stood up and asked if he'd mind finishing clean-up on his own so I could hear the discourse this evening. I particularly liked the day-four discourse, I told him. There was the story of Krsa Gautami.

'Maybe I'm more of a Dasgupta person than you think,' I said.

I took off my apron, hurried through the female dining hall and stopped at the loos to pee. It was pure nervousness. Nothing came. When I pushed into the hall, Harper was dimming the lights. But it didn't stop me seeing my diarist. GH hadn't found a space against the wall. He was cross-legged, on his mat. His head was turned towards the female side, looking for me.

'Men will always look at you, Beth. Always.'

'But what use is it, Jonnie, if the only person I want isn't willing to fight for me? What use is it?'

Look away. Fix your eyes on Mi Nu.

The servers never sit against the wall. We mustn't. We sit still in our regular places as if the long, dull discourse were a normal meditation session. Straight-backed as tombstones. A little cemetery of servers in three neat rows. Dead still. Dead pure. In this way we give the new students an example. Of what? Focus, concentration, other-worldliness? Or are we showing off? Was the Buddha showing off when he sat for days under a tree? Watch how still I can sit, how long I can sit. It's hard to stop pride creeping in. Kristin and Marcia were in their places. I stepped over my cushion and sat between them.

With the lights dimmed the video is bright. Dasgupta glows in a white suit on a plush red chair, pretty well a throne. It must have been hot when they recorded day four. Sweat trickles down his chubby cheeks. His face glistens. He pats himself with a white handkerchief. I settled myself and closed my eyes. 'Day four is over,' the voice began. He left a pause. Dasgupta loves pauses. 'You have six more days to work.' Even without looking I knew he was smiling and nodding, as he scanned the crowd.

He talked about the students' first *vipassana* experience. 'For the first three days you took refuge in the breath crossing your lips—*anapana* meditation. You were safe there, safe from your frenetic monkey minds, which you tethered to your breathing, safe from your bodies, which you kept in the background. But in *vipassana* meditation we go out to explore the full gamut of physical sensations. This is the field of *paññā,* the field of understanding, right understanding. This is the way to liberation. Now we use the concentration we have built up in *anapana* to go out and find sensation on every inch of the body, to meet experience, real physical experience, and to know it as it is. *As it is.* Not as we would wish it to be. *As it is.*

'This is a tremendous adventure, my friends. Sometimes pleasant, of course. Sometimes we can find very pleasant, subtle, flowing sensations in our hands, our foreheads, our chests. Then immediately we grow attached to them. We don't want to move on. Why should I move on, Mr Dasgupta, when I am feeling such pleasant sensations in my hands, like electricity, like warm water flowing over me? This is what I came to meditation for, after all, pleasant sensations. Very nice. Thank you so much, Mr Dasgupta, for your wonderful technique. It is making me so happy. No, no, nothing doing, my friends. That way you will only generate new *sankharas* of craving. Deep, deep *sankharas* that will multiply your misery. However pleasant a sensation is we must move on.

'And sometimes the sensations are painful. Oh dear. This is not so good. We find gross, intensified, solidified sensations in our legs, our shoulders, our backs, our ankles. We hurry away from them, we don't want to know them at all. What do you want me to explore these sensations for, Mr Dasgupta? Oh, they are terrible. They are painful, very painful sensations. You say you want me to experience these? What are you? A torturer? A sadist?

'And once again, my friend, you are multiplying your misery, you are laying down deep deep *sankharas*, this time of aversion. *Sankharas* of aversion. Yes. When we find unpleasant sensations we must show them the same indifference, the same equanimity we show to pleasant sensations. We must . . .'

I wondered then if maybe the diarist wasn't right and Dasgupta had been dead for years. How would I know? Now his voice is out there. Some podcast on a forgotten site. Or words that repeat in your head, years after they were spoken. You're soaking, Betsy M, soaking! Our minds are not strong enough to have the right relation to certain things. Children find it easier. It was unfair of Rob to say that. So offhand. So unfair. I'm not in tune with life. Otherwise I would have found it easy. I could have gone to meet it. With Carl's guitar, OK, I was in tune there. Or with Zoë, singing harmony. But not with life. Music isn't life, Dad said. About a million times. Music isn't life, Beth. Get serious. Marry Carl. Take your place in the firm. The family firm. I could explain it all to GH if I wanted. He would ask why I was in his room and I would explain all my problems. He will stroke me and calm me and make love to me. Like men do. I'll make fun of his pompous diary. I'll tell him how old he looks, with those wrinkles and the small stains on his hands. That drove Jonathan mad. He's looking at me now. I'm sure of it. His eyes are on me. He's marvelling how straight I can keep my back while he wriggles and struggles with his cushions.

Dasgupta had started his bit on attachment, on craving. We're getting close now. 'This is what we must learn, my friends, from our reaction to these pleasant and unpleasant sensations: that even wholesome things become dangerous attachments. Even the most natural relationships. And then, how strong that attachment is, how difficult to overcome. Let me give you an example. One day, in the town of Kapilavastu, Krsa Gautami, the wife of a very rich man, was plunged into grief when her child died. Her only son. You see, my friends, she could not accept that her baby was dead. She would not give up her baby boy for burial. "He isn't dead!" she screamed. "He isn't, he isn't!" She could not accept things *as they are*. "He can't be dead." No, no, no. Krsa Gautami was so attached to the future that she had projected for herself and her son that she could not accept reality.'

I came to try this story out on myself, I realized. To see where I am up to. I came to take this cut, and watch the blood.

'"Help my child," Krsa Gautami cried to the doctors. "You must help my child. I will give you anything, anything you ask.

My husband is a rich man." She ran around Kapilavastu pestering all the physicians. "Oh, crazy woman," the wise men shook their heads, "your son is dead. Can't you see? Are you a mad woman? He has been dead for two days now. You must give up his body for burial. It will begin to smell."

'Now, no doubt because of some merits accumulated in the past, some good action that this poor woman had accomplished, in another life perhaps, somebody told her to take her child to the Buddha. He could help her. Yes, Krsa Gautami had the great good fortune to go and meet Siddhartha himself.'

Dasgupta paused. I don't need to open my eyes to see him nodding and smiling, nodding and smiling.

'"Krsa Gautami," the Buddha told her after he had listened to her story, "you must hurry into town, knock on any door and ask for three sesame seeds. Just three small sesame seeds. Then bring them back to me."

'Oh, this is wonderful, Krsa Gautami thought. This is wonderful. The Buddha is going to use the sesame seeds to work a magic spell and save my child.

'"But . . ." the Buddha said.

'"Yes?" Krsa Gautami asked.

'"The seeds must come from a household where nobody has ever died. Before you accept the seeds you must ask if anyone has ever died in that house."

'"Yes. All right, all right." Krsa Gautami was in a hurry. She must get those seeds quickly so the Buddha could bring her little boy back to life.'

Dasgupta is brilliant at these stories. It's true what GH says, that he loves the sound of his own voice, but maybe that's why he's so good. And then GH certainly likes the sound of himself written down in his diary. I wonder if it was a relief when Dasgupta recorded these talks and could finally stop repeating them for every retreat. Or maybe he misses his own performances. Assuming he's still alive. It's so much fun to perform, really to be there with people watching you, falling under your spell, yelling for more. You shake your tits. You pout your lips. You dance dirty with Zoë, or beside Carl. Poor Carl. Couldn't dance to save his life. Now all I have is an old guy's eyes on my back. Can't he see I'm not relaxed at all? I'm rigid. I'm in trouble. Rigid with envy.

Krsa Gautami is knocking on doors asking for her sesame seeds. Dasgupta is great at doing the voices.

'"Of course, my dear, if the most Perfect One told you to ask for them, here you are. Take three *pounds* of sesame seeds, never mind three. What's that? Has anyone died here? Oh, but why do you want to remind us of our grief? My husband died in the spring. Our mother was carried off by a sudden fever. Many of our relatives passed away in the epidemic."'

I envy this woman in the story who is about to understand, about to be liberated. If she had gone to Jesus he would have resurrected her boy and she would have been back to square one, happy again, waiting to be unhappy, waiting for the next accident, the next illness.

Instead, she is about to understand.

'Then at last Krsa Gautami realized that there was no household in which no one had died. Death is universal. This was the Buddha's lesson. And she accepted it.'

Simple. Her grief was *so* simple. She lost a child. OK. But she still has her rich husband. Still has *herself*. She hasn't betrayed anyone, or been betrayed. She wasn't *responsible* for her child's death. Now she can give him a proper funeral. An expensive funeral. Fantastic. Now she can go back to Siddhartha and he will teach her Dhamma, he will show her the Eightfold Path to Enlightenment. Where's the problem?

I'M IN INTENSIVE CARE.

WITH YOUR MOBILE, BETH?

DON'T YOU BELIEVE ME, JONNIE?

TEXT ME THE NAME OF THE HOSPITAL AND I'LL CALL.

YOU DON'T BELIEVE ME. YOU WON'T COME.

BETH, I'M SUPPOSED TO BE DOING A MURAL HERE. I CAN'T FLY BACK AT THE DROP OF A HAT.

I NEARLY DROWNED. I'M NOT OUT OF DANGER. I'VE GOT THE MOST VIOLENT HEADACHE.

BUT YOU'RE TEXTING EVERY TEN MINUTES.

THEY WILL HAVE TO PUT ME IN A PHARMACOLOGICAL COMA. NURSE SAYS I SHOULD INFORM MY LOVED ONES.

CHRIST, BETH. ISN'T CARL THERE? AND YOUR PARENTS? IF THEY ARE, THEY WON'T WANT TO SEE ME. THEY WON'T UNDERSTAND.

I HATE CARL. I HATE MY PARENTS.

No reply. HOURS.

JONATHAN, THEY'RE GOING TO PUT ME UNDER NOW. I'M GIVING THE NURSE MY PHONE. SO SHE CAN TEXT YOU. IN CASE THINGS GO WRONG.

No reply.
No reply.
No reply.

IF YOU DON'T BELIEVE ME, MR ARTIST PLAYBOY, READ SOMETHING ABOUT DROWNING ACCIDENTS. MY BRAIN IS SWELLING! CONTROLLED COMA IS THE ONLY WAY.

No reply.

117

I WAS UNCONSCIOUS FOR TEN MINURES. IN THE SEA. IT WAS WILD. THE PERSON WITH ME DIED. HE'S DEAD! FOR CHRIST'S SAKE!

BETH, I LOVE YOU.

BUT YOU WON'T COME. WHAT KIND OF LOVE IS THAT?

GIVE ME THE NAME OF THE HOSPITAL, BETH.

SAY YOU'LL COME BEFORE I DIE. I WANT TO KISS YOU.

I NEED TO KNOW WHERE I'M SUPPOSED TO BE COMING, DON'T I?

Compassion is not some wishy-washy sentiment, Dasgupta is saying. It requires skill and intuition to understand what the person before you needs and how they can be approached. 'The Buddha always adapted his words to the person who was appealing to him.'

How does that square with using the same video talk for years?

Your diarist is not Jonathan. My back is aching. Go to meet the pain. You are not in love with him. My thumbs are tense with texting. I haven't touched a phone in months. My messages and his, back and forth, over and over, from the hospital bed, from the meditation cushion. Old shit, hidden behind pots and pans on a bottom shelf.

YOU'RE WITH YOUR WIFE, AREN'T YOU? WHY DON'T YOU JUST TELL ME?

I'M NOT WITH MY WIFE, BETH, NO.

Dasgupta is not my father. Ralph is not Carl. I owe him nothing nothing nothing. Don't drink so much, Beth. Don't smoke so much. You'll kill yourself. The surf is wild. I went into the sea to wash it all away. To *purify* myself. Mi Nu will have the skill that is real compassion. I open my eyes and watch her. When things get chaotic inside, open your eyes, Beth. Watch Mi

Nu. Beneath the bright screen she is pale and erect like cool wax. She is perfect.

An hour later, after the discourse was over, after the servers' *metta* was over, I said, I'm in trouble. I'm in such deep trouble. I can't serve. I need help need help need help.

Mi Nu sat on the dais with her head bowed, eyes closed. Cool, pale, erect. Like a candle burning with silence.

Work Diligently

Sttartt-tagain. Eight o'clock. And again. Two thirty. And again. Six o'clock. The guided sessions. The hours of Strong Determination. Day four. Day five. Day six. Dasgupta's disembodied voice invites us to explore our bodies. 'From the top of the head to the tips of the toes and from the tips of the toes to the top of the head. Indifferent to pleasure. Indifferent to pain. Work diligently, diligently. You are bound to succeed. *Bound* to succeed.'

I eat in silence, staring at the wall. I should skip a meal or two. My body screams for food. I should ignore it. Indifferent to appetite, indifferent to hunger. I cover up with baggy T-shirts. Tracksuit pants. I don't want to see myself. The weather has been mild and between sessions people walk round the field beyond the Metta Hall. Round and round, without speaking, without looking each other in the eye. If it's dry enough to lie down, I lie down. I miss the kitchen. I miss washing the rice and the beans. I miss peeling the potatoes, chopping the carrots. I miss spraying the crap from the dishes. I don't miss doggy Ralph. I don't miss Meredith, or Paul, or Rob, or Ines. I don't miss the chatter. The chatter was dragging me back to old ways. You came to the Dasgupta to forget; you thought you had forgotten. You thought you were cured. Then suddenly you were digging it all up again. Perhaps you needed to check what it was you'd forgotten. You weren't ready. You just wanted to sniff at it, but what you dug up crashed over you like a wave. You were sucked down and slammed on the sand and stones. Carl's voice calling, 'Beth Beth Beth!' Remember the tiniest bit of what you have to forget and at once you're hearing your name. Someone's calling your name. Loud. 'Beth! *BETH!*' He knows he's lost me. But he'd lost me long before. The French boys too, calling across the dunes. 'Beth! Come swimming!' The fly sheet of the tent flapping in the wind. The guy ropes humming. Tell me it didn't happen. Please, tell me it didn't happen.

The mind isn't strong enough.

I'm back to the first days again, that's the truth, I'm back to my very first days at the Dasgupta Institute. Except this time I know the technique. Thank God. I know where to find the breath on my lips. I know how to sit still, how to still myself, how to kill a thought quick. The tide is strong and the surf high, but my cushion is a rock. I can sit above it in stillness. My time at the Dasgupta hasn't been wasted. 'Work diligently, diligently. You are *bound* to succeed.' Oh, I believe so. I really do. I must have faith. Dasgupta's right. Diligently, I observe my breathing; diligently, I observe my body. Inch by inch, pore by pore. You are *bound* to succeed. You must. My scalp, my forehead, my temples, my ears, my nose, my lips, my teeth, my tongue, my cheeks, my jaw, my neck, my shoulders, my arms, my hands, my hands.

Move on, Beth. Don't get stuck with pleasure. Don't get stuck with pain. I understand now why Mi Nu wouldn't speak to me. We must not express our passions in the Metta Hall. We mustn't play the drama queen. Like the girl sobbing on *vipassana* day. Who does she think she is? To sob in the Metta Hall. We mustn't disturb others with our suffering, our specialness, our *angst*. There is no such thing as specialness. Follow my example, Mi Nu was saying. Watch me. I burn in silence. I don't need to speak to teach you. Head bowed. Darkness and silence. Mi Nu is a pale candle burning with darkness. These strange words, never spoken, help me more than Dasgupta's voice. Burning with silence and darkness. Burning nothingness. 'Move your attention through your whole body,' he says. 'If you are experiencing pleasant, fluid, subtle sensations, don't grow attached to them. Make an objective note, pleasant subtle sensations, and move on. If you find gross, intensified, solidified sensations, stay a while and observe them. Do not judge them. Do not develop even the slightest trace of aversion. These are the deep and painful *sankharas* of the past that are emerging. When they are gone, you will be purified, purified, purified.'

I follow his instructions. My attention descends the stairs from neck to lungs, from lungs to stomach, from stomach to hips, from hips to thighs. Then it slips. I've lost it. I'm off, moving through the pitch dark. Not walking, floating, blown along. No effort of mine, no decision of mine. Litter in the breeze. Now I'm brushing against a wall, scratching my face on twigs and thorns. Where am I? I'm trapped against a rock. I'm caught. The surface is rough, hard. Am I under water? Am I still breathing? It doesn't seem so. I'm not afraid. Fascinated, but not afraid. Beyond fear. Very calm. Very vigilant. Surrender, Beth, let yourself go, let yourself go into the darkness. Let it happen to you *now*, the thing that should have happened then. Whatever it is, let it happen. Oh, I understand why Mi Nu didn't speak to me. Come and talk when your question is ready, she was saying. You are still too confused to know what to ask. You are too upset. Meantime you must wash away your impurities. Wash yourself with darkness, scrub yourself with silence. A stream of darkness, a pumice of silence.

In the morning I arrive in the Metta Hall just after four. In the evening I leave at nine thirty. I am here before him, before anyone. At every session. At every session I leave after him. Four days and he will be gone. Four days three days two days one day. Blessing, acceptance, blessing, acceptance. GH will be gone. Then I can really start again, at the Dasgupta Institute. Start to bury it all again. Deeper this time. Like nuclear waste. Much deeper. And for ever. For eternity.

I rise as the morning gong clangs. No, *before*. Before the others are awake. I walk round the field in the pitch dark, stumbling on molehills, catching my sleeve on thorns. I would like to start living again but every time I try I am back in the surf. I'm a breathless thing tossed in surf. Not walking, or running, but tossed by the sea. Flotsam. I come early so as not to see him. I don't want to believe all this has happened to me. Life has happened. I stay late until everyone is gone. I don't need to open my eyes to know that. I can feel my aloneness. My diarist is not Jonathan, but he reminds me of Jonathan, he reminds me of who I was with Jonathan. Reading his diary I became Beth again. Smelling his clothes I felt intensely Beth. Beth must surrender. Beth must die. Ralph's doggy eyes are not Carl's, but they look at me the same way. The way boys always looked at

Beth. On stage, after the performance. I'll destroy Ralph like I destroyed Carl. Being Beth is killing and being killed, killing and being killed. When your question is ready, Mi Nu is saying, then I will talk to you. When you have cleansed your impurities in darkness, when you have burned away your *sankharas* in silence. But they won't wash, Mi Nu. They won't burn. I think the darkness fuels them, I think it feeds them, silence feeds the flame. My thighs are killing me. I've lost all my equanimity. I'm done. I'm finished. My back is killing me. My head is bursting, bursting, bursting.

At five past four I'm on my cushion. I am out of the room before the others are out of bed. I cross the wet grass in the starlight. As I walk between dormitory and hall, I try to be here, oh, really to be here, in the grounds of the Dasgupta Institute, to breathe the damp beauty of this place, to watch the rabbits hop off into the bushes. I love rabbits. I love their nibbliness, their twitchiness. I surrender to the rabbits, willingly, totally. I try to be here now, on the wet grass under the starlight before the dawn. Not on the beach, not in the surf. But I must hurry to reach my cushion before he comes. GH mustn't see my face, my body. I mustn't see him. GH isn't Jonathan, but if I went to his room and said, Hey, Garry, Hey, Graham, let's get the fuck out of here, he would say yes at once. What red-blooded man wouldn't? Two flaming Ferraris. He would grab his stuff at once. He would grab *me*. At once we would be a couple, he would adore me, then go back to his wife and daughter and pregnant girlfriend married to someone else. He wouldn't fight for me. I envy his girlfriend. I envy any woman who is with child. With child. There's one in the row behind me, a woman in her fourth or fifth month. I envy her, I envy the curve of her belly, I envy her complacency, why are pregnant women so complacent, so piously pleased with themselves, so invulnerable? A tall woman, overweight, plain, pregnant, and so pleased with the curve of her belly. And I envy a woman who can bury her dead child, yes, and go back to her rich husband. If only I'd had a child to bury. If only I was carrying a child, here at the Dasgupta. Like the woman behind me. Imagine. Swelling and filling out every day at the Dasgupta Institute. How everyone would envy me. Whose child? Jonathan's, Carl's? Who cares? How wonderful that would be. Giving birth at the Dasgupta. In the Metta Hall. Mrs Harper yanks the baby from between my legs, Mi Nu is watching over me, waiting until my question is ready, waiting for my surrender. When your question is ready, Elisabeth, then I will speak to you. I will explain everything. But my only question is, Why am I never ready, Mi Nu, why can I never think of my question? Why am I not carrying a child?

I'm first in the Metta Hall this morning. I love to be first. The whole hall is mine. The blankets and cushions stretch away in rows. The blankets are curled round the cushions where people dropped them from their backs. A wave of blanket curling behind every rocky cushion. I wade through them. 'Beth! It's too dark!' The silence makes Carl's voice louder. When I hear the sea I hear Carl's voice, I hear my name. 'Beth!' And the voices of the French boys calling, 'Come and swim with us, Beth. Come and swim naked.' They want to see my tits and pussy. OK! I want to see that big French cock. 'Beth, you're drunk. You've smoked too much. It's too late to swim. It's too wild tonight.'

WHAT AM I DOING ON HOLIDAY WITH SOMEONE I DON'T LOVE? WHY AREN'T I WITH YOU, JONATHAN?

Text after text.

YOU CAN ALWAYS GO HOME, BETH. I'LL BE BACK IN A MONTH.
GO HOME IF YOU'RE UNHAPPY.

I sit on my cushion in my loose T-shirt, my loose tracksuit pants. I don't look at my body. Dressing and undressing, I don't look. I don't want to see my body.

WHAT ARE THESE TWO FERRARIS FOR, JONATHAN, IF NOT TO FEED A BABY?

WHOA, HIT THE BRAKES, BETH.

I CAN'T MAKE LOVE TO CARL. I CAN'T.

I'M SORRY, BETH.

HE'S SO TENDER. I SHUT MY EYES. YOU'VE TURNED ME INTO A WHORE.

BETH, GO HOME. GO HOME, LOVE.

Four in the morning in the Metta Hall. It is so peaceful, so silent. I sit on my cushion and look out across the sea. Then the door creaks. The others are arriving. Quick. I wrap my blanket round my shoulders, pull in my ankles, join my hands, close my eyes. The breath crossing the lip. The in-breath. The out-breath. Right effort. Right concentration. Right understanding. The breath will still these voices. They will fade. Eventually. Waking in starched sheets with the tick of the monitor and the smell of medication, their voices are already distant. Carl. The French boys. I love hospitals, I love anaesthetics. I could live in a hospital all my lifeless life. If only I was ill. I envy the sick, I envy the dying. Children find it easier. I could live dying. And the dead. 'You're so full of life, Beth. You're bursting with life.' What a curse.

Other meditators are shuffling to their places, clearing their throats, arranging their cushions, settling themselves. The gong sounds for the start of the session. Four thirty. I bet his eyes are on me now. He's watching. I'm the kind of girl he wants. I'm stronger, though. I'm stronger than his eyes. I've shut him out. I won't go back. I don't care about his stupid diary. Day six. Day seven. Acceptance, blessing. Three days to go. I have escaped him. I have escaped my story with GH, the pompous diarist. When did you ever regret saying no, Beth? Never! I never regretted saying no to a man. But when did you ever regret saying yes? Ha ha. Never. I never regretted a fuck. No, not true. I regret it now. Now I do regret it. I regret saying yes. To every man I said yes to. I regret Carl. I do, I do. I regret Jonathan. From the bottom of my heart I regret him. And all the others. *All* the others. All the betrayals. I truly regret them truly regret them.

I BETRAYED YOU A MILLION TIMES, JONATHAN. I BETRAYED YOU EVERY CHANCE I GOT. EVERY SINGLE CHANCE.

I'M SURE YOU DID, BETH. I NEVER SUPPOSED OTHERWISE.

YOU'RE JUST AN OLD FART, JONATHAN. A FAILED FARTIST.

FAIR ENOUGH, BETH. I SUPPOSE I'M OLD ENOUGH TO BE YOUR FATHER.

Father. My disgraceful father. Sex is forbidden at the Dasgupta Institute. Sex is forbidden.

Sttart-tagain. Surrender again. There's no guiding voice at the morning session, no Dasgupta. I mouth the words to myself. Sttartt-tagain. Eyes closed on my cushion above the surf, I'm happy. Oh, I'm deeply happy! I love the mornings, the dawn. I love the crows scrabbling on the roof. I love beginnings. Beginnings. If he's watching me, that's his look-out. I can't feel them. I'm no slave to any man's eyes.

'Either you've got them eating out of your hands or you're threatening to kill yourself,' Zoë said.

Zoë kissed me.

I BETRAYED YOU WITH WOMEN AS WELL AS MEN, JONNIE.

I loved texting, loved getting him anxious. At all hours. Why should he be allowed to relax when I was away with the boyfriend I didn't love, when I was suffering my betrayals?

I'M SURE YOU DID, BETH. I'M SURE YOU DO.

Out of the blue he wrote: I ADORE YOU. Out of the blue. I ADORE YOU, BETH. ADORE YOUR SKIN, ADORE YOUR HAIR, ADORE YOUR EYES, I ADORE YOU AND ADORE YOU.

Zoë said: 'Tell him you've got another man's sperm in your pussy. That should wake him up.'

'I already did. I told him I'm fucking you too.'

We were in the hotel after the gig. I was crying.

'Drama queen,' she said.

People are fidgeting. Kristin has arrived to my left, Marcia to my right. Even without seeing, I feel who is there. I know them, I know the space. I know the vibrations they send, the way the air changes when they sit. Someone starts to breathe very deeply, rhythmically, behind us, some new student who can't find her breath. She's heaving like a bellows. We are preparing for *vipassana,* preparing to work diligently all day long: the in-breath, the out-breath. Across the lip. For half an hour at least, nothing but the breath. In and out. Preparing. A silver stream of breath parting an ocean of deep water. A silver lifeline through the dark. Somewhere it must reach the surface. Somewhere it must connect with the future. I DIDN'T BREATHE FOR TEN MINUTES, JONATHAN. TEN WHOLE MINUTES! I SHOULD BE DEAD. NOW MY BRAIN IS SWELLING. THEY HAVE TO PUT ME IN A COMA, OTHERWISE I WILL DIE.

Silence. My chest is rising and falling. Without breathing I watch myself breathe. It's such a gentle movement. A slight rising and falling of the chest, the diaphragm. The sea has calmed and the water is lapping ever so gently on the sand, rising and falling ever so gently, like a kiss, a caress. In the darkness the faces begin. A woman's face, distinct in every feature, generous mouth, pale skin, grey eyes in a web of wrinkles. Now a black man, a real Negro, looking up from far below, below the floor of the Metta Hall. He's resigned, tired, sympathetic. Now a little girl with honey blonde hair, right close up. A snub nose. She's about to smile, she's about to shake her head. If she does her hair will touch me. All these faces are very distinct. Very calm, very knowing. Is it me they're gazing at? I'm not sure. Maybe at someone beyond me, behind me. They appear and fade. Now a young man, now a Chinese boy. They're not there, then they're there, then they're gone. Faces glimpsed between the stars. You are lying on your back by your tent on the dunes. You know you shouldn't have come. You really shouldn't have come on holiday with a man you don't love, you shouldn't have told him you are pregnant. He is so happy. He is so near his goal. Marry Beth, Carl, marry Marriot's. You look up and find a face in the stars. Why did you tell him? It's already gone. But each face is too real, too present to be imagined. Who are these people? I don't know. Do they have anything to say? They are silent. Are they my past lives, come to watch over me? Beth's past lives? For Christ's sake! Are they lives to come? An old black man? Are they friendly? I feel they are. Friendly and equal. Yes, I feel they are all equal. No, they're *the same.* I'm not sure how it can be, but in a way they're all the same face. I am one of them. We are companions on a journey. I'm the same too. My face appears to them as they appear to me. Are we the Sangha? *Sangham saranam gacchami.* I take refuge in the Sangha, in the community of meditators. How can I become a

Dasgupta person? Is that the question I must ask Mi Nu? These are the faces of Dasgupta people. They have that look. I must take refuge in the Sangha. They appear and fade. I understand now why Mi Nu wouldn't speak to me when I cried for help. To blather out your story would plunge you deeper in. Isn't that what happens when you start to tell? You make things worse. You plunge deeper. Writing is forbidden at the Dasgupta. If you have chosen to sit in silence, Elisabeth, you have chosen well. So sit in silence. Don't ask for help. When you have betrayed and broken a lover's heart, then you have betrayed and broken a lover's heart. There is no remedy. When you have been betrayed and your own heart is broken, then you have been betrayed and your own heart is broken. You cannot have it back. When you have killed, you have killed. There is no help. Sit in silence and be still.

The world as it is, *as it is.*

Vipassana

'Are you all right, Elisabeth?' Mrs Harper asked, the evening of the fifth day. I nodded. I didn't break the Noble Silence, just nodded. There was nothing to say. Wasn't it Mrs Harper who warned me there was no God to forgive me, no God to punish me? When you have staked your life on a passion and it has gone wrong, what can you do but sit still, accept? You came to the Dasgupta to forget. You discharged yourself from hospital and came straight to the Dasgupta Institute, to another kind of hospital, with another kind of anaesthetic. You came to forget. You did forget. Then you remembered. A little bit. To check what had been forgotten: the beach, the sea, the French boys, the tent, the texts, the sea, the dark sea, the violent sea. Now forget it again. Bury it again, Beth. Bury Beth.

Breth.

How crazy of my diarist to suppose he could get his troubles out of his mind with a summary. One summary leads to another. As soon as you've said it you have to correct what you said. Mental proliferation, Dasgupta says. Painful projections. *Sankharas*. Say it again and you'll have to correct your correction. Is the third version better than the first? Is it more or less painful? Was the second the right one? Try a fourth. A fifth. Mum had at least ten versions of her life. All wrong. And a thousand combinations of the ten. Each new story guarantees another will be needed to correct it.

The Thirty Years' War was over. But not Mum's battle with Dad. I spent my childhood listening. My adolescence. My life. I joined in. No, I was already in. I was born in. I made their story more complicated, more exciting. I was part of their war. Part of Mum and Dad's talking. Part of their not talking. I knew more about Dad than Mum did. Less about Mum than Dad did. I tried to break the stalemate. Silly Beth. What about seeing it this way, Mum? What about starting again? It was just a mistake, your marrying. What's the point of trying to explain it to yourself? When your marriage has been a bad marriage, it has been a bad marriage. What's the point of the new twist, the definitive version? Who cares whose fault it's been? Every time you play a song it's different. None of them is right. You had a bad marriage, Mum. A crap marriage. Your life is ruined, Beth, you ruined someone else's life, you killed a living being. There is no way back. You chose the wrong man, the wrong job, the wrong songs, the wrong beach.

Shush.

The minutes pass. Four thirty to six thirty. I'm happy. I'm very calm. I have less pain before breakfast. Someone has got up to leave. Someone is arriving late. Not many sit the full two hours. Kristin gets up. She has to prepare breakfast. Then Marcia. Marcia hasn't farted, she hasn't been noisy. She's settling in. I want to laugh. Maybe Marcia is a really nice person. I have let my fellow servers down. I wasn't indispensable. I let everyone down.

'Was it the kitchen?' Mrs Harper asked. 'Was there some kind of problem with the other servers, Elisabeth?'

Yes, there was. The kitchen is too close to life, Mrs Harper. In a kitchen things start to happen. Words get said. A boy looks at you with doggy eyes. A woman bothers you with her pride. A man irritates you with his laziness, his snacking.

You tease the boy you trick the woman you snub the man. Reaction reaction reaction. *Sankhara sankhara sankhara.* Your mind begins to buzz, to burn. The tomatoes are too red. The carrots are too bright. The beetroot stains everything. A girl arrives and you begin to like her. She takes the mattress off her bed. You want to win her over. Why? Because she suffers? Because she's dignified? A woman arrives and you begin to hate her. You want to show your contempt. Reaction. Reaction. You try to bless her but you can't. You can't bless farts. Time to bail out, Beth. You are not ready for the kitchen. You open a door and find a man's diary. You can't resist. He adores his daughter. The thought drives you crazy. The girl has chosen the wrong man. He writes a letter to save her from her stupidity. He can't finish it. His head is full of his own mistakes. He is too full of himself to help his daughter. You ask a man what he does for a living and he tells you he gets paid to make dying children laugh. Children are more in tune with life. Children can laugh while they die. How can I get in tune, Mi Nu? How can I enter the stream?

Is that the question?

She is here now. It must be getting on for six. When Mi Nu arrives I open my eyes. Only for her. Only for a moment. She tosses her shawl round her shoulders and in a single movement sits and is still. I love to watch that. It's a graceful movement that accelerates to stillness, the way a good song swells to silence. A single moment, a single movement, and she is wrapped in stillness, cloaked in silence. Watching her, the words fade. The chatter fades. The questions fade. Now I am walking by a stream, wearing a long gown. My feet are bare in deep grass. The water bubbles through the grass, fresh and pure and full of life. It's beautiful. I'm happy. There are no banks, just the grass and the clear, bubbling water. I'm tall, straight, solemn. Oh, I'm so beautiful. My gown is bright red right down to my bare feet and a small smile curls my lips. I'm smiling. With each step I take, the hem of my gown brushes the grass and dozens of tiny, startled birds fly up all around me. They fly up in twittering clouds of turquoise, gold and white. They're very brightly coloured. And the twittering of the birds is the bubbling of the stream. They're the same sound. They fly up from my feet in the cool grass. Beautiful twittering thoughts. The green grass and the red dress are one. How can that be? How can green be red? Birds be bubbles? How can my feet be my hands and my hands be my feet?

Ananta pūnyamayī.

The chanting has begun. The oats are going into the pot.

Ananta gunyamayī.

Don't tell yourself there's only half an hour to go. You are here for ever, Beth.

Dharama kī nirvāna-dhātu. Dasgupta's throaty voice. Chanting and singing. I've no idea what it means. I'm suspended, floating in the sound. *Dharama dhātu, bodhi-dhātu.* Absolutely still, but not fixed. I've expanded across the whole hall. It's blissful. And I'm in pain again. I'm floating in blissful stillness, but my ankles are crushed on the floor. This is *vipassana.* The blissful suspension comes from the pain. It *is* the pain. Floating above the ground is being crushed to the ground. The chanting is harsh and guttural. The singing is sweet and fluid. The chanting is the singing. To say what I feel, I talk nonsense. I say a thing and then its opposite. This is what I feel. Deep down this is what I have always felt. I was always a thing and its opposite. I am Beth and I am not Beth. The in-Beth, the out-Beth. Something very distinct and very indistinct. I am everyone who is not Beth, everything that is not Beth. And I am Beth. *Sabake mana jāge dharama.*

I must stop using these names, Beth, Elisabeth, Marriot, Jonathan, Carl, Zoë. Names are shallow, names are divisive. We are all one. The chanting is in my pulse, the singing is in my skin. My body dissolves and flows. It flows from my cushion with the outgoing tide. Though my knees are burning rocks. My knees are fucking killing me. *Roma roma kirataga huvā.* I know this recording backwards. I know exactly how long is left before breakfast time and porridge and cereal and prunes and toast. I am here for ever. Now the verse *Dharama gaṅga ke tīra para.* Ten minutes left. Five. The chanting goes on for ever at the Dasgupta. It was here before the Metta Hall was built, and when the institute is forgotten and the recording lost the chanting will go on. Whether Dasgupta is dead or alive makes no difference. Dasgupta was always dead. Dasgupta is always alive. *Saba ke mana ke dukha mite.* The chanting came from long before and after. I don't know the words but my lips move to them anyway. My lips know the words. In a few moments it will end and the meditators will rush for their bananas. It will not have ended. There will be no bananas. The porridge will be terribly real, the smell of the porridge, above all the lumps in the porridge. Thank you, Paul, thank you, Rob. It won't be real at all.

135

'That's not me *at all*,' I told Jonathan when he showed me his painting. 'I never wear long skirts, I never wear red, I never walk barefoot. I'd be scared of dog shit.'

'This is as much you as any painting ever will be, Beth.'

'And the birds? I like the birds.'

'The birds are also you, Beth. And so is the stream. Perhaps especially the stream. Or perhaps especially the sky.'

'I can't see any sky.'

'I adore you, Beth,' he said.

How can something be what it is and its opposite too?

How can it be free *and* trapped? How can it be hard and liquid? How can life be blissful and terrible? How can that be, Mi Nu? How can a man adore me and not want me? How can love be hate and hate be love?

Saba ka maṅgela, saba ka maṅgela, saba ka maṅgela, hoya-re. For the closing verses a woman's voice joins in. It's as if she were there walking beside her man as he chants in his harsh, guttural voice. She sings beside her man, fluently and sweetly. I can see her swaying in her sari. *Saba ka maṅgela hoya-re.* She's not in time and she's not in tune, but it's absolutely right. It tears at your heart. How many times did I tell Zoë: a hair's breadth out of synch, a suspicion out of tune? It's through that tiny gap that life pours in, yearning pours in, passion pours in. That tiny wound between being in tune and out of tune. Tears are pouring down my cheeks. I will not cry in the Metta Hall. I am not crying. I am perfectly perfectly happy. I am no one. I can live at the Dasgupta Institute for ever. I can be free for ever of all attachment, free of all aversion. *Bavatu sava mangelam.* May all beings be happy. May all beings be peaceful. May all beings be liberated liberated liberated.

Sadhu, sadhu, sadhu.

The Dasgupta Manual

It isn't working.

If it was working I wouldn't be writing. I wouldn't be taking refuge in writing. I want to be in *jhāna*. I wanted *jhāna* to make me new. It hasn't. I have experienced *anicca* in my flesh, constant flux, constant flow, every atom of mind and matter arising and passing away, arising and passing away. It hasn't brought me wisdom. I have felt my body melt into air. I have walked out of the meditation hall and been one with the trees, the grass, heard great cathedrals of leaves rustle in my chest, seen my eyes blink in the bark, felt my head full of sky, my fingertips glow like petals. It hasn't brought me peace. I have lapsed into the humming of a bee, bumbling through the flowers. I'm not cured. I haven't achieved *paññā,* let alone *nibbana.*

You're a dumb girl, Beth, playing with things you don't understand. You go to the dining hall and everything solidifies, everything's gross. You're piling up cereals, piling up toast, piling up apples and oranges. Everything hardens. Your body is gross and hard. Your jaw chomps. Your throat swallows. Your stomach swells. Your mind is grasping and purposeful. These are Dasgupta's words. Grasping and purposeful. You must get the last piece of toast. You must get a place facing the wall. I don't want to look at anyone. I don't want to share with anyone. The misery comes back, Beth is back. Jonathan is back. Everything is the same again.

The breakfast, the bathroom. After a shit, I lie in the field hoping bliss will return. I love shitting. I love the smell and the bowels moving. We all have soft shit at the Dasgupta. I love wiping myself and pulling up my pants. Now bliss will return. It doesn't. I'm lying in the field but I might as well be back on the dunes, beside the tent, beside Carl. 'What's up, Beth? Come on, we're on holiday.' The gong sounds. I did wrong to Carl. I wronged him. I told him I was pregnant to cover my back. It wasn't his child. The gong calls us back to the Metta Hall. Start again. And again. Cross your legs again, Beth. Another hour, another two hours, another three hours of surrender. Work diligently, diligently. Behind closed eyes sensations open into landscapes. I am exploring a huge brown concave shell, following narrow red paths over acres of baked earth. It is very barren, very beautiful. I am moving along red paths inside a smooth sphere. Is it the world's crust, from within? The paths meet and divide meet and divide. Where are they going? Where am I? Inside my skull. I'm trapped in my skull.

After the evening discourse the students come forward to ask questions. Some of the students. The servers remain in meditation, waiting for the *metta*. It's been a long day. I won't open my eyes until he is gone, until the *metta* is over. A queue of students has formed, to bring their questions. The men to Mr Harper, the women to Mi Nu. Those who have questions. The others have gone. The others have stumbled exhausted to bed. Queuing, the questioners kneel. They bring their cushions to the front and kneel one by one before their teacher.

'Every time I switch from *anapana* to *vipassana* a terrible headache explodes inside me. Is it normal?'

'I don't understand how there can be no self if there is reincarnation. What is it that gets reincarnated?'

'What is *paññā*? Why is it so important?'

'What can I do to keep my back straight? I keep hunching up.'

'Why aren't we allowed to go out of the grounds for a walk? I need to move.'

I can hear the women muttering their questions in low voices. Mostly it's the same people every evening. There are people who ask questions and people who don't. Perhaps they want to draw attention to themselves, like kids sucking up to Teacher. I can hear the women's voices. Sometimes the men's. The men are louder.

'If there is no self, how can there be morality, how can there be punishment?'

I can't hear Mi Nu's replies. Sometimes I wonder if she does reply. Perhaps she just bows her head, invites them to look at her. I can hear Harper, though. He's embarrassingly loud. You can't help but hear. He drowns Mi Nu out.

'What is reincarnated is the accumulated karma, the accumulated *sankharas,* at the moment of death. Not a self, not a personality.'

'Morality is a natural unfolding of cause and effect. An unskilful action produces suffering as surely as a cartwheel leaves a track in the dust.'

I know the answers before he says them. The questions are always the same. The answers are taken from *The Dasgupta Manual for Teachers*. One of the course managers showed me. There is a manual and the leaders have to learn it by heart so that every teacher at every Dasgupta Institute all over the world can always give the same answer, the best answer, to the same questions that the students will always ask. It is hard to think of a new question, hard to say anything that might force Harper to think for himself. I wonder if my diarist will come forward and ask: Wouldn't you like to do the discourse yourself, Mr Harper? Wouldn't you like to become a guru yourself and the hell with Dasgupta? Suddenly I'm tempted. There seem to be a lot of students in the queue tonight. I can feel it when the queue is long. I'm tempted to open my eyes, to see if he is there.

A woman is speaking in a posh voice: 'I start exploring my body and everything goes fine until I get to my chest and then I lose it. I can never go any further down than my chest. Something blocks me. I end up starting again and again and again, as if the rest of my body were numb.'

I strain for Mi Nu's reply. I wonder if she also uses the answers from the manual. Her voice is low and follows a strange cadence, like a mewing, or a gurgling. *Anicchaaaah.* I hear the word in her weird pronunciation *anicchaaaah, anicchaaaah.* I'm so tempted now. What would be the sense of going to Mi Nu and asking a question that she could answer from the manual? At that point why not give us the manual to read? Why don't they post a pdf online so you can read it before you get here? I see myself opening my eyes to try to read her lips, to see the expression on her face when she replies. I'm sure her face is full of compassion, but impassive too, in that Asian way, caring and uncaring, loving and indifferent. I see myself opening my eyes but I don't open them. It's strange sitting here wondering if the urge to open my eyes will overcome the order not to, the order to keep my eyes closed until all the students have gone. I sit here wondering, wondering, observing my closed eyes on the brink of opening, but still closed.

I ADORE YOUR HAZEL EYES, BETH.

I kept that text for months.

Will I open my eyes, or won't I? Will the entity called Beth Marriot, a body made up of subatomic particles, *kalapas*, constantly in flux, constantly changing, open her eyes, its eyes, or won't she, won't it?

I don't know.

Or will someone else open my eyes? Another Beth. The Beth who is about to be. This second. This second. This, this, this, this. A man bathes in a river every morning—discourse day five—without realizing it is actually a different river. Yesterday's water is gone. Without realising he is a different man every time. Arising and passing away. Every atom of the body every second. Will my eyes be opened? Will they be my eyes when they are? The same eyes Jonathan adored? Perhaps my diarist is in the queue. Perhaps he isn't. I have a pain in my back now. It is a knife stabbed between my shoulder blades. It's not a problem. It's nothing beside the urge to open my eyes. Why? There must be some question that lies beyond all questions. Who is it decides when my eyes open? Is that it? A question that would make her stop and think, think for herself. How can I be like you, Mi Nu? Is that it? How can my eyes be your eyes, open when yours open, close when yours close? How can I become as pure as you are, as *safe* as you are? How can I make time pass without passing? If I hear a question from the men's side and I'm sure it's him, I'll open my eyes. Yes, I will. But why? Surely that would be just the time to keep them shut. There will be no story with GH. I've decided that. Anyway, how can you know it's him if you've never heard his voice? For a split second I'm back in his room, the moment when his face came out from his pullover: a bony, intelligent, manly face. He's astonished, he's amused. What will his voice be like? I'm listening for the men's questions over the women's. I'm listening for the voice of the man I will have no story with.

'What do I do if there's a part of the body I can never feel? The top of my head, for example. I can't find any sensation there at all. Or my ankles, or my neck.'

'Just concentrate on the area for about a minute,' Harper will say. 'Don't try to force the feeling. Don't be impatient. Wait a minute and move on. One day the sensation will come. There is sensation on every inch of the body at every moment. It's just that your mind isn't sufficiently concentrated. Keep working. Be patient.'

His voice has a confiding sound, which must be completely fake when you think he's repeating this stuff from memory.

Or maybe not. Maybe you can repeat from memory and be completely sincere. Maybe it's sincere *because* he's repeating truths he believes in.

'I'm sorry but I'm seeing these really ugly visions all the time. Images of violence. Rape, killing. I don't know where they come from. I don't know what to do.'

'Don't fight the visions or try to stop them.' I mouth the words as Harper speaks. 'Don't judge them or criticize yourself for having them. Take an objective note. Visions. Ugliness. Violence.

Then return to the breath crossing your lip. Return to *anapana* meditation until your mind is calm. Work on your equanimity.'

'I am sure that when I get home my wife and I will separate. I can't think of anything else.'

It's a bold, deep, desperate voice. It's him! I open my eyes wide. I blink and focus.

It isn't him. He isn't in the queue.

Honey on a Razor's Edge

Outside, I don't hurry to bed. I walk past the leader's bungalow to the field. It's getting dark and the hills have turned cold.
The North Star is out. I like this moment, between evening and
night. Others are walking the path that runs by the fence. Some
you recognize, some you don't. They walk slowly. There is the
small white-haired woman who was moved away from the wall.
She walks with her hands behind her back, head bowed. When
we crave, we don't crave the object we imagine we crave. I can't
remember which day Dasgupta says this. We are simply addicted
to craving. Attached to attachment. We need to crave. If it wasn't
this object, it would be another. It *will* be another. So why not
GH instead of Jonathan? Why not replace the artist with the
diarist? If you can't cure yourself, repeat. Plunge back into the
sickness. I was so alive when I was sick.

I walk down to the bottom of the field and then beyond
into the thicket where it's darker. It smells good here among the
bushes, it smells damp and earthy. The path that turns down

to where the wall is broken seems well trodden. The twigs and brambles have been pushed back. Someone's been skiving off to the pub. Actually, it's pretty easy to hop over the wall here and hike a couple of miles to the Barley Mow. With a bit of luck you could hitch a lift. On Fridays they have live music. I don't know what day of the week it is. I know it's day seven. A blessings day. 'Day seven is over, my friends, you have three more days to work.' But I can't remember what day this retreat started. A Friday, a Saturday? If they have live music I could borrow a guitar. I could ask to sing. The meditators do all the real work here, Harper says, after the *metta*. Serving is a holiday in comparison with sitting, the struggle of sitting. Our service is to make their meditation work possible. I would sing, 'Better Off On My Own'. 'That's the one made me fall for you', Jonathan said.

Now there's someone behind me, in the dark. There's a sound of scuffling leaves. But she's stopped. She's hurrying off. Must have seen me. I don't turn to look. I don't care who it is. Frankly I don't understand why people come to a place like the Dasgupta and take the vows they do only to break them and sneak off to the Barley Mow. I did it myself at the beginning. There is no *samādhi* without *sila*, no concentration without the Five Precepts. There is no *paññā* without *samādhi*, no understanding without concentration. There is no *nibbana* without *paññā*, no bliss without understanding, without the wisdom of experience. 'Why did you come on holiday if you don't want to be here?' Carl asked. Good question. He was getting frantic. 'Why do you keep fooling around with those Frogs, Beth? They only want to get their hands in your pants.' We had taken the guitars. He wanted to work out acoustic arrangements so we could do gigs without Zoë and Frank. Just us two. He wanted me to himself. He wanted to build a wall around me. It was too late. I wasn't there to be built around. I lay all day on my back in the tent, texting texting texting, and got drunk in the evenings with Hervé and Philippe.

'I'm pregnant,' I told him. 'About eleven weeks.'

Carl was thrilled.

HIT THE BRAKES BETH, Jonathan texted. FERRARIS ARE FOR SHOWING OFF, NOT DRIVING.

'Morality is part of the law of nature,' Harper always says, repeating Dasgupta's manual of best answers to common questions. I hope Mi Nu doesn't use it. Perhaps Mi Nu speaks in a whisper so that Harper won't hear she's saying things that are not in the book. 'An unskilful action leads to suffering as sure as a cartwheel traces a line in the dust.' I didn't tell Jonathan I'd missed two periods. That would have been even more unskilful than getting pregnant in the first place. If I told Jonathan, I would lose him. I had already lost him. I never had him. I THINK THE DOCTOR IS IN LOVE WITH ME, I texted. HE HAS GIVEN ME AN AMULET. IT'S SOME WEIRD INSECT IN AMBER. HE SAYS YOU CAN'T DIE WITH THIS AMULET ROUND YOUR NECK.

I'M GLAD, BETH. I'M GLAD YOU'RE IN GOOD HANDS.

Meredith and Stephanie were doing yoga stretches. Forbidden. They should be asleep. Kristin was on her slats, reading the *Bodhicaryavatara*. There are not many books in the Dasgupta Institute library. A dozen? I tried to read it, twice. The miracle is I learned to pronounce the title. Marcia was on her bed giving advice about the stretches, advice about breathing, advice about Buddhism. Thank God we haven't got Ines here as well.

I stood by the door. Kristin didn't look up when I came in. The lamplight is barely bright enough to read by. I wanted to join

146

the girls in their stretches, but couldn't. I didn't know whether to talk or to keep the Noble Silence. The others wouldn't start speaking first. You don't speak to someone who has left service to meditate. You don't intrude.

I stood at the door. It would be nice to talk, but then I would be back in the world again. I would make fun of Stephanie, I would crack jokes for Meredith, I would try to impress Kristin, I would start to smell Marcia's farts. When I'm silent, Beth is in the background. She hardly exists. If I come out of the silence, I won't be able to stop myself. I couldn't stop myself when I sent Jonathan those endless texts. I lost control. I totally lost control. It cost a fortune.

THE DOCTOR SAYS AS SOON AS I'M WELL HE'LL INVITE ME TO DINNER. HE'S QUITE NICE.

I'M GLAD, BETH. I'M GLAD.

'Who are you texting?' Carl asked. He never left my bedside. 'Who do you have to keep texting all the time?'

It was ten. I would be up at four. Or maybe not. Maybe your days at the Dasgupta are over. A voice spoke those words in my head. I'd heard them before. Stephanie is shapelier than Meredith. She has neater knees and thighs, squarer, sharper shoulders. But Meredith is sexier, bouncier. When she reaches forward to grab her toes you can see the tops of her tits. They're plump. When she crouches to stretch her back, her bum looks big and round. Marcia is watching. The girls sigh and murmur. Meredith giggles when she can't hold a position. 'When you have a position right you feel you could hold it for a hundred years,' Marcia says, lying on her bed. 'In fact, that's how you know you've got it right.' Says she who has to keep crossing and uncrossing her legs. Meredith's eyes catch mine. She wants

147

to know what I meant when I said I was in trouble. She wants gossip. Maybe she wants me.

Marcia has started to talk about yoga therapy for adolescents with behavioural problems. 'Some judges include it in their closing recommendations. It helps the kids handle their anger. They feel more embodied.'

Is Marcia a cauliflower or a cabbage, Stephanie? And what is the smelliest, most shapeless vegetable you can think of? I'm about to burst out laughing. Why? Why can't I be serious, like Kristin? Kristin is trying to make serious progress, reading Buddhist stuff in the dim light, looking for wisdom, trying to change. I should take off my mattress and sleep on the slats.

'Who's on breakfast?' Marcia asks.

Meredith has lifted her legs in a shoulder-stand and starts to scissor them back and forth. Her fleece drops down her back to her shoulders. There are love-handles, bright with sweat. If the skin was brown it would be Zoë's.

'You are,' Stephanie says. 'With Tony.'

'I think Tony fancies you.' Meredith giggles. 'He's been watching you.'

Meredith's saying what she thinks I'd say if I were speaking. She said that to please me.

'He's a professor, isn't he?'

A hint of a smile crosses Kristin's face now. I love that. I love it when she's distracted from her seriousness. I wish I'd caused that.

'What of?' Marcia asks.

'Romance languages.' Meredith's shoulder stand collapses.

'You know what my favourite line from the *Bodhicaryavatara* is?' Marcia says dourly. '"Sensual pleasure is like honey on a razor's edge."'

'Wow!'

'So I'll concentrate on the porridge.'

'And hope it doesn't come out too stiff and lumpy.'

'I should hope it won't come out at all.'

Meredith and Stephanie laugh. Actually, that was pretty good, coming from Marcia. Maybe she's OK after all. Everyone has wind sometimes. Meredith's giggling subsides. There are a few moments' quiet while she and Stephanie lie on their sides. Repose of the Buddha position. They look beautiful side by side face to face in the yellow light.

'What's that?' Kristin sits up. 'I heard a noise.'

Everybody listens. She's right. Scratch scratch. There's a scrabbling in the wall. I almost yell out, 'The mouse!' Instead I turn and leave. I mustn't speak. I won't. When I speak it will be because I've decided. Decided what? I've no idea.

Our dorm is an old building, a converted stable. Not converted enough to be honest. I pad down the wooden staircase and pull on my shoes in the porch. Outside there's a light over the door to the bathrooms. When I go in to pee someone in the next cubicle is heaving. Real grunts, barks even. But how can you be constipated on the Dasgupta diet? 'If you ever hear me on the loo, you'll be cured of any desire to live with me.' Jonathan laughed. It's disgusting how loud this woman is grunting, as if she were beating a dangerous animal. Ah ah ah! God. I hurry to wipe myself and get out. It's as if she were giving birth.

Could it have been Mrs Harper? Do the Harpers have children? How do Buddhists manage not to attach to their children? Probably there's something I haven't understood. Or maybe it's the pregnant woman in the row behind me. Maybe pregnancy constipates.

The female dining hall is dark. I go through to the kitchen. It's late. There's one red pilot light on the water heater and a yellow LED on the Rational Cooker. The female servers' room is at the far end on the left. I close the door, turn on the light and find a biro. No paper. I go back to the kitchen and pick up a wad of Service Report sheets. Imagine if I went through the male dining hall now, into the male grounds and over to Male Dormitory A, the fifth room on the right. Imagine I find him lying there asleep, snoring. All oldies snore. I shake his arm. Hey, Garry, Graham, Gregory, let's get the hell out of this place.

Now. I could do that now.

Instead I start writing. I can't leave the Dasgupta and I can't stay. So I write. Writing is in between things. In between doing and not doing. Writing is indecision, dreaming. A diary instead of a life. Let's write about what happens if he says yes. My name's Elisabeth, but lovers call me Beth. The diarist laughs. He's got some cigarettes in his locker and as soon as we're out on the road he lights up. I cadge one. It makes me dizzy and I ask him to stop a minute. We sit on a damp wall under clouds and stars. The wind is shaking the trees in big waves of sound. It's beautiful. Without waiting, I switch my cigarette to my left hand, put my right round his head and pull him into a kiss, a smoky kiss. 'I love how impetuous you are,' Jonathan said. We were in the cinema. *Match Point* is a terrible film. 'You ain't seen nothing yet,' I told him.

Now there's a sound. There's someone in the kitchen. I hide my papers under the tea tray. Someone is moving around the kitchen. I can hear plates, cutlery. It's eleven and gone. They should be in bed. Wait. I can definitely hear the sound of spoon on plate, spoon on plate. Someone's come for a midnight feast.

150

Marcia maybe. Honey on a razor's edge. Or Tony. The idea of Tony fancying anyone is ridiculous. He's past it. A professor of obsoletion. Is that a word? Obsolescence? The idea of anyone fancying Marcia is even sillier. She's an elephant, a sea elephant. Marcia would have had no trouble in those waves.

If I'm writing it's because it's not working. The meditation is not working. Or I'm not working at the meditation. Nothing is working. The seventh day is over. A day of blessing. You have three more days to write. Maybe writing will get me through. I can write about running away with him. For three days. That'll save me from running away with him. Then he'll be gone. Then I can start again.

I slip through the door. Why do I always walk around as if I was a burglar? Zoë noticed that.

'Beth, you're always moving around as if you shouldn't be where you are. As if you were cheating on someone.'

'I usually am.'

It's Ralph eating cereal. He hasn't heard me. He's at the work surface at the far end, face to the wall, bent over a big bowl of muesli and his BlackBerry, eating and surfing. Greedy pleasures. Attachments. Cravings. What a big head of long wavy hair he has. What a cute earring on a cute cute ear. I sneak up, ever so quietly. And he has an earpiece too! There's a tinkle of music. Music, food and porn. You greedy boy! His leg is moving up and down on the ball of his toe. Rhythm. His big head is swaying back and forth. He's so *into* it. He's so happy. Two feet away I stretch out my arms. One quick step and my hands are round his eyes.

'Don't move!'

I hold him tight.

'Who is it? Guess.'

151

He doesn't seem shocked. I can feel his face crease up in a smile.

'Bess.'

'Wrong.'

He laughs. 'It is you, Bess.'

'How do you know?'

'I know, yes.'

'I'm not Beth.'

'You are.'

'No, I'm not. Turn that music off. Pull it out.'

He takes out the earpiece.

'I told you, I'm not Beth.'

'Who zen?'

'Meredith.'

His head shakes. It's weird holding this big head as it shakes from side to side. I haven't touched anyone in ages. His neck is very strong.

'I'm not believing you. You are Bess.'

'Beth not Bess. Th-th-th! Pronounce it properly at least.'

He laughs. 'I told you it was Bess.'

'No, I'm not. But how do you know?'

There's a pause. He leans back slightly until his head is against my breasts. Pig.

'I just know.'

'Well, you're wrong.'

'I absolutely know.'

'You've been watching me, spying on me.'

'I am vorried about you, Bess. Everybody is vorried about you.'

'What are you doing with the computer? They're forbidden. You're surfing for porn.'

'Come on, Bess. It's email.'

The boy seems pretty damn pleased that I'm holding his head. Touching is forbidden but Ralph is delighted. He doesn't want to get free at all. He doesn't want to be liberated.

'To your girlfriend? Or girlfriends?'

'To my mum!'

'Oh, tell me another.'

'Read it for yourself.'

I lean over his head. His hair is freshly washed.

'I don't understand German.'

'Liebe Mutti. You are understanding zat.'

It's the smell of the boy who loves the shower, who loves being clean.

'Vant me to translate?'

I lowered my mouth right to his ear, his cute little silver earring. It's a tiny Buddha.

'Want a kiss?'

His body trembles. Fantastic. He really trembled and tightened.

'Bess.'

'I'm not Beth.'

He's super-tense.

'We shouldn't.'

'Then don't.'

I don't take my hands away and he doesn't struggle to get free. Or to move his head from my tits.

'Do you like me?' he asks.

'What kind of question is that?'

'A closed kvestion.' He laughs. 'Yes or no?'

'Would you kiss me if I were Meredith?'

'No.' There was no hesitation.

'If I were Stephanie? Stephanie's very sexy. Very French.'

'No.'

'If I were Kristin?'

'No.'

'If I were Marcia?'

He laughs. 'You know I vouldn't.'

'If I were Beth?'

He sighs deeply. 'We shouldn't.'

'Why Beth?' I ask. 'Why do you want to kiss dumb Beth? That girl's such a loser.'

I've got my lips right by his ear now. In his ear. It's amazing how handsome he is, what a pretty boy. I couldn't care less. The pretty boy every girl's mother loves. Please marry my daughter, Carl, please, before she ruins everything.

'Beth's a little scrubber, Ralph. Flashing her big tits around. They should tell her to cover up. She should wear a proper bra.'

'I like Bess.'

'Beth, th- th- th.'

'Bessth.'

'You're hopeless. Why not Stephanie? She's a nice girl. She's your age.'

'I like Bess.'

'Beth's a fucking drama queen. *Oh, I'm in such deep trouble.*'

He doesn't answer. He's very excited.

'That whole scene with Harper just to get out of a bit of cooking and washing up. *Oh, I'm sorry, I can't serve, I can't, I need to sit. Poor thing I am.* Just to get out of a bit of work. Beth's a cheat.'

'I like you, Bess.'

'I'm not fucking Beth!' I stamp my foot and pinch his ear, right where the earring is. 'I'll pull your precious Buddha off.'

'Ow, stop!'

'Maybe I'm a man.' I make my voice deep.

'You're not a man.' He's laughing.

'How do you know?'

He breathes deeply, hesitates. 'I can smell you're not.'

'Smell? All you can smell is the food you're filching. You're an animal! Coming here to steal at night. Filling your animal belly.'

Then I realize. 'God, you've even put a banana in your muesli. You've deprived the students of a banana. You're a pig!'

He's grinning. The skin creases under my fingers. 'It *is* you, Bess.' He's enjoying himself.

'I repeat, you've stolen a banana. You should be ashamed of yourself.'

'I was hungry. I couldn't zleep.'

'Hungry, eh? That's your excuse?'

He hesitates. 'Yes.'

'Craving, you mean. You were craving. You're a bad boy.'

I look around. The light's pretty bright in the kitchen. He's been eating cereal from a white bowl on a stainless-steel surface. His BlackBerry is glowing with his email to his *Mutti*. I lean down again and make my voice super-breathy and moist.

'Are you craving for a kiss?'

He sighs. He's very still now.

'I said, are you craving a kiss, Ralphie? Would a kiss help you get to zleep?'

'Ve shouldn't, Bess.'

'I'm not Beth.'

'As you like.'

'You're too scared, is that it? You don't want to store up some deep deep kissy *sankhara*."

'Bess,' he says softly. 'Please.'

'Please do, or please don't?'

He sighs again. I move my lips down his cheek, breathing ever so lightly.

He wriggles.

'OK, if you keep your eyes closed, Ralph, I'll kiss you.'

'We shouldn't. We took a vow. Ze Five Precepts.'

I'm laughing. 'For fuck's sake, do you want to or not? What kind of man are you?'

'Bess.'

'Beththththth! Listen, shut your eyes tight. After we've kissed I'll let you see who I really am. You're in for a big shock.'

I turned his head a little, crouched and took my fingers from his eyes exactly as our lips met. Honey on a razor's edge. His hands lifted to my sides. Very lightly. Very respectfully. I put my hands behind his head now and pulled him towards me. Our lips pressed together, then began to open. Now he was excited and began to push his tongue in. I let him for a few seconds, then backed off and ran.

'Bess!'

His chair scraped. I dashed across the kitchen and out through the swing doors.

'Please, Bess.'

'I'm not Beth!'

Just Observe

My cigarettes were in the side pocket of my backpack under the bed. The others sighed and stirred but didn't wake. The snorer was Stephanie. Who would have thought? Now there was the problem that I'd left four or five scribbled pages under a tea tray in the female servers' room. I'd have to go back. I felt in the pack to check if the lighter was there. Damn. Meantime the mouse was gnawing pretty loudly. I stopped to listen. Gnaw gnaw, scratch scratch. I grinned and listened some more. Why was I so pleased about the mouse? Like I'd found a friend at the Dasgupta Institute. But if I went back, I might run into Ralph again as I went through the kitchen. If he was still there. Did that matter? 'Life around you is a constant soap opera.' Zoë laughed. I'd shown her Jonathan's love bites on my neck. It must have been one of the first times we slept together. 'If you want, you can tell Carl I did it,' she said. I didn't understand. 'Carl knows I'm that way inclined. I'll say you thought it was just a hug and I went for you.' She squeezed me and sighed. 'Actually, Beth,

I wouldn't mind taking a lump out of your neck.' 'Oh, be my guest.' I laughed. Be my guest, I told the mouse. Go for it. I'm blessing the mouse, I thought. That was the feeling in my head. I'm blessing the fucking mouse!

Without a lighter I had to go back to the kitchen and use the gas. No sign of Ralph or his cereal bowl. A pity. Perhaps I should have gone the whole hog. Why not? Given him what he wanted. In the loos, or the servers' room. A good shag. The flame leaped up and nearly sizzled my hair. I rushed out through the female dining hall before the smoke could trip the alarms, then walked in the dark past the toilets, past the Metta Hall to the female teacher's bungalow. There was a bench outside beside the rose bush and I lay on it under the stars.

And inhaled.

'*Cher Jonathan, Je m' appelle Mariette. Je suis l'infirmière qui soigne votre amie, Élisabeth. Malheureusement, elle n'est pas sortie du coma. Je crains qu'elle puisse mourir à tout moment. Elle m'a dit de vous envoyer ce message, au cas où vous voudriez la voir avant qu'il ne soit trop tard.*'

With *vipassana*, when you have a pain, in your back, in your legs, you don't shy away from it, you don't resist or fight, you go to meet it, gently. You move the mind towards the pain and explore the shell it is locked in. That's the way with pains. They are gross, solidified sensations trapped in their shells. In a way, the shell is the pain. Nothing flows. Nothing moves. The pain is blockage, stoppage, paralysis. At most it throbs, it beats with an angry rhythm against the walls of its prison. Pulse pulse pulse. Or like a bee trapped in a box. But when you let the mind flow round it, patiently quietly, attentively, after a while—sometimes a long while—the shell begins to soften, it cracks. The mind seeps in, the pain seeps out. The two mingle together like river and seawater, pain perception, pain perception, perception pain. Suddenly it's gone. All the pain dissolves to mind, perception, pleasure, even bliss. This has happened to me many times at the Dasgupta. But not with memory pains. Then it's the opposite. When you break the shell around a painful memory the hurt buzzes out and stings everything. You thought it was a tiny thing, a tiny pimple of misery. Now it's poisoned your whole mind with its venom. And all the other pains come burning back. Your flesh is burning.

'*Chère Mariette, Ici à New York il est deux heures du matin. Pourriez-vous m'envoyer le numéro de téléphone de l'hôpital? Je tiens à parler au médecin.* Jonathan.'

An hour after that he rang. At least, the phone trilled. It was a private number. But who else could it have been? I turned the phone off and put it in the locker of the Dasgupta Institute with my wallet and iPod and went to take the vow of silence.

It's come on to drizzle. I'm smoking under Mi Nu's window. It must be midnight. And I love smoke. No, I *really* love it. I can feel it creeping into every purified corner of my meditative lungs, right down to the diaphragm, right out around the ribcage under the armpits, into the tops of the lungs and all around the throat. *Vipassana* has taught me to smoke better! I can feel it drifting up through the sinuses, muddying the transparency of my mind. About time. Too much transparency is too much. Take it as a burnt offering, Mi Nu. Take my purity sent up in smoke.

What shall I do?

It comes to me now that that's the only question I could ever honestly ask her. What shall I do next, Mi Nu? Where do I go from here?

That is the only thing I need to know. What is the other side of this blockage?

Who am I?

An owl called. What a lovely sound—tu-whoo—in the night. A spiritual sound. But it was getting damp. I was getting damp. I'd let my fag go out without lighting another from it. That was stupid. There was no point in smoking just one. Binge the lot. Get it over with. What is it decides that for months and months you keep the rules, you even enforce the rules, you spy on people, you make sure they stay in line, then suddenly you're breaking every rule you can, in the most obvious way you can, talking, kissing, smoking? Next it'll be shagging. How does that happen? Go the whole hog, I thought. Do it.

'I love how reckless you are,' Jonathan said. He must have said it a thousand times. It wasn't true. He loved how reckless *I seemed to be*, but without ever going the whole hog, without ever putting him in danger. Peeing between cars on Acton Vale, flashing tits in restaurants, blowing him in the cinema—there was never any serious danger. I didn't go to his ex-wife, his wife that is, and say, Look, your old pig of a husband is shagging me senseless every day, he licks my pussy inside out and likes to come deep in my arse. I didn't tell Carl, I'm leaving you for that paunchy old painter, the guy who always forgets to zip up. I didn't tell my father, Your old Rotary pal, the would-be Picasso, is porking me rotten. He's the man of my life. I didn't have the courage of my diarist's daughter, who is *giving up everything to be with her man*, whatever awful things he's done, however much he doesn't deserve her. The thought of this girl and what she's doing makes me dizzier than any smoke could: giving up everything, but *everything*. Total surrender. For love. I'm dizzy with envy. And your man says, Do it, Babe, come to me, Babe. I might be a useless criminal, but I won't let you down. I'll never let you down.

Jonathan only loved how crazy I was, because I wasn't crazy at all. I *played* crazy to please. I was neither fish nor fowl. I never have been. 'Did you like it?' Zoë asked. Her face was glowing and grinning and gazing. 'Did you like it, Little Beauty?' 'I don't know,' I told her. 'I just don't know.' What was really weird was being called Little Beauty by my bass player.

Tu-whoo. The owl again. The owl is a pure spirit. I jumped up, walked back to the female dining hall, crossed to the connecting corridor that leads to the kitchen, then doubled back through the male dining hall and out into the night again on the men's side. I've no idea where Ralph sleeps. Who cares about Ralph? Someone was coughing in the bathrooms, someone who needs to pee in the night. I thought I'd better wait till he was safely back in his bed and went to stand where they keep the garden tools in the open shed.

There were a few clothes lines for cover and I stood peeking out between damp towels and T-shirts till the guy came out of the bathroom and headed for Dormitory B. He stopped in the drizzle, breathed and looked around. It was Tony. He looked sad and stooped. Tony's a parsnip, I thought. A vegetable no one wants any more. A tired parsnip. Maybe I should have kissed Tony, shared my merits with Tony. He would have understood it was a joke. I went straight to Dormitory A and counted the doors down the corridor till I came to the fifth on the right.

What had I written in his diary four days ago? I couldn't remember. I honestly couldn't. Four days is an age at the Dasgupta. An age and a blink. It's four times ten hours of eyes closed sitting still on your bum. It's four times ninety minutes of Dasgupta's video discourses. And the chants. It's adzuki-bean stew, nut roast, curried tofu, baked potatoes with melted Cheddar,

161

dahl, dahl and more dahl. It's dozens of cups of Rooibos and herb tea. I hate Rooibos. And as many trips to the loo. Four days of drinking and eating and pissing and shitting and breathing in and out in and out endlessly observing the air crossing the upper lip, the in-breath crossing the lip, the out-breath crossing the lip. I'm not the same person who wrote whatever it was four days ago. He's not the same person who read it. Why write anything, then?

To see how much you've changed when you re-read.

I had a cigarette in my mouth but nothing to light it with. It felt good having it there, but frustrating. When I pushed my hair from my face it was sticky and dead. God knows what I look like. My period is coming any moment. I can feel it. I looked up and down the corridor. I listened. Very carefully, I pulled the handle towards me to keep the door shut tight, then pressed it down, slowly slowly slowly. It opened without a click. Burglar Beth. Zoë noticed how stealthy I was. She saw me more clearly than the blokes did. Now here I was again watching a man sleeping.

He's facing the wall under a couple of blankets, breathing easily, not snoring at all. It killed me that last night with Jonathan, how easily he breathed. I sat and smoked and watched. He knew it was over, I'm sure he did, and all the same he slept easy. I should have told him I was pregnant. That would have kept him awake. I should have told him I was going to keep the baby and tell the whole fucking world it was his and that he would have to pay for it. In cash. Then we'd have got some change out of him. Then he really would have had a reckless girlfriend. He knew it was over and went to sleep before eleven absolutely as usual so as to be up on time and fresh for his morning flight, his annual trip to New York.

162

Carl also slept pretty easily, except I never thought twice about waking him. We were in sleeping bags, on the dunes beyond Bayonne. You could hear the surf.

'Why are you getting texts in the middle of the night?' he wanted to know.

'From Zoë,' I lied.

'But it's three in the morning.'

'She's having some fantastic affair with a woman in Edinburgh,' I lied.

I lied and lied and lied.

Carl slept with his face towards me in a mess of curls. He breathed easy as an angel in the dark of the tent.

'I'm pregnant,' I told him.

'What?'

That woke him up.

'But that's fantastic!' he said. 'That's absolutely fantastic!'

Then lying down again he said he couldn't figure out how it had happened since he was always so careful.

'What are you saying?'

'Nothing. Hey, Beth, nothing.'

He talked for ten minutes and fell asleep again. Pretty well mid-sentence. He was chattering away and then he wasn't, he was asleep, breathing lightly and easily again.

Mr GH Diarist hasn't even stirred. He hasn't registered my presence at all. I haven't sneaked into his dreams or altered his breathing or anything. He's just lying there, time flowing over him like water over rock. Actually, I quite like being awake while others sleep. I could kiss him, if I wanted, or kill him. Or I could just observe. 'Just observe, my friends. just observe the sensations as they arise and pass away. Without a trace of craving, without a trace of aversion. Only in this way can you change the behaviour pattern at the deepest level of the mind. Only in this way can you come out of your misery.'

Except there's not much to observe, really. I lean over. His hair is thinning. His face is quite lean, but wrinkled round the eyes. His mouth is full and quiet. He hasn't shaved for a couple of days. Why bother at the Dasgupta? He's stubbly. Not much else to say. A man. An ordinary man. I could go into every room along this corridor and watch them all sleeping, all the men. That's a nice thought. To be there while they sleep. To watch over sleeping men. Their stale breath. Maybe run a fingertip over their stubbly cheeks. Or I could sit on the floor beside them and meditate. I could sit like a statue beside each sleeping man. Like an angel. My men.

Why do I want to do that, Mi Nu?

I would feel strong and calm and happy meditating beside the men as they sleep, if they would let me do that. Or I could be a little mouse in the men's dormitory, gnawing away in the dark. That would be fun. It drove me wild that Jonathan slept so easily on our last night together. But what did I do about it? I sat and watched over him. I gnawed round him. I felt motherly is the truth. The stupid stupid truth. Jonathan was a baby. Anyone could see that. He left his wife and reverted to being her baby. He was the child they hadn't had. She had the keys to his studio and brought him food when he wasn't there, brought him clothes, even booze. I felt more motherly to Jonathan than to the baby in my belly. And to Carl too. I felt motherly towards Carl. Even when I ran off to go skinny-dipping with the French boys. Maybe especially when I ran off. I was staggering with drink and dope. This will save you, Carl, I thought. This is going to save you so much shit, so much shit. It will all be washed away on the tide. Beth's shit. The French boys couldn't believe it, that I was up for a swim in a sea like that. *'C'est dangereux, bien sûr.'* They couldn't believe how high those waves were. 'Your cocks have shrunk to nothing,' I yelled. 'Shrunk to nothing, shrunk to nothing.'

Will I ever have a child, Mi Nu?

At least that might be a new kind of question for her.

There is nothing in this room but his clothes on the floor and the diary by the bed. Diaries. A pile of exercise books. It's too dark to read in here. Jonathan's room was stacked with paintings. I don't know if he was a good painter. There was something childish about his pictures, a kind of stupid longing. You looked at them and felt filled by a sort of yearning. It didn't mean anything. There was no connection with anything real, no chance of anything really happening. They were girls dissolving in abstract backgrounds, surreal collages. Clever, but stupid. Stupid *because* they were so clever maybe. There was something I didn't understand. The cleverness was being used for the wrong thing, perhaps. Like when a musician wastes his cleverness on some tricky syncopation instead of concentrating on the song. The painting he did of me was different, though. It was more solid and fleshy than the others, more real, except for those silly birds flying up from my feet. They were tiny birds with really bright colours.

'The birds are you too, Beth,' he said. 'The birds are my surprise that you exist.'

'Give it to me,' I said.

He thought a moment. 'After I've shown it in New York. I'll make a copy.'

'No, now.'

'It's on the catalogue, Beth. I have to show it.'

'By the time you get back from New York it'll be over between us.'

'Why, Beth?'

'I've got other fish to fry. I'm not the kind of girl who waits around.'

He was quiet.

'You too. You'll shag anything that moves. I know you will.'

'Come with me,' he said then. 'Come to the airport and get on the plane. Come to New York.'

'You should have asked before. You can't ask me the night before the flight.'

There was a pause. Our life was in that pause, in the carefully tidied space between his paintings and his bed. Jonathan was an amazingly tidy man. But he didn't fight for things.

'I guess I'll go and fuck Carl,' I said. 'In his tent in France.'

He didn't say anything. If he had grabbed me by the wrist, if he had said, Let's go and get your passport, Beth . . .

If I went and got one of the kitchen knives, the one that whams the celeriac in half, I could kill this man sleeping here now. This unfaithful diarist. How many men could I kill along the corridor before they stopped me? Two? Three? Four? All unfaithful. Bank on it. All diarists. But the night is passing. I need to light this cigarette.

Grabbing the top exercise book, I sneaked out.

The Second Arrow

Vipassana shit has a special smell. Sort of sweeter, but staler. It lingers. At first I thought it was the diet, the oats, the veggies, no meat, no fish, no booze. Now I think it could be the thinking we do here. If mind and body are one why shouldn't our shit smell of our thoughts? Anxious shit, laid-back shit. Anyhow, the female servers' loo is the only place where I can smoke and read through the night. It stinks.

What a lot this guy's been writing, though. I can't find the line I scribbled. Something about pain. It must be way back. Or it was in another notebook. Flicking through the pages, it doesn't seem to matter where you start. He hammers on like a drum solo at a druggy festival. Sometimes I find a few words I could have written myself. I mean, *really* could have written myself, as though we were the same person. I used to think that about Jonathan sometimes, that we were the same deep down. We had started to speak the same, think the same. Or I had started to speak like him. Now I wonder if we ever met.

Dawn session surreal. Since we started vipassana my body confused as my mind. Hands swapping over, left right, left right, mouth detaching from my skull, merging with my stomach, parts of my body disappearing for long periods, then resurfacing, like those exotic islands explorers kept losing and finding again. My knees behind me. My shoulders in my thighs. Cramps aches stabs burning pleasure pain happiness sadness hopelessness bliss all fading in and out of each other through calves ankles spine everywhere.

Just getting used to all this when L barges in. She looms up inside my skull like a shadow on the wall in a Hitchcock movie. I want a dog! she yells. She must have a dog. She needs to substitute me with a dog. Because a dog she can train. A dog she can trust. She can't trust me. I betrayed her. She's through with men. She wants a dog! Me shouting: But Linda, I am a dog! Can't you see? I've always been your little doggie.

Lighting fag two from fag one, I remember Carl always complained I treated him like a dog. Carl, do this, Carl, do that. Meantime I've started to bleed. I'll have to go over to the main loos and pick up some tampons.

Mum drove Dad crazy with cats. Five cats.

What a relief to read, though. Someone else's shit. Read read read. I always hated reading. So the wife's called Linda. It's good to have a name for her.

Vipassana vanity. Heading for lunch, young bloke, tall, pale, sitting in lotus position on the bench outside the dining room in deliberate full view of everyone with his hands upturned on his knees, thumbs and forefingers joined, eyes ecstatically half closed. Jim Carrey in Ace Ventura. How many times with Susie? Almost made up for the awful lunch. What did they do to that nut roast? Dunk it in turps?

Yep, Ines fucked up big-time with the nut roast. Maybe I was indispensable after all. Lotus show-offs are two a penny at these retreats. Girl a couple of months ago used to block the stairs to the servers' bedrooms. Meditating supposedly. Her spread knees pretty well touched both walls.

Meantime, I would like to learn not to feel superior to everyone, though I don't suppose I ever will. Actually, I'm already thinking how superior I am, wanting not to feel superior. And how superior of me to have recognized this paradox. And to have admitted this stalemate. And so on and on. Seems there is no escape from my superiority.

What a prick!
But this is one of the bits I could have written myself.

You're lying on the sofa and I touch your foot. You withdraw it. You turn away. Same thing in bed. You're turned the other way and I touch your foot with mine. I want at least our feet to be together. You withdraw. I'm sleepy, you say. Leave me alone. Same thing with your hand over the table. You pull it back and lean down to stroke the dog. You turn away from me to the dog. I touch your shoulder while you're cooking and you shake my hand off. You don't want me. So why do you want to keep me? Why? Why can't we separate? What is wrong with us?

169

This was me with Carl in France. Definitely. I couldn't bear for him to touch me. But how can you avoid a man in a tent? Why is everything in this diary about me?

Day 6. Signed up for appointment with the retreat leader, name of Ian Harper. Pure curiosity. Not expecting him to help me really. A ten-minute slot in his bungalow living room. Guy seeing him before me wouldn't meet my eyes as he came out. Sombre, with heavy jowls, bushy eyebrows. Harper in an armchair. Pink and proper. Grey jersey. Personnel officer for Waterstones sort of thing. Ordinary middle-class decor, table chair sofa, shelves with CDs. Somehow old-fashioned. Not sure why. Me in an armchair opposite. He asks how I'm getting on. Can I feel the breath on my lips, can I move my attention through my body finding sensation on all its various parts, can I keep still in the hours of Strong Determination?

Vipassana for Dummies.

When I open my mouth to answer I wonder if any sound will come out. I haven't spoken for days.

It depends on my mood, I tell him. My voice feels thin, a bit high-pitched. I say I'm experiencing drastic mood swings. Euphoria. Depression. Sometimes I can hold the position, cross-legged, if I manage to concentrate on my breath, or some sensation somewhere. Then it's quite pleasant. There's a pleasant glow. Sometimes I have to move every few minutes. I'm in agony. I can't understand how I ever sat through ten minutes, never mind a whole hour. I can't understand those people who sit there seraphic, as if time didn't exist. They are already in eternity. The leader on the women's side, that Asian woman. Like a statue carved in air.

He nods sagely. He's bored.

'The truth is,' I confide, 'there's a bit of a crisis at home at the moment, with the result that I keep on and on thinking of what I'm going to be getting back to when I finish here. It's hard to concentrate.'

Silence. He doesn't want to go there. He doesn't want to hear about my marital crisis. Hard to blame him. Absolutely neutral, he asks me what I do for a living.

'I run a small publishing company. Unfortunately, we're on the brink of bankruptcy.'

He does his sage nodding again. He doesn't want to know. I can't tell if he's really watching me very carefully or if he's just waiting for the ten minutes to be up. Why does he do this job? Is it a job? Does he get paid?

I ask: Is there any way the meditation can help me? I tend to panic and I'm afraid I'll really panic next week. Then I'll do the wrong thing. There will be tough decisions. Can meditation help me?'

He blinks. Maybe I've finally come into focus.

'Did you come to the Dasgupta to run away from this situation?'

It's an aggressive question, but he manages to make his voice relaxed and peaceful, as if it hardly mattered.

'Let's say, to get some distance, before the shit hits the fan.'

'You suffer in these situations?'

'I do.'

'Why?'

'Well, who wouldn't? I'm losing everything I've ever worked for. It's my company. I built it from scratch.' Then I

tell him: 'At the same time I'm splitting up with my wife. I'm going to lose my home.'

I wish I knew I was splitting up. I wish it was decided and done. Over.

He sighs. After a short silence, he asks: 'Do you know the story of the Buddha and the second arrow?'

'No.'

I'm beginning to feel angry.

'A student asked the Buddha a question very similar to the one you have asked me.'

His voice is precise, bureaucratic, as if recorded, but I suppose there is something kind in his face. It's hard to describe. An impersonal kindness, if that makes sense. I try to pay attention.

'The Buddha replied to the student with a question of his own: 'When someone is struck by an arrow, is it painful?'

'Yes', said the student.

'And then another question: 'When this someone is struck by a second arrow, is it painful?'

'Of course it is,' said the student.

'Then the Buddha said, "There is nothing you can do about the first arrow. Life is dukkha. You are bound to encounter suffering. However, the second arrow . . ."'

Harper hesitates.

'"The second arrow is . . . optional."

He stops, end of story apparently. I have the impression he has told it a million times.

'Optional? The Buddha said optional?'

'Yes. Optional.'

'I'm surprised the word was around. In those days. In Sanskrit?'

Harper raises an eyebrow. He smiles. 'Optional,' he repeats. 'The second arrow is optional. Meditation can help you with that choice. You can decline the second arrow.'

Long silence. Maybe a whole minute. Finally he says: 'You have four more days to work. Maintain sila. Develop samādhi and paññā. Above all, build up your equanimity in the knowledge of anicca, the law of impermanence. Work hard and you are bound to feel the benefits. Bound to.'

I could have strangled him.

Pretty good description of Harper. When I first came here I thought the guy was too ordinary and boring to be running the Dasgupta. Like an accountant, a job-centre info officer. Even when he sits to meditate he looks like a council employee who's lost his swivel chair. He came into his office one morning and found they'd put a *zafu* there instead. Then suddenly you find another side to him: you realize there's a deep calm behind the nerdishness. He changes. For a few seconds you get an inkling of why he's running a meditation centre. I suppose this is the Buddha body inside him that's supposed to be inside us all. A calm Buddha body beneath frenetic, chain-smoking, wired-up Beth. Can you imagine? Mi Nu is the opposite. Mi Nu never comes back from her Buddha body. A statue carved in air is good. Just occasionally there'll be a grin, a sexy flounce, a flash of appetite. Amazing because you never expected it.

Walked round the field so often I decided to go for it in the dark after the last meditation. Needed to be on the move instead of alone in the room. So fed up with thinking about what happens when I get home after the retreat. Walked across the field in a dark mist, then into the little wood at the bottom. Completely blind. How many years since I did something like this, feeling my way between trees at night, blundering into things? Twenty? Thirty? Surprisingly like the meditation, come to think of it, never quite knowing where you are, even though theoretically you're somewhere entirely familiar. Inside yourself. Just that it's dark. Maybe you don't know yourself at all. Then where the path comes out of the wood back into the field I suddenly brushed against someone coming the other way. What a shock. In the pitch dark and silence. For one split second I was frightened. I didn't see or hear him coming at all. That's strange. I presume it was a him since we were on the men's side. Anyway, whoever it was was as surprised as me, I heard him catch his breath, but we both observed the vow of silence and he hurried on. Then the truly mad thing: I suddenly thought that he was me. I'd bumped into myself! In the dark at night. Then we'd split in two and he'd disappeared. God, I wish. I wish I could. Though then I suppose I'd have to decide which of the two mes I wanted to be.

I love walking in the field at night too. When it was still cold, a couple of months back, I'd take a hot cup of tea in my hands and stand in the pitch dark sipping it and smelling the steam. Still, in eight months here I've never managed to bump into anyone. And my eyesight is awful.

Day 7 Three things at war:

1. Experience of sitting in silence: the breath, the mind sinking into the body, the body drawing the mind through it, like sap. Definitely something new. Worth coming for.

2. My thoughts resisting this, clamouring to get back to misery and melodrama. Huge desire to wipe my whole mind-slate clean. How?

3. Dasgupta's evening explanations of what is going on in my head, in all our heads: our physical and mental pains are 'the consequence of accumulated karma or sankharas following the principle of conditioned arising'.

Not much clarification there.

Forgot to mention the high point of the day: a Band-Aid in my salad. Must have been wrapped round somebody's finger. I was taking it to a server to complain, then relented. Didn't want to break the Noble Silence. The silence is the best thing about this place, like a cocoon. I would never have imagined the intimacy, eating together in silence.

Meredith's plaster in the gentleman's Waldorf salad. She's hopeless.

The second cigarette is not as good as the first. I'm already hawking.

Conditioned arising is a funny expression. Nice title for a novel maybe. Nothing is absolutely itself. Everything arises as a consequence of certain conditions. Nothing is independent or permanent. Ergo, to get rid of something all you have to do is remove the conditions for its arising.

Easy.

Buddhism is an optimistic way of life, says Dasgupta with his droll, gala-evening smile. There is suffering, but there is also an end of suffering, a path that removes the conditions that allow suffering to arise. I'm getting to like him, the way you do get to like an old fraud. So much of what he says is rubbish, so much is self-regarding, but it makes sense, in its way. It makes sense that a man preaches against self-regard in a self-regarding way. Why would he be aware of the dangers of self-regard if he wasn't so insufferably self-regarding? Full of self-regard he preaches against self-regard, and acquires adoring disciples. Convenient. Maybe I've said this already. Half the writers I publish write indignantly against pride and arrogance, then get more indignant when people take no notice.

Blessed are the poor in spirit, says Jesus, spiritedly.

I like Dasgupta's glistening cheeks and his immaculate white outfits on the red armchair. He wears gold cufflinks. I like the way he preens after getting a laugh from his crowd. It must have been an American crowd, to judge by the cackles. Mainly women. Or, at least, it's the women's voices you hear. On the video you don't see anyone but Dasgupta. Perhaps the men don't respond because they sense the banter is meant for the ladies. Do gurus get a leg over from time to time, the cock arising in response to certain conditions? I haven't had an erection all week. Not surprising with no T and no pornography.

Is this all men ever think about?

Jonathan reckoned modern civilization couldn't survive without pornography. To be condemned in public and enjoyed in private, he said.

176

So, no conditions, no sweet arising. Maybe it takes a Buddha to see the obvious.

No woman, no fuck.

No fuck, no children.

No marriage, no divorce.

No bottle, no drunk.

No business, no bankrupt.

No gun, no shoot.

No birth, no karma.

No karma, no birth.

The aim of Buddhism: to avoid the conditions for arising again, for being born again.

Opposite of Jesus. Always wanting people born again.

In Buddhism the very fact of being born is a sign of failure. Old karma kicking it all off again. Sorry, kid, you screwed up.

What a welcome. Every start a bad start.

There's optimism for you.

On the other hand, being born human is better than being born animal. You can develop sila, samādhi, paññā. Glass half full after all.

Because of man's superior consciousness.

Does anyone believe this guff?

We must make best moral use of being human because the chances of a human rebirth are equal to those of a blind turtle that rises to the surface of the ocean only once every hundred years finding, by pure chance, that he has poked his head through the single narrow yoke floating up there on the surface.

What is this all about? Why a yoke? What sort of yoke? Do yokes lie on the surface of oceans waiting for blind turtles to stick their heads through them?

What kind of turtle can stay under water a hundred years?

How many of them must there be when you look at all the human life around you?

Did they mean joke?

What is this story?

Actually, it's quite pleasant thinking about this crackpot Buddhist stuff instead of my own miseries. Maybe I should launch an esoteric religions list as ultimate escapism—Beginner's Guide to Tantric Meditation. A Hundred Reincarnations To Avoid At All Costs.

Bet there's a market.

I'm enjoying this too, Mr Diarist. Maybe if you and me just got together and chatted and smoked and had a quiet drink and a game of pool we could forget all the shit that has been driving us mad.

No daydreams of sex now the curse has arrived.

It never bothered Jonathan.

First time we made love I was bleeding like a pig.

He said . . .

Stop.

Breathe.

The time I came to get my stuff having said I was leaving. I was leaving for ever. She had cooked big tomatoes stuffed with couscous. She had bought a bottle of whisky and chocolates. Susie was excited about an audition. I sat in my chair and ate the tomatoes and the couscous, which was flavoured with nutmeg and pinoli. I sat in the garden on the bench beneath the wisteria and poured a shot of whisky, chose a chocolate. I never got up again. Maybe that is what bourgeois means. Birthright sold for a few liqueurs.

Then the coldness. The rancour.

Mum used to make Dad steak tartare when he threatened to leave. And shush the cats into the spare bedroom.

Dream. I'm on the floor wrestling with some kind of man-animal-monster that is also part of me, in me, and I'm trying to push him away, but it's dark and I can't see what's me and what isn't. It's a wild struggle. I'm making a superhuman effort to push this creature inside me, indistinguishable from me, away from me. Woke in a sweat with the word 'exorcism' on my lips. Exorcism, exorcism. Not ready yet. I don't feel ready. So many dreams. All intense. The locked room with the broken Christmas tree. The car crash.

My dream is I'm walking along the seashore with Jonathan. The breakers thunder and rush right up to where we're walking. He has his arm round me and we're in love. It breaks my heart, that dream. It sets me back weeks.

Suppose for the sake of argument I'm reborn as a newt. Of course I don't know I was previously a man. I don't know I was previously married to L. Relief. I don't know it was Everests of negative marital karma that led to this humiliating downward transformation. Prince to newt. Actually, I don't feel transformed or humiliated at all. I don't even realize I've been spared the frog. I'm a newt. I'm very happy slithering in and out of the weedy pond. Don't even have to decide between earth and water. I'm amphibian. It's a great life being a newt. Dukkha is for humans. Humans suffer, not newts. Humans make themselves miserable with their thoughts, their need to decide things. Newts are in nirvana from day one. Without even trying. Is there anything that makes me suffer aside from my thoughts, my impossible decisions? Nothing. I have a dreadful pain in my back. That's not suffering. I have merciless haemorrhoids. A joke. Not a yoke. My haemorrhoids are old pals. Give me a lobotomy and I'd be happy as Larry. If I don't want a lobotomy, it means I don't want happiness, or Larriness. I don't want nirvana. I want to be alive and suffering with a messy, mixed-up personal story. My little intruder with the cute cantaloupes was spot on there: 'You love your pain too much.' She really did look

Cute cantaloupes!

At least I remember what I wrote now. It must have been in the previous exercise book. In four days he's finished one and scribbled half another.

Who would ever think of returning as a newt?

Zoë said everyone over forty had haemorrhoids. She was thirty-three.

interestingly animal, with that funny, screwed-up little mouth and long teeth. Small hands, dirty nails. Not unlike T in a way. An odd sort of nibbliness.

Too bad this diary paper isn't absorbent. I could tear the pages out, clean up between the legs and flush.

My mouth is *not* screwed up. It's pursed.

'Pretty pursed lips, my sweet little rodent.'

I'll use some bog paper for the moment. There's always plenty of bog paper at the Dasgupta.

Judging by where she sits she must be a server. So still and straight-backed, hour after hour. I wish I could.

How much did she read? Do they check our rooms? Surely not a woman in the men's, though.

Anyway, that's definitely what they're trying to teach here. Stop identifying with your pain. Detach, de-dramatize. When they asked the woman who was crying to leave the meditation room, the first vipassana session, I was worried for her, sobbing away, some kind of breakdown, and Harper just tells her to leave if she can't stop crying. In his super-dead bureaucratic voice. How can he be so uncaring? I'm thinking. Then I saw the sense of it.

You love your pain too much.

Stop crying. Stop dramatizing. Concentrate on the breath going in and out of the lungs. A matter of the utmost importance for you.

Newts don't cry.

Damn, I've finally seen that's what he meant by the second arrow being optional. How slow can you be?

All our marriage I've been afraid. That's the truth. Did you know how terrifying you are, Linda? Your coldness, your rigidity, your rages. Have you any idea? Or is it just me? You've been married to a spineless weakling, a newt, when what you needed was a man.

I live like a widower haunted by his wife's angry ghost.

Very funny. There was a spider on the floor today between my cushion and the guy to my left. Didn't know what to do since we've taken the vow not to kill any living creature. Couldn't communicate with this guy, who seems a much more experienced meditator than me since he never seems to move. The spider didn't know which mat he'd prefer to climb on and neither of us could shut our eyes and just let him go where he wanted. Why not? What could happen? It went on and on, the spider moseying back and forth, back and forth. Must have wasted half an hour watching a creature that is completely harmless, waiting no doubt to be reincarnated as human so he can take his first step on the Dhamma path. Eventually the guy behind us saw the thing, got it to climb on his hand and took it out. Hard to think the spider was suffering any more than us, or in any way inferior to us. It must be quite fun spinning your way down from the roof and disturbing the meditators.

Spiders don't bother me at all. I could meditate with spiders crawling all over me. But I remember a wild scene with Zoë in a motel bathroom.

Question: can we keep the conditioned arising theory and dump the reincarnation?

You have no self. Last night's video. What you experience as self is an amalgamation of five basic chemical elements (forgotten what they are). Constant fluctuation of said elemnts, or aggregates, conditions the circumstances in which, at any one moment, consciousness arises. Hence instability. Hence difficulty making decisions. Hence difficulty knowing who you are.

Makes sense.

In my case, then, what are/were the conditions that led to how things are in my head now? The conditions of this arising that is me.

How did it all begin?

When I met her across the table at Dad's office party?

Bright red mouth, flowery smell.

She was immediately, but immediately, the mother I wished I'd had. The one who would find time to notice me, to love me.

I was immediately, but immediately, the child she was leaving it very late to have. The child she needed so she could feel she'd lived.

Nothing clear in our heads, of course, but definitely a sense of destiny.

She saw the danger. One drunken fuck and she fled.

I couldn't let her get away. A guy with five older brothers isn't going to hear a woman say she needs an older man.

I tracked her down, laid siege to her phone, stood under her window.

'What you need is a child.'

'You're too young.'

'And you can't wait.'

She'd had an unhappy time with a married man. She drank too much. She was interesting. I could help her. I fell in love with the story of helping her. She had the money to help me. And the expertise.

Fatal meeting of needs. Conditioned arising.

Newts, real newts, don't have to deal with any of this. Newts don't have mothers who ignore them, or who they think ignored them. Newts don't live in stories, projecting and planning and regretting and reconstructing. They don't tell and retell. They don't shoot second arrows. Newts slide in and out of slime catching insects on their tongues. Wordless, worryless. L and I had to concoct the most elaborate stories to justify the folly of a twenty-three-year-old male marrying a thirty-nine-year-old female. I was a brilliant young man, much older than my age, in need of money and stability to launch an adventurous publishing house that would mark a turning point in English literature. I really believed that. She had recognized my genius, she had cash, she would withdraw from the law courts, bring up her baby, support my project, Wordsmith.

Mum wept. She couldn't believe it. She couldn't suspend disbelief.

First time Mum noticed me was when I escaped her. And fucked up big-time.

So. Susie born into a story of special love, special achieving, special denial. A tall story. If Susie and I weren't amazingly special we couldn't justify L's having blown her career, L's having blown her family money for Wordsmith, L's having withdrawn from the world. She had invested in us and we were locked in her investment. We had to yield. A high return.

L obsessed by achievement: mine and Susie's, not her own. We mustn't let her down. Otherwise she starts drinking again. We have to succeed to stop her drinking herself to death.

Everyone else disparaged. Everyone else despised. We her only contact with the outside. Accomplices against the world.

Conspiracy of three. She the queen bee, we the drone and the worker. She at home, we roving. She the mind, we the body.

When I was criticized she defended me. She was counsel for the defence. I needed her.

When I was successful she was envious, critical. Counsel for the prosecution. I needed to be rid of her.

When she understood I was looking at young women, she loathed and despised me. Judge and jury.

She had nourished a viper.

Her bowel problems. Her constipation. Her rages.

Communication went out along with sex. No fuck, no talk.

How can Dasgupta imagine that the mental trap we are in can be nullified just by stepping back from attachment and identification? It's not a question of a second arrow but of third fourth tenth twentieth hundredth thousandth arrows all shot ages ago, all dead on target.

San Sebastian.

I am locked in a story and can't wish it away. It won't dissolve because I say, 'Story story not my story.'

It's not a play I can get up and walk out of.

Or, rather, it is a play, but I'm one of the paid-up actors. They don't let you leave. Or if you do you die of hunger.

Disappointed with me, L suffocated Susie. If Susie took piano lessons, L also took piano lessons. To help her daughter, to outshine her daughter. If Susie studied Spanish, L also studied Spanish, with better results. To show her husband how much genius and potential had been sacrificed when she gave up her career for me, for Susie.

Then she drank for a couple of months.

Susie took up dance because L couldn't. L is too awkward. L has a bad hip. Susie excelled in dance rejoiced in dance gloried in dance because her mother couldn't dance, although to compensate she soon learned everything there was to know about choreography. L soon knew every opening, every career track in the world of dance. L bought the clothes, the shoes. L drove her daughter to dance classes and back, talked about her to everyone she met. L promoted her at every possible opportunity.

L didn't dance: she dazzled. With dance talk.

L stopped drinking to admire her daughter dancing.

I feel ill.

I feel there is nothing between us but the awareness that there is nothing between us. It's the only thing we share. The knowledge of defeat. What intimacy.

That makes it more and more important to achieve.

Do L and I really care about Susie, or is it that we don't want to have to tell people our daughter is a failure? Susie's failed. We don't want to have to tell people. We can't enthuse about our daughter running off with a middle-aged alcoholic facing a gaol sentence for manslaughter. Our marriage hangs together thanks to shared pride in Susie's success, career success. Without that, L's sacrifices were in vain. Our daughter's beauty and success justify our continuing (gangrenous) marriage. Gangrenous, paralysed, mouldering.

Is that it?

Is that what Dasgupta means by deep, deep sankharas?

I must do everything I can to get Susie to change her mind so we can keep our old stalemate going.

Stalemate. Stale meat.

Is that it?

Reminds me of The Keeper. Hero embalms whole family to keep everything as it is. House and home exactly as it is.

If Wordsmith goes under, we'll definitely lose the house. Lose the bay window. Lose the garden. Lose the wisteria. I love the wisteria. Meditating this morning, strange moment, I unlatched the back gate, smelt the jasmine along the fence. It was so present. I brushed aside a few leaves and went through to the terrace. I was home. Safe at home. It was so intense.

If I had come to the Dasgupta twenty years ago, maybe there would have been some point. How can I detach in the middle of this drama that obliges me to be myself? I can't change the conditions that long ago determined how my consciousness arises. My wife won't let me. The banks won't let me. The bookshops won't let me. My authors won't let me. I can't tell the banks, sorry no self. They're not familiar with the doctrine of anatta. They tell me what my responsibilities are, they show me where I signed on the dotted line. You are your signature.

The Keeper was definitely the best book Wordsmith ever published. Should have won the Booker. We was robbed!

Is this why Susie's doing it? Not because she loves the bloke, but because she's understood that her success is the only thing that keeps her parents together? She wants to blow us apart with this disappointment. She can't choose her successful life because she feels we created it more for ourselves than for her. She damages herself to give us the coup de grâce.

Is that it?

The conditions of her arising. And falling.

Or is it that you don't want to believe in her passionate love? Because you're so incapable of it yourself. Passion shames you. Because when you should have walked off with T, you didn't. You were in love with T and did nothing about it. You let your love die because you didn't have the courage. You see Susie committing career suicide for love and you feel humbled, humiliated. You see the beauty of love, real love, sacrificial love, and you see your utter, utter failure to love.

She'll save him and they'll live happily ever after. Maybe.

Wasn't the enigma in *The Keeper* that the three victims were embalmed years apart? The grandmother before the son, the son before the mother. So first the son, then the mother must have accepted the presence of a corpse/corpses on an armchair/armchairs around the house, for years, before falling victim themselves. Bizarre. But fascinating. Accomplices becoming victims. Even after seeing another accomplice become victim.

So what if the author borrowed the plot from some old fairy tale? Everybody else does. Wordsmith wouldn't be on the brink if they'd given it the Booker.

Dasgupta says we must avoid mental proliferation/speculation/daydreaming/second arrows etc., but how can I not speculate on the motives which are prompting my only child to throw away her talents to be with a drunken criminal the other side of the globe?

Is that inappropriate attachment?

Perhaps it's our fault. She runs off for love because her parents show no love. She loves passionately because our togetherness is embalmed venom.

I should surely pay attention to something if it's my fault.

Or is she clinically mad? Have her sectioned?

How can I benefit from the teachings of Dasgupta until this drama is behind me? How can anyone who is as involved in life as I am, as mixed up with others as I am, as bound to others hand and foot, how can such a person benefit from Dasgupta's simplistic precepts, how can such a person MEDITATE when his wife is exploding in his head, his daughter is singing in his ears, his mistress is breathing on his neck, his wisteria is beckoning, his jasmine drenches the air with perfume, his beautiful lawn begs to be mown?

If only it was over. Truly over. The child dead, the mother eventually realizes she'll have to bury him and let go. Pain is not pain when there is no alternative.

Maybe there's really only one arrow, the second.

The first was hardly an arrow at all.

How can a newt suffer?

Talk about indecision. I can't even decide which way to cross my legs now. Terrified before Strong Determination that I'll choose the wrong position and be in awful pain. Do I tuck in the left first or the right? Meanwhile the guy behind me suddenly has a cold. At one point it felt like his wheezing was right inside my chest.

Dreamed of T. We were making love. Normal lavish rejoicing. Unbelievably vivid. Don't know where my body ends and hers begins. Utter serenity. Until I realize we're at home. We're on the sofa at home, for God's sake. L is walking by, she's calling to the dog. Susie is tugging her sleeve. 'Mum, look at Dad and Teresa. Look at Dad and Teresa! Why don't you look, Mum?' Susie knows. 'Why don't you see?' But L doesn't turn. L doesn't want to see. L's calling the dog. 'Charlie. Charlie!' And the dog is T's husband. T's husband is L's dog!

'I'm pregnant,' T is saying. 'I'm going to have your child.' No, she's already had it, it's already there on her bosom. A tiny newt is crawling up her cleavage to suck on her nipple.

That's my boy.

Bizarre moment after two-thirty session. I'd just about held my position to the end. I'm getting to my feet, fighting pins and needles, when suddenly I'm transfixed by the sight of my blanket that I'd let fall from my back on to the cushion. I honestly can't move for staring at the folds of my grey blanket. I'm fascinated by how complicated all the curves and wrinkles are and the way the light plays over the whole tangle and by the realization that no blanket will ever again fall in exactly that conformation. An intense awareness that the moment is unique, that all moments are unique.

Yeah, wow, yawn. But this is another bit I could have written myself. We all get these moments at the Dasgupta.

The thing about The Keeper was definitely the house. He wanted to keep the family together because he loved the house. The point of the novel perhaps was to capture the essentially bourgeois spirit of the embalmer. The serial killer keeps a beautiful garden. The neighbours are admirers. 'Very able with roses and climber plants,' someone tells the BBC. 'Quite the artist.'

I love the bay windows. I love the old fireplace. I adore the rose arch.

And the irises.

190

In the end all those murders never made much money.
I'd have done better publishing porn.

The loo is full of smoke. Time to open a window. Cig four already. Two to go. But I feel calmer now. The more upset my diarist is, the calmer I feel. Maybe that's why Jonathan read all those miserable books. Cormac something. Thomas Bernstein? The more other people are in the shit, the more the reader breathes easy.
Don't think Mrs Harper would approve.

Started crying in the field. I was on my back in the grass.
Suddenly the thoughts turned to tears, the thoughts streamed out of my head in tears. Kept muttering, I love my wife I must escape I hate my wife I must escape I love my wife I must escape I hate my wife I must escape. Life is unfair unfair unfair unfair unfair unfair unfair unfair.
   Instructive.
   So there I am on my back in the field weeping and I realize I'm weeping for JOY. Yep. Lunatic. This meditation stuff has driven me mad. I'm a hopeless failure but I love life. I've thrown away my life, my marriage, twenty-five years, but I'm full of optimism. Criminal. Meditation should be banned. Definitely. It is dangerous for a mind to be left in silence for long. We need music, we need the radio, we need the television, we need parties. Even books. Good news, bad news, anything. Actually, nothing better than bad news. A tsunami an earthquake a flood volcano bomb anal rape female circumcision torture scandal atrocity. Send a donation write a letter post a comment make your point say your piece anything but this silence alone with your thoughts.

Not just me but all of us. Think. 150 people all desperate together in the same room. 150 desperate silences in the same room, ferocious seething cancerous silences.

300 stiff legs, stiff ankles, sore knees.

All the stories. Think of all the awful stories revolving in all these sick heads. Worse than my Master Murder list. Dissolve them in acid, silent acid, acid silence.

Whatever you do, don't write them down. Don't publish!

Or maybe no, write them down the better to destroy them. Good idea. Paper can be torn up. Computer files can be erased.

Instead of a publishing company, an UNpublishing company.

Gap in the market!

'My dear young man, this is a very interesting novel you have written, extremely poignant; the account you give of your hero's decline into poverty, old age and perversion is at once moving, disquieting and deeply, deeply disturbing. Anyway, I'm pleased to say we can offer you a contract to destroy this story in all extant editions typescripts electronic files and whatsoever other relevant media. Our offer will be for world rights of course. We undertake to keep the story out of print worldwide for at least ten years from the date of signature. Our boast is that our titles are all surrounded by the utmost silence and secrecy; under no circumstances will your name as author appear in any publication. No, my young man, neither you nor anyone else need ever be troubled by this moving story again.'

The author has exercised his moral right.

What do stories do but glamorize pain? That's true of all the novels I've published, all the pretentious sagas I hoped would change the face of English literature. They glamorize suffering. Only a life with suffering is glamorous. That's obvious. Starting with Christ. Physical suffering love suffering spiritual suffering. No suffering, no glamour. We're in love with dukkha. That's the truth. Head over heels in love with pain. Pretending we want happiness, we go prospecting for misery, like paupers panning for gold. Our lives have to be moving stories. No triumph without adversity. Long adversity. The longer the better. Angela's acid ashes. And the seduction is in the adversity, not the last-page triumph. The seduction is in the sentiment that clings to adversity. Oh, poor thing. Oh, poor David Copperfield. Oh, poor Little Nell. Oh, my generous heart having these generous feelings for these poor people.

Let's catch some tsunami with our supper.

Tsunami salami.

Dasgupta teaches emotional calm. The girl cries in the quiet of the meditation room. She has a story to tell, a novel to write. All too soon she'll be running to the publishers with her typescript. How many misery memoirs will be waiting on my desk when I get back to the office? Then her pain can be made public and everyone can hold it in their hands, savour it, caress it, fold back the page and sigh, Oh, what intense feelings, oh, what infernal dilemmas, oh, how noble the human soul! Oh, what a fascinating life!

Dasgupta says, My friends, the last thing we need is your unhappy story, the last thing we need is an account of your pain.

We need silence.

If you can't stop crying, please leave the room.

Harper was right not to enquire into my difficulties, to dismiss me with a simple injunction. Don't shoot that second arrow, mate.

Leave the room. Put down your pen.

The second arrow is the pen.

Of course!

Second Arrow Publishing. Brilliant!

A profitable unhappiness.

The cute little girl was absolutely right. Oh, I could kiss her. You love your pain too much. How can she be so young and so wise? You love your pen too much. Your pein. Oh, I could kiss her wise little rabbity lips.

Publishing should be banned. Forbidden. Publishing is not a right livelihood. Not part of the eightfold path. Harper should have said something. Should have said, Students, you'll never get to nirvana by publishing.

After this retreat I go home, I wind up Wordsmith, I tell Susie her life is hers to do what she wants—absolutely whatever you want—I tell L it is over between us. Linda, it's over. It is truly over. And T. I tell T it's over too. Terry, it's over. I only needed Terry to stay with Linda. I'm a disgrace. Charlie is a fine man. Take care of your husband.

Everything's over.

I wish.

And what then? Where am I?

Broccoli

Jonathan had no mood swings, no indecisions. I could get up now, go back to Dormitory A, take off my jeans, stretch out in bed beside my diarist. 'Just looking in your eyes now,' he wrote on a beer mat 'is the most beautiful moment of my life.' That was our best evening together, the one before the last. Not for a second did he think of changing his plans. I could storm into his bedroom and shout, 'What a shit you are, Mr Diarist! What a twisted mixed-up worm!' I could dump his diary in the bin and forget about it. I could sneak it back to his bedside with a word of wisdom. 'Just let go. GH. Let go of your big ego.' I do feel compassion for him and his wife. They're lost. I feel compassion for my parents. They will never be happy together and they will never be happy apart. Talk about people embalming each other. Marriot's was a funeral parlour. It would have been death to marry Carl.

But I thought you *wanted* to die.

Two moths are fluttering against the lightshade in the female servers' room. Why have I stopped killing insects? It's creepy how they bang and scrabble against the paper globe. It's mindless. All Dasgupta lightshades are Ikea. One moth drops to the floor, twitches its filthy wings, whirrs up again. Jonathan killed flies by clapping his hands. He never got angry or irritable, except when you tried to talk about his wife. 'My ex-wife,' he said. 'Ex marks the spot.'

It's very still in here. Except for the moths. They're creepy the way they seem to look for death, but I do feel compassion for them. I feel lost. Maybe I should kill a fly or two, just to get back in the saddle. Maybe that's what I need, to shag and kill and be brutal: fuck Ralph, fuck up Ralph, tear up the diary, swat these stupid moths, write some obscene graffiti with menstrual blood. DASUCKTA!

It's two a.m. and Beth's at a turning point.

With nowhere to turn.

Do I leave this place or do I stay?

Nothing. Stuck.

Say I went to bed and listened to the mouse gnawing, to Stephanie snoring. I could. I could do that. What does the mouse want in that bedroom? To gnaw our toes? To nibble our ears? To pee on our bedding? Or just to be there, to share our company?

What do animals do all day? What are these moths doing, really? How do they *know* what to do?

Their bodies tell them.

A sort of nibbliness! Rabbity. The teeth, I suppose.

Say I went back into the kitchen and pigged out on yesterday's leftovers. I could do that. It amazed Carl how much I ate after concerts. We were so sweaty and smoky and drunk and alive. Sausages. Pizza. Kebabs. Then sex. Sometimes I hardly knew who with. Carl was always up and down, happy or depressed.

He wanted so much to marry me. He could already smell our babies. They were puppies or baby rabbits. Carl wanted to change the straw. He was a sweet little boy in need of a pet. It should have been obvious I wasn't the one. I do feel compassion for him. He was a fantastic guitarist. So slick. So clean. So talented. But he would have accepted a job at Marriot's any day. Marketing. Perhaps he already has. Perhaps Carl is working there now, for Dad, selling Marriot's synthetics. I feel compassion for him. I feel compassion for myself. I envy my diarist's pregnant girlfriend. Teresa. Nice name. God, I envy her. Think. All she has to do is let her creature grow. Let her body do its thing. Like the mice, the moths. Woman in the row behind me. Who cares who the father is? I didn't care, really. I just didn't want to bring up a child with Carl. It was obvious Jonathan would never accept one. I could go to Mi Nu and ask, Why do I never know what to do? Time ticks by and everyone is sleeping or busy. The moths are busy, the rabbits are busy. The mice are busy. My diarist is dreaming demons. I never know what to do. I can't sleep. I didn't let my creature grow, Mi Nu. I failed to love failed to love.

I could masturbate. Yep. I could pull down my jeans, my panties, stretch back in the armchair, smell myself, lick my fingertips. That drove Jonathan wild. He nibbled my knuckles. Please make yourself come, Beth, please please please. I love it when you come.

No, I couldn't.

With the curse as well.

I could check my email. Out of the kitchen, left towards the main door, then right and I'm in the office. They won't have a password on the PC. It's not in the Dasgupta spirit. Or something like, BEHAPPY. User name: ALLBEINGS, password BEHAPPY. I cross the kitchen, go into the office, turn on the computer, check my mail. Servers are allowed occasional Internet access, if they ask permission, if they don't visit the wrong sites. To keep in touch with their nearest and dearest, of course. I used to dream about it the first month at the Dasgupta. It was one of the hardest things to get out of my head. I open my mail and his name pops up. Scores of messages. Jon Jon Jon Jon. I want you back, Beth. I want to live with you. I want to paint you day in day out. Please. Forgive me for not believing about the coma. Forgive me. Beth. Come back, Beth. I need you, Beth.

There will be mails from Carl, mails from Zoë, mails from Mum, from Dad, from the producer, the manager. Where are you, Beth? Dear Elisabeth, where are you? Betsy, what's become of you? You don't have to do this.

Forgive me for not believing you, Jonathan has written. Just looking in your eyes that evening . . .

I got over these fantasies months ago.

Apparently not.

'If there are thoughts, daydreams, unwelcome mental projections, gently return your attention to the breath, to the in-breath crossing the lip, the out-breath crossing the lip . . .'

You're lucky you still have a breath.

Maybe Hervé will have written. *Il ne faut pas te sentir coupable, chere Elisabeth. Ce n'est pas ta faute si nous sommes venus nous baigner avec toi.*

Did Philippe die, Mi Nu?

Is an induced coma a form of embalming? Is he still there in the hospital bed?

'They asked you to go in the sea, Beth, not you them.'

Carl was by my side, my bedside. I kept my eyes closed, texting beneath the sheets.

'They're only inducing the coma, Beth. It's a controlled thing. He'll recover. It's not your fault. And thank God it's not you.'

But I was planning to kill myself, Carl. No, I didn't say the words. I couldn't speak to him. And killing yourself is something you should do on your own. Not with two nice French boys. They would never have gone in the sea without me.

Not on a night like that.

They would never have gone with me if they knew I was planning to kill myself.

Carl sat by my bed for days. The perfect boyfriend. 'Think about the child, Beth,' he said. 'For Christ's sake. Think about us.'

I lost the child, Carl. Haven't the doctors told you? I didn't speak. I kept my eyes closed. I had a perfect boyfriend and I'd completely failed to love him. I tried, I couldn't. I betrayed him. I cheated him. Every evening making love in the tent, I tried to be there, really to make love, I think I tried. I couldn't. I couldn't love. My only plan was escape. If he wouldn't disappear, then I must. I must dissolve in thin air. Or walk into the sea.

Instead the child vanished.

I'M IN INTENSIVE CARE, I texted. THEY ARE GOING TO INDUCE A COMA. IF YOU LOVE ME, COME BEFORE IT'S TOO LATE.

It's not true I could check my email. I couldn't. Maybe I'll never look at email again.

What if the news were all good, though?

Beth, Philippe's out of coma. He's asking after you.

Beth, 'Better Off On My Own' is number one. Everyone's looking for you. Everybody wants you. Where on earth have you buried yourself? We have bookings for every major festival. We have contracts for two new CDs. We have money for a house.

I'm sorry, Carl, that's not what I want any more.

I'm sorry, Carl, I'm not me any more.

This is the wrong email address for me, Carl.

I've escaped, I've disappeared.

Dear Elisabeth, I'm afraid Dad's cancer has come back. He's very poorly. Whatever your reasons for disappearing, do please come now. It's unkind not to.

There's no way I can check my mail.

Why can't the moths leave be? Can't they feel they're destroying their wings, scrabbling at the light, pressing their bodies where bodies can't go?

The moths are a torture. I feel compassion for them.

My pen is pushing and scrabbling where I can never go. Pein. Nice word, Mr Diarist.

An hour ago I was just fine, reading his diary. I was enjoying his troubles.

A week ago I was fine, living the Dasgupta routine, accepting the Dasgupta rules.

I was fine washing rice and kichada beans.

Fine chopping celeriac.

Fine mashing potatoes with soya milk.

Fine spraying crap off dishes.

Writing, I push myself against a hard place, without getting anywhere, but without really suffering either.

Does that make sense?

Maybe I mean, without any chance of dying.

I stood up, went through the kitchen and switched on the lights. They hadn't cleaned up very well. My throat was raw from the cigarettes. And I was getting sticky. There was a bowl of chopped cabbage that should have gone in the cold room. The tea-towel covering it was filthy. Vikram would go ballistic. I put on a clean tea-towel and moved it. Imagine getting locked in the cold room. You're someone else's left-overs, freezing to death.

I loaded a trolley and took plates and bowls and cutlery into the dining halls for breakfast. The female hall. The male hall. I turned all the lights on. I checked the cereals, the spreads, the milk, the marge, the butter, the honey, and replenished them. I could do these things in my sleep. I don't need to make a decision to check if there's soya and dairy, sesame seeds and ground nuts. I don't need to be someone. The Rooibos has run out on the men's side, the hummus on the women's. If only there was more to do. If only I could serve and serve and serve. Serve and serve. Night after night. Day after day. A nobody. If I could wash someone's clothes, polish someone's shoes, cut someone's hair, cook someone's meal, iron someone's shirts. Like Mum did for Dad, not loving, just serving. 'Like hell I'll iron your shirts,' I told Carl. I couldn't love him. I did try. Maybe I didn't. What do words like 'try' mean around words like 'love'? 'I don't do laundry,' I told him. 'I don't do meals. I definitely don't do ironing. When we're famous we'll live in a hotel. We'll be waited on hand and foot.' Why did I stay with a boy I didn't love? That's the weird thing. For years. Why did I treat him so badly? The pleasure of serving people at the Dasgupta is precisely that you don't know them, like hotel guests. This person is not your father. He's not Jonathan. He's not Carl. Not a mother or a girlfriend or a sister. You expect nothing back. You don't feel resentful. Their being nobody becomes your being nobody. Not knowing them you don't know yourself. You're a server serving. Serving mankind, serving yourself. Being nobody is serving yourself.

I put the trays for the dirty dishes on the table by the door. Then the plastic bucket for the cutlery. First the women's side, then the men's. It's good there are two sides to serve. Twice the work. The first days as a server I kept doing kindnesses for everyone. I'd run off and get a clean knife for someone who had dropped hers. I'd fetch a heavy blanket for a meditator who was shivering. It was a sort of show. Very Beth. I wanted to make myself known, to say, Here's Beth, serving you! Big grin on my face. Here's Beth, helping you to meditate! That makes me laugh now. That isn't service. Service is doing only what is required, facelessly, no more, nothing personal. Let the woman eating go to the tray and get herself a clean knife. Let the meditator go to the back of the room and get herself the blankets she needs. Personal is poison. Personal distracts. Invites relationships. I wish I could serve more and more and more, in the dead of night, always in the dead of night, in complete silence, unheard, unseen, unpraised, unloved. Serving. I don't want to be loved. I mustn't be loved. I don't want to fail to love the person who loves me. I don't want anything.

May all beings visible and invisible be free from all attachment.

May all beings be liberated, liberated, liberated.

I want to be one of the invisible beings.

Mi Nu is becoming invisible. One day we will see right through her. She won't be there.

I put out breadknives and crackers. I measured the oats for the men's porridge and the women's porridge. I love to smell the oats on my fingers. I put prunes and lemon slices in a pan to warm. If only there'd been more to do, I would have gone on for hours. I wasn't tired. It was like setting up for a concert when you've arrived too early. Take it slowly. The drums the amps the mikes the leads the wah wah. I loved setting up with Zoë. We bumped into each other and giggled. Sex was so childish with Zoë. I was so childish.

Now I remembered the serving spoons for the cereals, for the stewed fruit. I made up bowls of oranges and apples. The apples were a deep waxy green. I took them one by one from the box in the cold room, rinsed them and dried them at the sink. I even polished them with a clean tea-towel. They looked good. And the oranges glowed beside them. The orange of the oranges made the green of the apples greener. How healthy fruit is. After concerts we ate crap. We rushed to whatever crap place would fill us with junk and booze. What do you expect? But now I was bleeding like a pig. I was uncomfortable with sodden wads of TP between my legs. I must go to the main loos and get some tampons. You're an unclean woman, Betsy M. They should segregate you.

Jonathan was the only guy I ever knew who didn't mind blood on his dick. Nothing fazed him. Nothing changed him. Not blood, not passion. There was nothing doing with Carl on menstrual days. If only the Red Army had invaded France that week. No sex, but he'd go all concerned and caring. 'How are you feeling, Beth? Will you be able to sing, Beth?' Carl liked a girl to be weak, he loved me fragile. A fragile Beth with puppies and baby rabbits to look after. Jesus. I went to the loo which still smelt smoky. If only I had another pack. If only you could chain smoke for eternity. Chain smoke, chain drink, chain fuck. Why not? If it has to be *dukkha,* go the whole hog.

I went back to the kitchen and looked for the recipe book. Time was passing. A month away will pass in a blink, Jonathan said. He actually smiled. I found it on the small fridge, then made a cup of chai instead. I rinsed a pot, filled it from the kitchen boiler, stirred in ginger, cloves, cinnamon. I'd never have dreamed of drinking this brew before I came to the Dasgupta. No fennel seeds, though. Someone must have put them away in the wrong place. We were in a pub in Edinburgh and one of the bands invited me on stage. Someone had recognized me. We did a pepped-up cover of 'Girls Just Wanna Have Fun'. The crowd was stomping. I was weeping as I sang. I was laughing. My voice was booming. I cupped the mike, "'Oh-o-oh-o-oh. When the working day is done, girls just wanna have fun.'" It wasn't true. I wanted Jonathan. 'Just looking in your eyes now . . .' he scribbled on his beer mat. He was ecstatic. People couldn't believe I was with such an old guy. The next night, back in London, he was in bed before eleven for an early start.

'I have other fish to fry,' I told him.

Vikram's Vipassana Cookbook. Food for Meditation. Cool Cooking for Cool Karma. The servers always made jokes about the folder with the recipes. We imagined a cover illustration with Vikram sitting cross-legged in the bratt pan.

I turned to day nine. Tofu and broccoli stir-fry, steamed kale, mashed potatoes, a mixed salad, soya mayonnaise, two dressings. I went into the cold room to see if anything had been prepared yet. The spuds. There were two plastic boxes with peeled potatoes in cold water. Nothing else. I went to the fresh-supplies shelves, found a box of broccoli and dragged it out to the counter.

It's incredible how tightly they pack broccoli, how good it looks in the box. There's a layer with heads down and stalks up and a layer with heads up and stalks down. Looking in the box, you see the heads in rows and between each foursome of heads a fat stalk poking up from the layer beneath. It all fits so neatly it looks like a jigsaw. You can't lift one out without pulling them all up. They're locked there. To move them you have to break one, at least one.

I wondered how they did that, whether they had a broccoli-packing machine, or just people pushing them into place. The heads were a fine dark dull green and the stalks were pale and rubbery. It was an unbroken pattern that you needed to break to cook them. It seemed a shame.

I waited a moment before pulling one out. How could they fit together so well, even though, being living things, they must all be different? At least slightly. Not made to fit together. Not like factory things. I felt weirdly mesmerized looking at the dark broccoli heads and pale broccoli stalks. My breathing went softer and I was suddenly aware of it. I had the feeling I was seeing something that wasn't the broccoli really, even though, as Dasgupta would say, when you are looking at broccoli, you are looking at broccoli, nothing else. I shook my head.

'Break up the broccoli into small twigs,' the recipe book said.

Why did it bother me that I'd have to break one and take it out of the pattern, if the whole purpose of pulling them out of the cold room was to chuck them in the pot? I didn't know if I was blessing them, or adoring them or studying them. Or if they were just in my head. Why bother tugging feelings this way and that to fit this word or the other? Who cares what I was doing? Mum used to give us tons of broccoli because it was great against cancer, and as soon as he'd turned fifty that was exactly what Dad got.

I grabbed a stalk and yanked.

'Elisabeth? Elisabeth, what on earth are you doing?'

I had found a pair of scissors to snip the branches into a big metal colander with the tap turned on over it. The running water must have masked her footsteps.

'I couldn't sleep, Mrs Harper.'

What was *she* doing here?

I went on working as she drifted nearer. She was wearing a baggy green nightdress. She always gives that strange impression of moving on wheels. You couldn't see her legs. I snipped the broccoli into the bowl under the fluorescent light in the big empty kitchen. We understood at once there was a tension between us. It was the same tension I used to get with Mum. Love and impatience. Maybe I couldn't speak to Mrs Harper because of her motherliness. It wouldn't be like that with Mi Nu, I thought. Or with GH. I would definitely be able speak to GH, if I decided to go that way. He is as fucked up as I am.

I felt angry with Mrs Harper that I couldn't talk to her. I wanted to yell. I went on with what I was doing. The broccoli offered the tiniest resistance, then the scissors snipped. The little branches tumbled into the colander where the running water frothed over them, shifting the pale stalks and dark heads this way and that. I said: 'I love touching vegetables and washing them. It calms me down.'

She reached over and turned off the tap. The water gurgled away. The broccoli sucked and drained. There was quiet. I could hear her wheezing now. She must have a cold. Eventually she said: 'I'm sorry you can't sleep, Elisabeth.' Her voice is kind and heavy with regret. I hate that. I hate regret. Mum's regret. Carl's regret. My regret.

Jonathan never regretted anything.

I picked up another head of broccoli and snipped harder. It's the rubbery resistance then the sudden snap that drives you wild. Like baby's fingers.

'Sometimes when we meditate more intensely, as you have been doing for the last three days, Elisabeth, we find things getting harder rather than easier. We find we have more pains rather than fewer. And more thoughts perhaps. It gets harder to sleep.'

I knew when she stopped speaking she must be looking at me in an inquisitive way. She wanted me to confirm what she was saying.

I snipped the broccoli.

'The reason is that our stillness, our *sila, samādhi, paññā* have allowed the deep *sankharas* of the past to rise to the surface, the things that really pain and trouble us. It is part of the process of purification we spoke about. You should feel encouraged rather than disappointed.'

I hadn't said I felt disappointed.

I picked up a fresh stick of broccoli, then stopped. Something was coming to a head, but what? And when exactly? Something was about to change, about to change. Oh, but I'm always about to change and never do. I was not going to cry in front of Mrs Harper.

'It's my period,' I told her. 'I'm bleeding like a pig. I'll have to go and get a tampon.'

That was true.

She wasn't convinced. She waited, watching. It began to get on my nerves. In the end I asked: 'Why do you pay me all this attention?'

She stood watching, very solid, very soft.

'You don't talk like this to the others. To Kristin. Or Ines.'

She was silent.

'Is it because I'm a bad girl? You want to convert the bad girl.'

Mrs Harper smiled. 'We have no desire to convert anyone at the Dasgupta, Elisabeth. You know that. I'm not even sure what the word means. I don't want to change your mind about anything.'

'My friends call me Beth,' I said.

I wondered if she had got a whiff of smoke. I wondered what she was doing in the kitchen at three thirty a.m. Was she after a snack? You could see she didn't starve herself.

'Ian and I have the impression that although you have been at the Dasgupta a long time, it is not because you want to be here, but because you are afraid of leaving. We would like to see you choose to stay with enthusiasm, or go with courage.'

I could have killed her. Ian and I. Ian and I.

'Why don't you just ask what my problem is?' I demanded. I slammed down the scissors. 'Why don't you ask? How can you pretend to help me without knowing anything about me? I could be a serial killer for all you know. Or a nymphomaniac.'

I looked her in the eyes. I meant to shoot arrows. If they hit home she didn't show it.

'I suppose we're concerned that you might do something disruptive to get yourself thrown out. Because you can't take the decision yourself.'

'Like what?'

She smiled gently. 'Hard to tell. Smoking on the premises. Going to the pub. Visiting the men's side.'

I stared at her. She was standing with her back slightly curved, her hands linked over her big belly. What if I rushed over and whacked her in the mouth?

I picked up the broccoli again and made five or six quick snips.

'You don't know anything about me.'

'You're standing in front of me, Elisabeth. With your scissors. At night. In the kitchen. Cutting broccoli.'

'Beth.'

She said nothing.

'That doesn't mean you know me.'

'You're here,' she repeated. 'Now. What does it mean, to know someone?'

I thought how nice it had been working in the kitchen, alone, and how agitated I was now. Her calmness was driving me wild. I needed a scene. I should chuck the broccoli at her.

'Why don't you ask me something? Ask me what's bothering me. Ask me why I feel bad.'

'You said it was your period.' She hesitated. Suddenly I was anxious she might really ask.

'What are *you* doing here?' I said quickly. 'I'm bleeding. What's your excuse?'

She sucked in her lips, smiling.

'Do you need a bowl of cereal, like Ralph? He was here earlier. He eats like a horse.'

Mrs Harper turned, trundled to the water heater, took a mug and a green-tea teabag and filled it with steaming water.

'I've got a sore throat. I need some tea.' Again she hesitated. 'You asked why I don't want to know what's bothering you, why I don't ask you. But if you think about it, Elisabeth, why would I want to hear about your *sankharas?* How would that help? My knowing. Your past *sankharas* are not you. I'm not a psychologist. I have no expertise in analysing someone's life history. You've been here a long time now. Your stories are no longer you. You can let them go.'

'Just like that?'

I took a piece of raw broccoli and pushed it into my mouth. It was tough and cold, like the thing the dentist pushes between your gums.

'If you start telling me your past you'll go back to whatever unhappiness there was. You'll get involved again.'

I bit my lip. Something was in the air.

'Maybe if I tell someone I can get it out of my system.' She fished the teabag out of her tea and sipped. When she turned to the counter I saw her broad back, her big backside.

'Let's try an experiment,' she said brightly. 'If you really need to, you can tell me your story, but why not tell it as if it had happened to someone else? Someone called Elisabeth. Someone you used to know before you came here.'

I found I was shifting my weight from one foot to the other. Something trickled down my thigh. I needed to get to the bathroom.

'That's stupid. It's stupid pretending not to be who I am.'

'I said it was an experiment. It can't harm, can it?' She dipped her face to her cup. Her lips were sipping and smiling.

I tapped the scissors on the counter. It was an incredibly slow conversation. A chat in slow motion. The trickle moved slowly and stopped. She was watching me over the top of her tea. Her body wheezed slowly, her breasts, her flabby stomach. Waiting for a stab from my scissors maybe.

Then I said: 'I'd rather tell Mi Nu.'

'Ah.'

She nodded, as if we'd made progress. She didn't seem hurt.

'If I have to tell anyone.'

'Elisabeth, as I said, you don't have to tell anyone at all. It was you who talked of needing to tell.'

'I'd rather tell Mi Nu.'

'Well, *do*. She receives people after lunch. Make an appointment.'

I couldn't understand why I was so wired up, why I was gripping the scissors so tight.

'I can't,' I shouted. 'I keep trying to tell people but I can't. I get scared.'

She sighed deeply.

'What have you got to lose, Elisabeth? What is at stake?'

I was praying the morning gong would interrupt us. It must be nearly four. I really needed the bathroom.

'Well?'

'She won't be able to help me, will she? It will be a waste of time. She'll despise me.'

I dropped the scissors, put my hands on the counter behind, jumped up to sit on it and started to kick my heels on the cupboard door beneath. Thump thump thump. I could get one of the knives now, I thought. They were on the wall. I could grab one. We'd both be bleeding.

Then Mrs Harper said a beautiful thing. 'Elisabeth, Mi Nu will help you just by being there and listening. Mi Nu helps all of us just with her presence.'

She paused. 'I sometimes think that to look at Mi Nu is to look at *vipassana* itself. Watching her is all the instruction anyone needs. You are quite right to want to talk to Mi Nu. And don't worry, there's no question of her despising you.' She laughed very naturally, as if we were at a nice tea party. 'I doubt if she'll say much, though.'

I was surprised, like I'd betrayed someone and they didn't mind.

'Isn't Mi Nu fantastic?' I jumped down from the counter, feeling really cheerful. 'You know, though, sometimes I think all I need is a good hug.'

I shook myself in a shiver like a dog and looked straight at her, grinning. We were about a yard apart. The trickle moved again.

'Would you hug me, Mrs Harper?'

She let her tongue slip over her lips and set down her mug. 'The Dasgupta is not a place for hugs, Elisabeth.'

I felt evil.

'I know it's against the rules.'

'I'm afraid, it is, yes.'

'Does that mean you'd hug me, if the rules were different?'

She stood, unblinking, slow and pale and swollen in her baggy nightdress.

'Even with your husband you don't hug?'

She shook her head.

'You don't?'

'We took a vow, Elisabeth. For as long as we're at the Dasgupta.'

'So why are you married?'

She wasn't smiling now. After another sigh, she said slowly: 'There's more to marriage than physical contact.'

'Like what?'

She didn't answer.

'Do you have children?'

Again she shook her head. She didn't want to talk about herself.

'What did you do before coming to the Dasgupta?'

She thought a moment, as if she could hardly remember. 'I was an insurance executive. In Hartford, Connecticut.'

'Hug me.'

I moved towards her. The trickle was down at my knee.

'Please, Mrs Harper. It's been ages. Hug me tight.'

When our bodies were almost touching, she opened her arms. I could already feel what a warm, soft, motherly embrace it would be. As her hands closed around me I wriggled free and ran.

Equanimity Is Purity

What did the Buddha do about the bathroom? I mean when he decided to sit for as long as it took to be enlightened. Did his bodily functions stop, under the Bodhi tree? And what shall I do about my bleeding? Do I have to get up and change my tampon every few hours? Is enlightenment a kind of endurance test? You sit and sit and sit till it happens?

It's raining now and the only sound in the Metta Hall is the dripping from the roof. Plosh—one two three four—plish—one two three—plosh. You concentrate on body and breathing for twenty-four hours at a stretch maybe, letting go, letting go. Or forty-eight hours. When there's pain you don't react. When there's pleasure you don't react. Or a week even. Leaving behind all attachment, all aversion. Layer after layer after layer, deeper and deeper. Without even a trip to the bathroom? Without food, without water?

I'm tempted now to turn and look at the drip hitting the carpet. Why? Why do I count the seconds between the drops:

three, nine, five? What could there possibly be to look at? If I didn't have eyes there would be no danger of distraction. I'd be resigned to sitting in the dark. If I didn't have ears I wouldn't listen for the drops and count the intervals between. Why do they vary so much? The rain sounds steady on the roof. But sometimes I only get to three between drops and sometimes I count to eight. If ever I reach enlightenment, these temptations will disappear, I know that, these questions will be gone. The drops will splash on my consciousness and slide off like rain on rock. I'll ask no questions. Or they'll just fall through my mind without splashing at all. There'll be no friction, no distraction. I'll hear them and not hear them. Is that what enlightenment means? Something will change and I'll see clearly. I'll know what things I've been between here at the Dasgupta Institute, what the past was before I came here and what the future holds after I leave. Enlightenment would set me free.

I wonder if nature is always irregular: heartbeats, raindrops, my periods, waves at sea. 'It's not natural to have a perfectly regular beat,' Frank used to say. 'It's too mechanical.' He and Carl argued for hours. The excitement was in the shifts of tempo. Frank always tapped on the rim of his snare while he spoke. He never put his sticks down. But not planned and rehearsed, he said, intuitive. 'That's the difference between live music and recordings, Carl. Things happen, right there on stage, right as you're playing, things fuckin' happen. You're alive!'

I was on Frank's side. But Carl wanted to rehearse with a metronome. He'd leave the band if we didn't, he said. He wanted to play in a serious band, not with kids on a night out. He wanted to play the concerts as if we were using a metronome. He wanted total predictability. A guitarist could only improvise,

215

Carl said, when he knew exactly what space he was working in. How could he play his solos if the beat was all over the place? Zoë said she needed an absolutely regular beat, otherwise she got lost. Zoë was always lost.

Playing 'Mean Hot And Nasty', Frank let things speed up. It's that kind of song. Once, seeing Jonathan at the back of the hall, I really went for it. He didn't often come to hear us. I pulled the mike in close and turned the temperature way up. *Expect no mercy, baby, don't ask me to behave, cos I'm mean hot and nasty, mean hot and nasty, like you can't believe.* Frank must have felt my excitement and raised the tempo. I could feel the pulse start to race. We were crashing along. *Mean hot mean hot mean hot and NASTY, YEAH!*

Afterwards Carl was furious. Said it had fucked up his best riff. We were a bunch of fucking amateurs. Zoë hadn't noticed. 'Great gig,' she kept saying. She was streaming sweat. 'Great when you bumped all round me, Beth. You were wild.'

PRETEND TO BUMP INTO US, I texted Jonathan, WHILE WE'RE LOADING THE VAN ROUND THE BACK. I'LL TELL YOU WHEN. PRETEND IT'S A BIG SURPRISE.

That was the time Carl and Jonathan sat at the same table. The only time. I was so excited to have them there. We were in Soho. Jonathan got in a couple of rounds. Gins. He was always generous. He kept praising Carl's solos and Carl played music prof explaining the harmony singing in *Now maybe, but never again. Love me now, Babe, then never again.* He kept an arm round me. *Build me a sandcastle, before the tide turns. Love me now, then never again.*

We were on a bench against the bare brick wall. It was a semi-basement place off Wardour Street. From time to time Carl kissed my hair and whispered the words of the song. And while he held me I was smiling into Jonathan's eyes diagonally across the table while Zoë, beside him and opposite me, kept rubbing my feet between hers under the table. She'd taken her shoes off. Zoë knew about me and Jonathan, but neither of the men knew about me and her. They couldn't see our tangled feet while they pontificated about roots and influences. Carl thought I'd written the song for him, of course, when actually I'd written it for Jonathan, who didn't know Carl had come up with the tune and the last line. *Now is for ever when I'm with you.* God. At one point Zoë leaned across to me, grinning, and whispered, 'Whore!' I was in paradise.

Afterwards I slept with Carl, thinking of Jonathan and Zoë. I felt grateful, grateful, grateful. It was a great evening, a truly great night. I was a lucky girl. 'Some people set little store by *sila*,' Dasgupta says in the video day seven. 'Some people imagine you can build up *samādhi* and *paññā* without morality. Nothing doing, my friends. Nothing doing. There can be no concentration without *sila*, without the Five Precepts. No wisdom without morality. And especially no *samma samādhi*, no *samma paññā*. Right concentration, right understanding. Oh, you can have *intellectual samādhi, intellectual paññā*. You can learn what Dasgupta says in his discourses, or what some wise man has written in a book, and even memorize it, even believe it. You could take an exam if you liked and prove you know everything about it. But without *sila* you will never experience *samādhi* and *paññā* in the body, in physical reality. You will never know them at the deepest level of the mind, so that they really change your life. Why not? Because without morality the mind is divided and disturbed, without *sila* the mind cannot settle, cannot concentrate. This is why a monk has such an advantage on the Dhamma path. In a monastery it is easy to maintain *sila*. There are no temptations. It is easy for a monk to avoid unskilful acts.'

Is there any point in Beth trying for enlightenment?

Is there anything wrong with trying even if it's pointless?

I would love to have an undivided mind. I would love to be completely focused, the way when you sing sometimes you become the voice, you are the sound vibrating in your chest and there is nothing outside the sound. I would love to feel like that all the time. But I love to break the rules too, to break *sila*. I'm glad I kissed Ralph, I'm glad I smoked those cigarettes. I'm glad I went into my diarist's bedroom. I'm glad I got Mrs Harper to hug me. I bet I could get Meredith into bed if I put my mind to it. There's something piggy about that girl. I regret all my betrayals. They made my life insane. But it was fantastic having three lovers at the same table. All happy to be with me. All enchanted by little old Beth. It was a great night when I drank with Jonnie and Carl together. And it was great that Zoë was watching.

Plosh, plish, plosh. The students new and old are all at lunch. I'm not eating. I'm alone in the Metta Hall with the raindrops. I think I'm alone. I haven't opened my eyes. I haven't opened my eyes for seven hours. I have never sat so long. I have never been so long without peeing. I feel no urge. What's happened between my legs? Is the cushion soaked with blood? Seven hours is a lot. I won't look. I can't feel anything.

From time to time I slip into a deeper trance. I've no idea for how long. A sort of stillness gathers behind my nose, my eyes. Then I know it's beginning. Then every breath I take, or every breath that takes me, is a wave creeping up across the sand. I feel it flow from my feet to my knees, from my thighs to my crotch.

Then out again when I breathe out. I'm sitting on the beach and the water laps back and forth up my legs as I breathe in and out. And the tide is rising. The water is higher with each breath. I am breathing the sea into my lap, into my belly, my chest, my lungs. A warm sea. A gentle sea.

Under water, a current starts to flow in my flesh, in Beth's flesh. The calves first. It's a soft stirring in sludge, the thick sludge of muscle and bone. Gradually it grows stronger, it's pulsing. Then my forehead starts to buzz, my wrists fizz off in atoms, and suddenly I'm moving. Suddenly Beth is the current, not the sludge. I'm mist drifting on low hills. I'm dew falling through twilight, snow settling on pine needles. On the dunes at Bayonne it drove me crazy how beautiful the world was, how incredibly beautiful, and me not part of it. I'd never realized. How fresh and sweet the air was, how *whole* the universe of hills and sand and sea, of grass and shells and water. But I wasn't part of it. It was beautiful and whole *because* I wasn't part of it. Being me meant exactly not being part of everything I found beautiful and whole. Everything was seamless, where grass turned to sand in the dunes, where sand turned to sea and sea to sky, and breeze to silence, but I was quite separate, separate from the world and, worse still, separated and torn up inside myself, my body in Carl's sleeping bag and my mind in New York, lying on the beach but yearning to be on stage bumping Zoë, yearning to show my father I was a success, to show my father I didn't need Marriot's, I didn't need his help, his sarcasm, and all the time I was thinking: This baby will ruin any chance you have for a singing career, Beth, this baby will nail you to a life you don't want, to a man you don't want, this child isn't part of you, Beth, it isn't, it isn't anything, it's an accident, spit it out, shit it out. Then I was talking crazy with Hervé and

Philippe, I was bragging and lying to Hervé and Philippe, I was playing dumb girl on holiday, I was drinking and smoking with Hervé and Philippe. Wine, dope, pills.

Carl was furious and went off to the tent, then came back again. Carl kept joining in and backing off. He couldn't leave me alone, but he couldn't share me with anyone either, he had to have me all to himself. Carl wanted me to be one with him, always with him. Never with anyone else. 'Take your clothes off, Beth,' the French boys said. 'Let's go in the sea. Let's go in nude. Swim to the buoy and back. I dare you. I dare.' Pulling down my jeans I felt the wind between my thighs and heard the crash of the surf and I wanted to be part of it, or to have it tear me apart for ever.

Let Me Change

I've been to the bathroom. First another long spell of *jhāna,* wandering through the rooms of my body, opening doors, climbing stairs, standing at windows where it is always sunset, then suddenly I was present again, I was back, thinking. That's how *jhāna* ends. The stillness splits into words again, separate words, everything turns sharp and distinct and I'm thinking again and time is motoring on. I suppose enlightenment must be bringing back the peace of *jhāna* into this nowness, bringing wordless, timeless wholeness into this ordinary stuff of deciding and doing. I don't see how that's possible. I can't imagine it. But I would never have imagined *jhāna* if I hadn't learned the Dasgupta technique. I would never have imagined the stillness and the currents in the stillness. Mi Nu must know. What does enlightenment feel like, Mi Nu? I could ask her. That would be a good question.

I suppose I was half hoping that when the course managers realized I'd been sitting there since four a.m., all day without a break, without breakfast, without lunch, they would tell Mrs Harper and Mi Nu and someone would come and touch my shoulder and remind me that fasting is forbidden at the Dasgupta Institute. I would be forced to get up and eat. I didn't know if I wanted this to happen or if I was determined instead to sit on till enlightenment, or till doomsday, or at least until some serious change, something that would finally get me out of this trap I've fallen into—but that's stuff the diarist said—no, I didn't know what I wanted, but I half hoped that Livia or Mrs Harper would come over and force me to eat. I would enjoy eating, even if I'd be angry with myself afterwards for not sitting till I dropped.

They didn't. No one came. No one touched my shoulder. Maybe it's because Mrs Harper won't have anything more to do with me now. She's scared because I attract her so much. 'Your body is awesome, Beth,' Jonathan said. 'You terrify me.' But suddenly I was on my feet anyway. Without deciding anything, barely out of trance, I was on my feet. The hall was full, full of sighs and a sort of soft, pulsing quiet. Things get much quieter on the last days of a retreat. People go in deeper. They've learned how to sit and be still. Kristin was to my left, kneeling, arms loose at her sides. Marsha was slumped forward. Then Meredith, Stephanie. Everybody was in his or her place. I didn't turn to look at the men's side. Surprisingly, my legs were fine, my feet were fine. I didn't have pins and needles, even the bathroom didn't feel urgent.

Outside the clouds were breaking up. The sunlight was dazzling on the wet path. A fresh breeze touched me everywhere. It moved under my clothes like gentle hands. Then I was filled with sounds. There was a bird chirping, rustling leaves. The bird was inside me. The leaves rustled in my fingers. I picked my way between the puddles to the loos, but it didn't feel like that: it felt as though the path shifted as it came to meet me; it was snaking this way and that to make sure Beth didn't get wet. Sweet path. And the handle drew my hand up towards it and opened the door to pull me in and it was only when I was actually sitting on the seat that I realized I had hardly bled at all. No blood. Weird. When had a period of mine ever been so short? Unless the meditation had put it on hold and now the blood would flow again.

I peed, or the pee came. Didn't shit. I shivered and wondered what to do. I was cold now. Still, I was very clear in my mind, very calm. You have sat eleven hours, Beth, and nothing has happened. Nothing major. Eleven hours. So what to do? Go back to the meditation hall, push on. Go to the limit. It seemed the only way. Either I reached some giant change in my head, or I left the Dasgupta and plunged back into life. One way or the other I must make something happen.

I stood in the entrance, looking across to the lines where people hang their washing. I still hadn't taken down my panties. Five pairs. They'd be soaked again with the rain. The clouds were coming fast across the hills and the sun had gone again. GH wouldn't be able to break free of his wife, I thought. Something about the way he wrote told me he wouldn't. He would be lost without that unhappiness. Your story becomes you. There's nothing else. That's what happens if you go on for years with something like that. My parents *were* their marriage, their shouting match. Or the guys who just keep on trying to make it in music, who can't decide to give up. If he actually makes a decision, he'll die, I thought. Or he won't be the same person. Jonathan said he'd left his wife, but he hadn't really. 'We see each other once a week for dinner,' he said. I bet there was more to it.

I bet she came regularly to his flat to sit among his things when he wasn't around. That's why she came the day I was there, nude in bed. To sit with his smell, his aura. 'I'd like to fight for you, Beth,' Jonathan said one day. 'I'd love to be the man who fights for his girl. But I'm not.' And what he must have meant was, even if he had left his wife, because they lived apart, at some level they were still married, still attached, still caring for each other. As soon as he had stopped living with her, he told me one day, he had stopped hating her. He didn't want to hurt her, he said, any more than was necessary. They had dinner together once a week. He didn't look forward to it, he said. But it wasn't like when they were married. He didn't mind. I bet they went on holiday together too. I bet she was in New York with him when I was sending those texts.

Maybe she read them.

'So there's no hope at all for me,' I asked. 'Even loving you the way I do?'

'None, Beth. None in that department, I mean.' He laughed.

'So why do I stay with you?'

'Because you're crazy, Beth. Because you're afraid of your life with Carl. You're trying to break away from Carl. But you can't quite decide.'

'OK, so let's do something really crazy,' I yelled. 'Really fucking crazy.'

I grabbed him and kept him inside me when he came.

'That was mad, Beth,' he whispered.

For me, not for him.

I stood on the step outside the washroom and looked across to the dormitories and the ragged flowerbeds. They wouldn't keep me much longer at the Dasgupta. I had to make something happen. If I'd had a bit more success with the music, it would be easier. I could go back to that, to being a musician, a singer. If we'd made a bit more money. If we'd had just a smell of real business. What was driving me mad with Carl was what would become of us if we weren't successful. Two nobodies. 'Ambition is a hard master,' Jonathan said one evening. Artists were destroyed by ambition, he said, even more than businessmen and politicians. 'Very few artists are a match for their own aspirations.'

Maybe that's what we let go of, I thought now, when we are drawn into *jhāna*. We let go of our ambitions, of all the things that eat us up. But they are waiting for us again when we come out. Our monsters are always lying in wait. We can't escape them. Not that they lurk or hide. They're standing there, whips at the ready. As soon as the stillness breaks up into words, your ambitions are there telling stories of success and failure. Mainly failure. Get on with it, Beth, get on with it, or you'll die a nobody. Show them you have the courage, Beth, show them you have what it takes. When I leave the Dasgupta I'll *have* to be successful. I'll have to have a hit. Otherwise who am I? On the other hand, I can't arrange the songs without Carl. Carl was so good at arrangements, even though he only went through the motions of trying for the big time. Carl was going to do just enough to say he'd tried, he'd had a go, he'd used the metronome, then as soon as was decent he'd give up and marry me and take a job in Marriot's. He even went fishing with Dad. In Oxfordshire somewhere. 'I like fishing,' he said. 'I get good tunes when I'm fishing. I get good riffs, waiting for the fish.' Dad had wanted a son to take over the company and no son came. My sisters married nerds. Beth was bait for the future managing director.

'Carl's a nice guy,' Jonathan said after the evening in Soho.

'He's a great guitarist,' I said. 'He's great at arranging the songs.'

Jonathan thought. 'He is a talented guitarist, Beth. You'd know that better than me. But he doesn't have your balls.' He laughed. 'Carl isn't ruthless. He isn't going anywhere.'

'Am I ruthless?'

Again he hesitated. 'You are, Beth, yes. I think you are.'

'And you?'

He smiled again. Jonathan could say terrible things with a smile on his face. 'You should ask my wife.'

'And what would she say?'

'That I've always put my work first, always. That I married young because of my work and had affairs because of my work, that I left her because of my work and stayed with her because of my work. She'd say I adore you, Beth, because of my work, but won't fight for you, because of my work.'

We were in bed, which is pretty well where we always were.

'Was it worth it?' I asked.

He thought quite a while about that. What I loved about Jonathan was that he really did think about things when you asked a tough question. He did try to tell you the truth, even if it wasn't the truth you wanted to hear. 'Yes and no,' he finally said. Then he said: 'Judge for yourself, Beth. I have this studio, don't I? A nice enough place. I paint. Well enough. Pretty well, actually. And from time to time I sell something. From time to time. I have the price of a taxi when I need one, the price of a restaurant. I have you, Beth. Tonight. Tonight I have you. But no, I haven't changed the history of painting. No, I'm not on everyone's lips.'

'Who cares?' I snuggled up to him.

'I do,' he said at once. He didn't have to think about that. 'But the question isn't really, was it worth it, the question is, could I have done otherwise? And the answer there is, I don't think so. It's impossible to be categorical—how can one know?—but I really don't think so.'

'What if we had a baby?'

'We won't,' he said.

'But what if we did, Jonnie? After what we've just done.'

'We won't,' he said.

'You mean because you don't want one. You'd make me have an abortion.'

'I wouldn't *make* you do anything, Beth. I couldn't, even if I wanted to.'

'So what makes you so sure?'

'Because you don't want a child, Beth. You don't want one, and least of all with me.'

'But what if I do?'

'You don't,' he said. 'And since you don't, you won't.'

In the female servers' loo I washed my hands and took a fresh tampon, the last in the pack. Now was another moment when I could walk over to the men's side and leave a message in GH's diary. 'Given that you'll never be able to leave your wife,' I could write, 'why don't you stop tormenting yourself and make the best of it?' Or I could take my clothes off and lie in his bed and wait for him. That should be enough to get me thrown out of the Dasgupta.

'You look amazing,' Jonathan said. He didn't forget to paint my teeth into his picture, or the explosion of hair.

'You look *fantastique*,' Philippe said. 'Your tits are *fantastiques*.'

'I can't believe you'll be breastfeeding,' Carl said. 'I can't wait.'

Carl could already smell the milk. He was already changing the nappies. On the beach there was a gale. All the red flags were up. Stepping out of your jeans, you knew you shouldn't be there. It was wild. We were drunk and doped.

'Scaredycats,' I shouted. 'You're scared scared scared.'

The boys were shivering. 'No, *pas du tout,* Elisabeth. *Pas du tout.*'

We held hands and ran towards the surf. It was huge.

I can feel the hard sand under the balls of my feet, dry first then damp, the sting of the spray as the sea comes towards us, now the water is frothing at the ankles, freezing the knees. 'To the buoy and back!' The surf was shining slightly as it rolled in, but beyond the ocean was black. The breakers roared. 'The buoy and back! The buoy and back.' Maybe in the distance Carl was yelling, 'Beth!'

I walked up the path to the Metta Hall. This would be the last time. I hadn't drunk any water. On purpose. I hadn't eaten. I will sit all night, all tomorrow, all tomorrow night. For as long as it takes. Without a break.

'Why are some people ruthless and some not?' I asked Jonathan.

'I don't know, Beth. I really don't know.'

I will sit as long as it takes to change. I won't get up. If they force me to get up, I'll leave the Dasgupta at once. I'll shout and scream. I'll tell them Ralph kissed me, Mrs Harper hugged me, GH keeps a diary, plus a million things that aren't true. I'm going to change my head, or go crazy trying.

I slipped off my shoes, opened the door and closed it quietly behind me so it wouldn't disturb. But even the tiniest click has an effect. There were a hundred and forty people in there, towards the end of an hour of Strong Determination, some erect, some slumped, cross-legged or kneeling, some hugging their knees, one or two on chairs at the back, and when the door closed that tiny click shivered through every one of them, as if a pebble had been dropped in still water, and as I walked along the rows towards my place, stepping carefully between one mat and another, there were stirrings and sighs to each side of me, as if plants under water were swaying as I waded by.

I don't think I'd ever walked into the Metta Hall when everyone was so concentrated, so peaceful. It gets like that around day eight. All at once I felt I loved them. I was happy. I really loved them all. Even Marcia. And before sitting down I turned and looked around. Mrs Harper's big head was bowed. Mi Nu was ghostly, floating. Across the room my diarist was hunched forward, his chin on his chest. It seemed he might fall on his face any minute. I looked at the girls. Meredith was solid and solemn. Kristin was kneeling. She was sitting on her heels. I could never do that for a whole hour. Kristin's pushing herself. Her pale lips were parted. For a moment I thought of touching them, I could lay a fingertip between her lips to feel the breath flow in and out. Would she mind?

I sat down and assumed the toughest position I can, a tight half-lotus. I shall not shift from this posture till something happens, till I have reached some change. I don't care if this is the wrong spirit. I will not shift till something budges, till deep inside me something breaks or opens or dies or is born. I won't eat won't drink won't piss won't shit.

I sat still, placed my hands palm up on my thighs. I took a last look round before the plunge. A last look. Then I realized

I was crying. There were tears in my eyes. I felt so happy, so *ready*. At last. Everybody was sitting so beautifully. Even Marcia. I remembered the fourth evening—was it the fourth?—when the white blankets and the grey had been the sea, the blue cushions, the white blankets, and now all these people were sitting in the sea together. We were sitting in the surf. All these good people were rocks in the surf, sitting solid against the tide. Bless them. Bless them.

Before closing my eyes I looked awhile at Mi Nu. I would take inspiration from Mi Nu. I would only open them again when I had become like Mi Nu. If ever a person could sit still in the sea, right in the surf, that was Mi Nu. She was sitting slightly above us on the teacher's raised seat. The blanket draped over her shoulders made a triangle, a lighthouse, a buoy. It was a big off-white shawl tossed around her shoulders, falling straight to her feet. Tilted slightly downward, her face glowed. Her face lights the way for those in peril. She lights the path between the rocks. Then for the first time I understood that her beautiful Buddha stillness depended on the chaos around it. The Buddha sits up there so still, so serene, because the world around him is chaos. Or the world is chaotic because he sits so still. The Buddha needs the world chaotic and the world needs him still. Something like that. The lighthouse needs the stormy sea. Its light is there because the waves are dark and rough. Mi Nu needs me, I thought then. That was a strange idea. To sit there so serene and pure and still Mi Nu needed Beth Marriot, she needed my mess my pain my filth.

If only we could swap places.

I closed my eyes and at once felt hands take mine. I'd known this would happen. They were soft, boys' hands, but strong.

Mine were resting palms up on my thighs, but they were also being pulled towards the sea, we were running across the beach towards the surf. It was cloudy, but there was the moon somewhere, behind a cloud, or gleaming in the surf. Then I was in. Their hands let go but I ran on and plunged. 'Stop, Beth. Don't.' They let go. They saw the surf was huge and stopped. The red flag had been up all day. The breakers were monstrous.

'Stop, Beth, stop!'

I flung myself into the wave. It crashed like a wall. I was slammed on the sand, tossed this way and that, tossed and turned and tumbled, then suddenly, violently, dragged outwards. Stronger hands took me and tossed me out to sea and another wave crashed and another and another and I wasn't trying now, I wasn't floundering, I wasn't fighting, I was waiting, waiting for change. Let me change, I screamed, let me change, let me change.

Never React

'The ninth day is over. You have only one more day left to work.'

The words surprised me. People had come and gone, gone and come. The vents under the roof turned on and off to bring us air. You felt a low humming in the belly, the faintest draught at the roots of the hair. Five minutes, then it stops. Dasgupta talked about multiplication. I sensed the flicker of the video. The hall was full again. The *law* of multiplication, he said. The seeds of the banyan tree are infinite. The tree is huge, the multitudinous seeds are tiny, but each contains another huge banyan tree, which again contains infinite seeds, infinite banyan trees. Likewise with *sankharas,* the painful formations of the mind. Every unskilful action carries the seed of endless multiplication, endless mental misery. This is the law of nature. One betrayal spawns a thousand others. The karma grows and grows. Where will there be an end? When will we be free?

My body reassembled itself. It had come apart in the surf. My nose floated off from my face. My lips swimming away like eels. Let them go, let them go. My eyeballs shifting back and forth in the shingle. My skin flapping and tumbling with the seaweed in the long wash of the tide. How to stop this mad multiplication? Dasgupta asks. How to come out of our misery?

Hour after hour, even deep in meditation, the old stories came back. It had never happened before. Previously I had been safe in my trance. I could hide. But now Jonathan, now Carl filled my mind, this wild concert, that drunken night, Zoë, Dad, Mum. I thought the sea would purify, now each tide brings more wreckage.

'How to stop the *sankharas* multiplying?' Dasgupta asks. I sit in my filth and his voice flows through me.

'By not giving these seeds of misery a fertile soil to grow in, my friends. That is the answer. By denying them nourishment.'

And is the sea a fertile soil? I've been turning in this water for months. Shouldn't it have washed me clean?

'It is so easy,' Dasgupta says. 'This is what the Buddha understood. It is so clear, so easy. If we stop producing new *sankharas*, the old ones float to the surface and evaporate. It may be painful, my friends, but it works. It's automatic. It's the law of nature. Or like an old-fashioned clock: as soon as you stop winding it up it winds down. Like a spring released after years of tension. Just stop producing new *sankharas*, new attachments, new aversions, stop winding up the clock of your misery, stop throwing new filth into the wash.'

I threw myself into the sea. Why did they bother saving me?

'Suddenly everything is so clear,' Dasgupta says. 'If only we will accept things *as they are,* not as we would wish them to be, if only we can stop producing new *sankharas* of craving and aversion, then we can break out of this cycle of ignorance and misery. Then we can be liberated.'

Dasgupta believes what he's saying. He's not a fraud. But when I tried to stop I made things worse.

'You must master the present moment,' Dasgupta says. 'The future is child of the present. Master the present and the old *sankharas* will unwind. Master the present and the future will be happy, the future will be peaceful. You will be liberated.'

How? I have held my half-lotus for hours. The twilight is deepening. I feel it. The video is coming to a close. I know these videos. I know how Dasgupta's voice changes when he is near the end. Now he's talking about the angry old man who went to the Buddha to protest that his teaching distracted people from their prayers. '"Thank you, but I will not accept your gift of anger," the Buddha told him. "Take it away, old man. It is your anger, not mine. I do not want it."

'Master the present moment, my friends,' Dasgupta says. 'The present moment. Do not accept gifts of anger. Do not react to pains and pleasures, provocations, promises. Do you see? It's *so* easy, once you have understood. Do not react to pleasant thoughts or to negative thoughts. That is the way of ignorance and limitation. Observe your breathing. Observe sensation. Observe thought. Just observe, just observe, don't react, never react. Work hard at the technique and you are bound to succeed, oh, bound to succeed.'

If the present moment is a crashing sea, how can I master it? If the surf around me is churning with filth, how can I not feel aversion? My baby is there. She is tossed up on the sand, swept away by the next wave. How can anyone master anything? The present is an angry sea. I have sat still and breathed and observed my breathing, observed my body, observed my thoughts and the present moment has overwhelmed me, the sea has overwhelmed me, my aching ankles have overwhelmed me. I am beaten, beaten, beaten.

The only thing to observe is my failure.

'Bavatu sava mangelam.

'May all beings be liberated, liberated, liberated.

'Sadhu, sadhu, sadhu.'

It was over. The meditators left the hall. Those who had questions to ask lined up before Harper and Mi Nu. There is no need to open your eyes to understand these things. I can feel the people getting to their feet, shuffling this way and that all around me. Now there are low voices. Some questions are muttered, others I can hear easily enough.

'Is *anicca* a name for a single energy force, or more in general for any kind of change that takes place in nature?'

'I am sure I did something terrible in a previous life. How many lives does it take to work off the bad karma of something really awful?'

'My husband cheats on me. Sometimes I think I'm using meditation to live in denial. What would the Buddha say?'

It goes on for twenty minutes, maybe half an hour. I never hear Mi Nu's answers. Harper repeats his formulas. 'Whatever you did in a previous life, the way of Dhamma is always the same. There is no need to torment yourself.'

Then the questioners are done and the *metta* can begin. 'If I have offended anyone in today's Dhamma Service, I seek pardon of him or her. I seek pardon of him or her.'

Dasgupta's voice feels closer and quieter in the *metta*: the recording has a sort of throaty intimacy, as if he knew he were addressing his band of faithful servers and no one else; he doesn't need to persuade.

'If anyone has offended me in today's Dhamma Service, I ppardon him or her, I ppardon him or her.'

May all beings, visible and invisible, visible and invisible visible and invisible . . .

The *metta* was over and the servers took their cushions to kneel before the leaders. I stayed put. I stayed separate, marooned on my cushion. Motionless. I have been motionless all day. I am turning in the surf, with all the filth the tide is bringing, and I am entirely present and motionless here, sitting still while the servers get together for their final meeting. Surely now, I thought, someone will intervene. Someone will remind Beth Marriot that eccentric behaviour isn't permitted at the Dasgupta Institute.

No one touched my shoulder. No one intervened. Perhaps I have become invisible. Perhaps I really am out in the surf, beyond help, beyond the reach of those who love me. I felt the sea drag me out; it was a strong, sure pull. Where was the buoy? Perhaps I could grab it and hold on. The waves were huge. I had hurt my shoulder. Lifted over a crest, I glimpsed the beach. Philippe was diving in. He was coming after me.

'Oh, definitely better,' Ines was saying about the kitchen. 'We'll be perfectly in control when it's time to go home.' She laughed. 'It's been so much fun.'

Vikram said that the rule about servers eating separately in the male and female servers' rooms was not being strictly observed.

Livia asked if the other servers could please report it if they saw a student sneaking out of the grounds. There had been two absent the whole afternoon. They were neither in the Metta Hall nor in their rooms.

Harper said: 'Tomorrow we lift the vow of silence. I know one or two of you have a boyfriend or girlfriend among the meditators. Please do remember to keep the rules about physical contact. There must be no touching inside the grounds of the institute, and of course you are still not permitted to go outside until the retreat is over.'

After a short silence Rob spoke up and said it seemed excessive to him. It was natural to hold hands, he said. Or shake hands. Natural to hug.

'It's the rule,' Harper said calmly. 'We wish the Dhamma campus to remain absolutely pure.'

'Do the invisible beings obey this rule?' Rob asked.

'I believe they do,' Harper said. He was serious.

'And the rabbits?'

This was Meredith's voice. Meredith was taking the mick out of Harper! Was something going on between her and Rob? I'd thought she was after Ralph.

'It is a rule of the Dasgupta Institute that there must be no physical contact inside the grounds,' Harper repeated.

But what is the point of my sitting in a half-lotus, eyes closed, if in fact I'm eavesdropping on the servers?

There is a point. I am still hanging to the thread of breath on my lips, I am still observing the heat in the palms of my hands. I can't give up sitting with nothing changed.

'Let's close with a few minutes' meditation,' Harper said.

They sat. We sat. Five final minutes after a day that began seventeen hours ago. An hour can be the blinking of an eye at the Dasgupta, and the blinking of an eye can be an age. When the servers get up to go, I thought, they will insist I leave the hall with them. They will tell me I need to sleep. I didn't sleep last night.

'May all beings be filled with sympathetic joy.'

'Sadhu, sadhu, sadhu.'

People were on their feet. They were heading for a last cup of chai, a last chocolate biscuit. It's funny to think the male servers have a store of chocolate biscuits. I don't care what's going on with Rob and Meredith. It's not my business.

The doors closed and I was alone. They had left me to sit through the night. Alone. I couldn't believe it. Unless someone has stayed to keep me company. Somebody is in the room with me now, ready to sit beside me through the night. Mi Nu. Who else? Mi Nu is sitting so still my antennae haven't picked her up. Suddenly, like a terrible itch, I felt I must open my eyes and check if Mi Nu was there.

Don't.

It makes no difference if Mi Nu is here or not.

My body had reassembled, but all wrong. Returning to the stillness behind my nose, I found it was planted in my stomach, I was breathing through my navel. My lips were in my forehead. I wasn't surprised. You'll never be the same, I thought, when I woke in hospital. I was on a drip, I was full of tubes. My right leg was bandaged. You'll never go on stage again, never sing again, never dance again. Why was that my first thought in hospital? Beth will never go on stage again. The baby is dead. Pocus are dead.

It makes no difference to me what is going on between the other servers. It doesn't matter if Mi Nu is here or not. I am in the Metta Hall, after the final meditation, the closing *metta*. I am here to sit through the night to find enlightenment. Or something. I will sit still all night and all tomorrow. Sail on. Master each single moment as the night passes. Want nothing, react to nothing, whatever is thrown at you, whatever thoughts arrive.

there's nothing wrong with me? When I know that as soon as I move I'll be fine again. As soon as I react I'll be fine. I'll be beaten, but fine.

Don't move, Beth.

Would Mi Nu move? Does Mi Nu ever have to go through this stuff?

This pain doesn't throb. It doesn't sting or stab. It's just enormously achingly present. It's black. I know it's black. It's a black rock. Getting heavier, getting denser. I feel sick. If I don't move I'll die.

Then die, Beth. Don't move and die. Feel calm about dying. Accept dying. Let it happen. Pain is just pain. Just a barrier. There is always something the other side of pain.

Wait, Beth.

Don't panic.

How long has it been going on? I've no idea. All grand thoughts have gone. Enlightenment, change. All memories have gone. Mi Nu has gone. The Metta Hall has gone. Just this huge rock, this vast rock in my chest. Let it crush me.

Then it moves. Oh, Christ, it moved. It's moving. Just observe. Don't smile, Beth. Observe.

The pain had started to push upwards. It was on the move. Like an animal inside me. It knows where it's going. It pushes up into my neck. Jesus. There's no space for it. It can't pass. It's too big. I'm swelling. There really is something inside me pushing to be out. A creature is pushing up through my neck. Now my head. There's a sort of core of scalding paralysis pushing up through the left side of my brain, behind my eye. My eye is swelling now. My left eye is swelling. It's horrible. But weirdly beautiful too. I know relief is coming. We're almost there. How do I know? Just observe. My eyeball will explode. Let it, Beth. Don't fight. It's the size of a football. It's awesome.

It's gone.

A sudden rush of deflation, liberation. It's gone. The pain rushes out through the socket behind my eye. Deflates. Everything is fine again. In a second everything is absolutely relaxed. No pain, no pressure. Tears are flowing. Just observe. My cheeks are wet. Don't react. Don't rejoice. Don't ask yourself if something important has happened. All sensations are impermanent, Beth. The pain was, the relief is, impermanent.

Anicca, anicca, anicca.

Stillness. At last only stillness in the Metta Hall. It is midnight. Right now. For some reason I know it is midnight. The stillness deepens. It is like soft breathing on dark water. It's beautiful. I have never known such stillness. The mind floats on stillness, on emptiness, like feathers on a dark lake. It is vast and still and utterly empty, blissfully empty.

God.

I opened my eyes. Oh, at the best moment I stopped. Why? How long had it lasted? A second, an hour, a lifetime? I felt scared. Or just too present, too *there*. The hall was in darkness. A faint glimmer came from the high windows. I was alone in a sea of cushions. Nobody had stayed behind.

Why had I stopped? Why was I scared?

I got to my feet and felt shivery, but not stiff. My body was relaxed. My breathing was soft and easy. I had seen out the pain. I had pushed myself to the limit. Then right when everything was perfect I had stepped back.

I had failed again, failed to stick to the plan.

My blanket round my shoulders, I walked between lines of cushions to the porch. Mine were the only shoes left. It was nice of them to let me stay in the Metta Hall alone, to give me this chance to sit through the night alone.

Why hadn't I stuck it out?

An owl hooted. I looked out into drizzle. The air was cold and damp on my face and hands. The owl called again. Tu-whoo. It must be close. There must be a family of owls round here. All beings visible and invisible. Perhaps I had heard it in my trance. Perhaps it was the owl called me out.

I lifted the blanket over my head. I hate drizzle in my hair. I hate the stickiness. Despite this sudden change of plan, I felt calm. I wasn't going to be angry with myself. I had seen through the pain. At least that.

Tu-whoo-oo.

All at once the Buddha smile formed on my lips. The corners of my mouth turned up and I smiled, involuntarily. I smiled for the owl. I blessed the owl. Maybe you did the right thing, Beth, I thought. Maybe the owl did the right thing calling you out of there. Why did I like those words so much? All beings visible and invisible? When the owl hooted it was inside me, or I was inside it. There was a vibration. The owl is Mi Nu, I thought. Meee Nooo, meee nooo. It was the sound of an invisible being, calling me out of the Metta Hall. That's why I smiled.

I walked round the hall, away from the dormitory blocks. The rain fell steadily on the grass and bushes. The puddles gleamed.

Mi Nu

The bungalow door was unlocked. Sex is forbidden at the Dasgupta Institute, there's no need for locks. Everyone here has taken
the Five Precepts. They will not steal. They will not harm another
living creature.

It was dark in the porch. I kicked off my shoes and put them
by the wall. I had to reach out and touch to find it. I pulled off
the blanket and shook out my hair.

Where was the door into the house? I reached out and my
fingers found the handle at once. I just put out an arm. As if I
had lived here for years. Strange.

The passageway opened to my left, lit at the end by a dim
light, just above floor level. I took a step towards it. There was
definitely a smell of incense. Something lemony. And the light
was smiling. The light was the Buddha, an orange Buddha on a
low table with a bulb inside.

Then came the growl. I stopped. It was the same I'd heard
when I escaped from the Dhamma recording. There was a

growl and a wheeze, like a kettle. A whimper, like a seagull. My heart was racing. I almost ran. But the stillness of the Buddha held me. Don't react, Beth. Be calm. The quiet of the corridor reassured me. The quiet of the incense. I love incense. Jonathan sometimes lit incense when he painted. Every painting has its smell, he said.

I padded barefoot another step or two. The sound came again. The growl. Almost a snort. What was it? I had reached the Buddha at the doorway. Beyond must be the main room.

I looked in. The place was really large. But how could it be? I had no sense of where the walls were. Was there a face? High up? I stopped. It might be a picture. Or more than one. I couldn't make it out.

I took another couple of steps and banged into a bed. My shin. So much for emptiness. It was a low single bed. I waited for the pain to go. Someone sighed under the blankets. Only the hair was visible. A gleam of black hair. I had found Mi Nu and she was asleep. Fast asleep in her bed. There are only single beds at the Dasgupta Institute.

I pulled off my T-shirt and top, my jeans and pants. I let my clothes fall to the floor. Was I bleeding? I don't think so. I didn't check. I lifted the sheets and slipped in. You're reckless, Beth, completely reckless. She would wake, horrified. They would throw me out. But I needed to be beside her.

As soon as my body was under the bedclothes I started to shiver. I get that after meditation. I find a warm place and shiver. The body beside me stirred and growled. She whimpered. I was so surprised. I almost burst out laughing. I had to clench my teeth. Mi Nu was snoring! What a weird snore. Worse than Jonathan's. Like a little pig and a little bird in one. A grunt and a tweet.

For five or ten minutes I lay still trying not to touch Mi Nu in the single bed, trying not to laugh when she snored. She was turned away from me. I lay right on the edge. I observed my breath, I tried to relax. I didn't want to scare her. Then the snoring stopped. I couldn't hear her breathing at all. Had she woken? She would be frightened when she woke. She would jump up and shout. Mi Nu wouldn't be used to people climbing into her bed.

She'll wake, I told myself, and you'll be thrown out of the Dasgupta. You're doing this *on purpose* to be thrown out. For months I had wanted to get Mi Nu's attention, to hug Mi Nu, to melt into her, to share that strange light she has. But Mi Nu will never hug anyone. I was clutching at the moon. If you were going to get into anyone's bed, I thought, it should have been your diarist's. Or Ralph's. Or Meredith. Then there would have been some piggy pleasure.

I was on my back and as my eyes got used to the dark I began to make out the faces high up on the wall. Pale faces with crowns, with snakes, with jewels. Posters, I suppose. It seemed strange to hang them so high. Almost on the ceiling. Perhaps the roof was slanted. I was safe with Mi Nu. Unless she went wild when she woke. What if I was bleeding? I should put my pants back on. I stared at these pale, floating faces high up in the dark. They were all smiling. But solemn too. When my hands and feet had warmed I turned and snuggled up to her back. There's no point getting into a bed and not touching.

She wore a cotton nightdress. Her body was still and cool. Very carefully I pushed my face into her hair. I wriggled my front against her back. My hands were on her shoulders.

I breathed a warm scent. It was fresh bread. Her hair smelt of fresh bread. Five minutes passed. Ten. It was a torment to be beside her, a torment of pleasure, of worry. Still she hadn't woken. She hadn't tensed. We could lie all night like this. I could sneak away before the morning gong and no one would know.

'Who is it?'

The voice was so soft. How could she have woken without starting or turning?

I waited but she didn't repeat the question.

Then I whispered, 'Beth.'

She didn't turn. She was silent. Touching is forbidden at the Dasgupta Institute and I was naked, pressing against her nightdress.

In a low voice I said, 'I need to ask you a question.'

She didn't reply. So now was the moment to ask something deep, something that would justify my being there. I couldn't think. All those clever questions I'd had and now I couldn't remember one. My heart was beating loud. She was absolutely still and soft. I was touching her, but it did not feel as if she were touching me.

Then she sighed and said: 'I was wondering when you would come to see me, Beth.'

I didn't know what to say. Mi Nu had woken and she hadn't kicked me out. She was going to let me stay. She'd even been expecting me!

'We've all been wondering,' she said.

'Wondering what?' Suddenly feeling incredibly happy, I just forced my arms round her thin body and hugged. 'What, Mi Nu?'

It seemed an age before she answered: 'We've been wondering when you would decide to leave.'

'But I don't want to leave. I haven't decided anything.'

There was another long silence. In the darkness I heard a faint tinkling. As if tiny bells had been stirred by a draught.

'Who are the people up on the wall?' I asked.

'What people?'

'The faces. The women.'

She hesitated. 'Parvathi, Kali. They watch over me.'

'Are they goddesses?'

'That's a word people use.'

'I wish someone would watch over me.'

She didn't reply.

'Actually, I haven't decided to leave at all.'

I was holding her, but she wasn't there. Or she was, but not really in my arms. Then I thought I must be practical.

'The truth is, Mi Nu, I killed someone. Someone died because of me. I don't know what to do. I need your help.'

My hands were clasped tight around her, but she wasn't really there. She was lying beside me, but not in my arms. She was all around me somehow and I was the only thing in the room that was not her.

'I want to be like you, Mi Nu. That's what I came to ask. How can I become like you?'

She lay quite still.

'You're perfect, Mi Nu. When you meditate, you're like the moon. You shine. How can I be like that? I feel you know things I should know.'

Her body shook a little. She was laughing.

'Is the moon perfect?'

'It's beautiful,' I insisted. I felt very earnest and excited.

My little pillow-prattler, Jonathan used to say.

'I always think you're like pure moonlight when you meditate. I want to be like that.'

She sighed. 'You are craving, Beth.'

'It can't be bad, craving to be pure.'

'Craving is craving.'

She slipped from my arms and out of the bed. There was no chance of clinging on. She tossed a shawl round her shoulders, stood beside the bed. She was frowning, but in a friendly way.

'Stay under the blankets. I'll make some tea.'

She was gone. Again I heard a faint tinkling in the darkness. She must have one of those hanging mobiles that turn in a draught. It was sad she had left the bed, but at least she wasn't kicking me out. Maybe she'd get back in and we'd drink tea in bed together. I looked around. Catching the orangey light from the Buddha in the passageway, the faces high up glimmered. Every smiling face had a crown, a necklace, earrings that dangled.

Mi Nu was taking an age. Had she gone to fetch Mrs Harper? There was no sound of water or kettles. No lights went on. What if I had climbed into GH's bed? Or Ralph's. I could have made love. I was aching to make love. But I thought Mi Nu could help me. Has anyone ever really helped me? I've done everything alone. Now I wanted help.

She came back with a tray. Perhaps she hadn't been long at all. Perhaps I'd dozed off. I'd been awake so long. She poured out a cup and put it on the bedside table. She sat on a low stool and crossed her legs.

'Drink. It's good hot.'

Had she realized I was naked?

I pulled myself up slowly, dragging the quilt with me. The tea was some herb stuff. Mi Nu seemed shadowy, lifting her cup to her lips, sipping, lowering it, lifting it again. We drank for a while. Then I put my cup down.

'I was pregnant and I made sure the baby died. I did it on purpose. I tried to drown myself, to kill myself and the baby. Instead another man died trying to save me.'

I stopped. She seemed to be looking at the floor by the bed.

'I was going out with a bloke, a really nice boy, we'd been together three years, but it wasn't his baby. The father was an older guy, he was married as well. I was in love with him. I was really in love. He didn't care. Maybe he cared a bit, but not really. Even when I pretended I was dying. I told him I was dying to get him to help me. I wish I hadn't done that. I was too young for him, I suppose. He was successful. He already had a life. I felt like I was nothing.'

Mi Nu was quite still and calm, exactly the way she is when she takes questions after the evening discourse.

'I can't go back.'

She said nothing.

'If I go back I'll just mess up with men again. And women. I've had things with girls too. You know Mrs Harper tried to kiss me?' I laughed. 'She's really attracted to me. I think she really likes me.'

Mi Nu swayed. Sitting on the stool, legs crossed, her slim body rocked gently back and forth. I think it was this inner rhythm that separated her from the people round her. It was a secret she had.

'I'd mess up. That's why I want to stay here. Only I must learn to meditate better. My head's all over the place.'

Mi Nu sipped her tea. What was she thinking? The more she was silent the more I was shooting my mouth off.

'I want to be your friend,' I said.

'But you already are, Beth. We are all friends at the Dasgupta.'

I sat up straighter and the quilt slipped.

'Sorry.' I pulled it up. 'No, I mean, I want to know all about you, where you were born, what your family are like, whether you ever had boyfriends. Or a husband. Or even children. You know? The whole story.'

She smiled. 'Is that all?'

'It'll be enough to be getting along with.' I laughed. Maybe I was making progress. She liked me. 'Please tell me.'

'There is no story,' Mi Nu said.

I thought a moment. I was trying to be serious. In a way I knew what she meant; I'd even thought this about her myself. All the same I couldn't help insisting.

'Everybody has a story. I mean, you were born in a different part of the world. So there's the story of how you came to be here. Tell me about that.'

She was shaking her head, smiling. 'I've put all that behind me, Beth.'

I sighed. She was looking at me, trying to see if I understood.

'You are young, Beth. All the same there must be parts of your life you don't think about any more. An old school friend. A holiday with your parents.'

'Quite a few boys.' I chuckled. 'A singer is sort of obliged to seduce everyone.'

Mi Nu said, 'We soon stop thinking about most of the things that happen to us. They don't leave much impression. And this can be true of the memories that torment you too. You can look to the light beyond them. Let *anicca* do its work, enter the flow and let yourself change.'

This was a bit hard for me right then. I'd been awake a long time.

'I don't want to forget everything,' I said. 'It would be like not knowing who I am.'

She smiled. 'So, who are you, Beth?'

I tried to think of a good answer.

'I'm a mess, I suppose. But a good musician. Or, at least, I'm good on stage. I give people their money's worth.'

Mi Nu waited, sitting in the shadow with the glow from the passageway behind her.

'I can't play again, though, after what happened. I feel I can't. That's the trouble. I mean, I don't know what to do for the future. My mum and my sisters are so proper. All church and don't do this or that. I'm more like my dad. He's ruthless. Their religiousness drives him nuts. But he never helped me. Dad was always having affairs with his PAs, and Mum wanted me to be his PA so he wouldn't be able to—she tried to commit suicide once, she stuck her head in the oven—so then I got roped into the office doing Dad's secretarial work. I hated it.'

I stopped. I couldn't figure out if Mi Nu was really listening, or if I was just making a fool of myself.

'There's a dream I keep having. I'm walking hand in hand with a man. We're escaping, we're happy, except then the road goes through a tunnel and the tunnel is blocked with snow. How can it snow in a tunnel?'

I hadn't talked this much in ages.

'Another dream I get is I'm in the tube with my guitar on the way to a concert. I try to go up the escalator, only it's a down escalator and I look at my feet and see I'm barefoot.'

I waited.

'I bet you have beautiful dreams.'

Still she said nothing. She could make her face completely expressionless.

'You know, when I left the meditation hall just now, I heard an owl. The sound seemed to get right inside me. Woo, woo. And I thought it was you. I thought the owl was you. Mad, I know. That's why I came here.'

She cocked her head slightly.

'Then when I came in, do you know you were snoring? Actually, it's a pretty funny snore you have.'

She smiled. 'Is that so?'

'When I got into bed I was really worried because my period's due. I mean, I wouldn't want to dirty your sheets.'

The smile didn't fade. I couldn't tell whether she thought she knew me through and through and was being indulgent, or whether she couldn't make me out at all. Or it just didn't matter to her whether she knew me or not.

'Did I do the right thing coming here, Mi Nu? Please tell me I did the right thing.'

She asked: 'Do your parents know where you are?'

'No.'

'They must be anxious.'

'They could find me if they put their minds to it. In fact, I can't believe they haven't. You can find anyone in this day and age.'

'Why do they have to find you when you could tell them where you are?'

'If they want me, they can find me,' I said.

'Are you punishing them?'

'I never think of them.'

'And these men? Are you punishing them? Would you like them to come and find you?'

'I'm through with men.'

Mi Nu sighed. She was looking at me very steadily. Then she said: 'I think it's time to change your name.'

'What? What do you mean?'

'It's time to leave these unhappy moments behind. You've changed. You're not the same person. It's time to be different.'

'I wish I had changed.'

'Tomorrow we will give you a new name. But you should sleep now.' She smiled. 'Take rest, Beth. Sleep.'

I did feel terribly sleepy all of a sudden.

'And you?'

'I'll sit here. I'll watch over you.'

I smiled. 'I wish I could kiss you, Mi Nu. I wish you'd let me hug you. A goodnight hug.'

She laughed out loud. 'You're a bad girl, Beth. You're a bad girl. Go to sleep now.'

They were Jonathan's words, exactly.

Lisa

Someone leaned over my shoulder and asked, 'So, when do I get my reader's report?'

It was not the sort of voice I'd expected. High-pitched for a man. Very South London.

I went on eating and he sat beside me. He put his hands on the table. There were small age stains, more hair than you'd want.

'What did you think of the food?' I asked.

'Some days nice, some days so so.'

'You can't remember which?'

He thought about it. 'I remember a good curry. Did you do that? An honest baked potato. A horrible nut roast.'

'The porridge?'

'Never touch the stuff.'

'The toast?'

'Nice if you could get it warm.'

I was eating chocolate whip. My lips must be dirty.

'Let me finish and we can go for a walk in the field.'

'I'd like that very much,' he said.

Older men are so polite.

I'd woken in a mess of blood, in my own bed. How had that happened? Had I mucked up Mi Nu's bed too? I'd definitely fallen asleep there. Had she chucked me out? There was a strange gap in the night, like when you're meditating and you can't feel anything between your head and breasts. You don't have a neck. You don't have shoulders. Your mind isn't focused enough to feel them.

The other beds were empty. I got up and stripped off the sheets. I mustn't feel aversion. Confront your slime with equanimity. Now there was a buzz of voices. I went to the window. People were hurrying out of the Metta Hall, chatting and laughing. It must be lunch already. Day ten. They had lifted the vow of silence.

I'd slept a long time. But then I'd been awake a long time before that.

It's time to change your name, Mi Nu had said. It would have been so good to wake up in her bed and find her watching me. What kind of name? I like Beth. It was typical that I had gone to see her right when I didn't have a proper question to ask, when I couldn't think of anything smart to say. Do I have to have some weird Oriental name to become like Mi Nu?

I cleaned up in the shower then went back for the sheets. There's a plastic cover on all Dasgupta mattresses. Good job. But I needed to know if I'd dirtied Mi Nu's bed. How can I speak to her without knowing how we left each other?

Gathering the sheets, I remembered how I'd once stained Jonathan's sofa. It must have been the second or third time we made love. He had a big blue sofa in his studio and the blood was brown and smeary, like wet rust. I was upset. Jonathan put a finger in it and rubbed it round his mouth. He turned the cushion over and laughed. 'Life is all dirtying and cleaning. Of the two, I prefer dirtying.'

'But your place is always so tidy.'

'The better to muck it up, Beth.'

Going down the creaky stairs, I thought, Jonathan and Mi Nu are the same person. I said it out loud: 'They're the same person.' What a stupid idea! How do these things come into my head?

Outside everyone was talking ten to the dozen. That's how it is when the Noble Silence ends. There'll be about a minute's hesitation, as people come out from the Metta Hall. They know they can talk now, but they're not used to the sound of their own voices. They open their mouths and close them again, think a bit. Then they take the plunge and that's it. All of a sudden everyone's spilling out their experiences, pains, complaints, impressions. Now they can't talk fast enough. They can't stop themselves. A hundred and fifty motor-mouths. I did the same after my first retreats. Later you start to feel superior, you learn to stay detached. When people are silent they seem so dignified, so considerate. You don't know where they're from, what class they are. You don't criticize. You're not tempted to flirt. Then on day ten, eleven o'clock, all of a sudden, yap yap yap yap yap. Northern, southern, foreign. Downmarket, posh, smart, dumb. You want to stop your ears.

What name would they give me? I wondered. And would they send me away afterwards? I liked Beth because Mum hated it. Elisabeth was the good girl they wanted me to be. Beth was rock and rebellion, the name I gave myself. How could they let me stay after seducing Mrs Harper and climbing naked into Mi Nu's bed? It was strange, though, that she hadn't been upset. Mi Nu hadn't been upset that I hugged her and she hadn't been excited either. Maybe that was how she was like Jonathan. I couldn't touch her. And maybe calling myself Beth had become a kind of trap. Beth *had* to be young and rebellious. But now those days were over. The Beth days. Was changing names the price I'd have to pay for staying at the Dasgupta?

I didn't want to start another retreat.

I didn't want to leave either.

In the laundry room the washing-machine was busy and the floor stacked with plastic baskets. There was a mix of clean and dirty smells, soap and soiling, and every basket had a label on top: 'Tea towels day 9'. 'Aprons day 9'. 'Harpers day 8'. 'Maintenance crew day 8'. Had Mi Nu told Mrs Harper about my visit? Would she mention what I'd said about Mrs Harper trying to kiss me? I put the bloody sheets in a basket and filled out the label. 'Beth, sheets, day 10. Sorry'.

On day ten there is an evening meal as well as lunch, to prepare people for the world again, for their departure the following morning. I went to the kitchen to help. Important things were about to happen, but I wanted to be back in the routine for a while. I needed a breather. Coming in from the service entrance, I'd barely got my hat and apron on when Kristin told me Rob and Meredith had done a runner. They'd been on breakfast together but cleared off. There'd been no porridge. Now there was an extra meal to cook, twice the normal washing-up, and two less people to do it.

The news cheered me up and I rushed around chopping leeks and stacking dishes. Rob and Meredith had absconded! Nobody could see the point of their screwing off on the last day, with only one more night and breakfast to go. What was so urgent? They'd let down their friends at the busiest moment. For what? A few hours.

'Maybe we weren't really friends,' Ines said.

Ralph asked me to help him with the chocolate dessert. The day-ten treat. We checked the ingredients. I felt happy now, I felt myself again. Then I was just coming back from the cold room with the soya milk when he upended a two-kilo tub of cocoa powder into the big tin basin. He just opened the thing and tipped it upside down. Wham! It sent an explosion of powder to the ceiling. It was so thick we could barely see each other. We were breathing chocolate.

'Bless you.' I reached through the cloud and pinched his waist.

'Sugar!' he complained.

'Actually, cocoa.'

Kristin burst out in one of her roaring laughs. It was definitely day ten.

Then, waiting till Mrs Harper was in earshot, I said: 'I've got it. Meredith needed *the morning-after pill.* That would explain the hurry. She needed a prescription.'

Mrs Harper was staring through the glass of the Rational Oven. She didn't even turn round.

'They couldn't be *that* stupid,' Marcia said.

'Whatever the reason, it was not respectful,' Ines said. 'What if everyone ran off?'

Paul felt personally let down, he said.

'Breaking rules together can be a way of confirming love,' Tony pronounced. 'Alliance against the world kind of thing.'

Stephanie said she was *d'accord*. 'Rob is in love.'

'See what happens the moment Beth turns her back.' I laughed.

Mrs Harper said, enough, we must concentrate on our work, we mustn't be distracted by speculations and gossip. 'They have let us down, but we don't need to ask why. We will manage.'

Ralph plugged in the big whisk. The recipe said to stir in the cocoa by hand but with ten litres of soya milk it would have taken an age. We moved to the window near the plugs and I held the basin while he pointed the shaft.

'Ralph, don't turn the thing on before the whisk's well in.'

He sent me a pained look.

The liquid swirled white and brown. Ralph was solemn, moving the heavy motor round and round while I kept the bowl still. I could see the concentration in his jaw. There was a veil of cocoa on his young man's stubble. Honey on a razor's edge. The heavy mix was lifting and falling in soft slaps. Under cover of the noise, he asked: 'Can I kiss you again, Bess?'

Glancing round, I dipped a finger in the mix and dabbed it on his mouth.

'No.'

'Bess,' he moaned.

'I'm not Bess. I'm not even Beth.'

He smiled. 'You can't tell me you're Merediz now.'

'You should have run away with her. She was after you first.'

'I like you, Bess.'

'From now on,' I said, 'you must call me Lisa.'

Geoff

When the vow of silence is dropped the screen in the dining hall is folded away. Men and women can mix. The servers eat with the meditators. Heads lift, people look you in the eye. It's back to regular body language. Harper sets up a table in a corner to take people's donations. You can pay with a credit card or cash, as much or as little as you want. There's no fuss. They don't tick off names or try to figure who paid what. The Dasgupta really is a free institution.

When we'd got all the food done and served, I found a place at the end of a table and listened to their conversations. There was such a buzz in the room. Somebody was convinced she'd levitated. One man was telling a story about how he'd sleepwalked and tried to get into the wrong bed. He was sharing a room with four others. He sleepwalked a lot. Then there was the problem that with the vow of silence he couldn't explain himself to the bloke he'd woken up.

Everybody laughed.

'Never heard so much bollocks in all me born days,' an older woman said. 'Karma bollocks, reincarnation bollocks, nirvana bollocks.'

I ate my risotto slowly. The woman saying 'me born days' and 'bollocks' had a posh accent. I let the grains dissolve on my tongue before swallowing. Rice turning into Beth who would turn it into shit soon enough. *Anicca*. Lisa, I mean.

From now on I am going to be Lisa. I sat listening to the hubbub. I was swimming in noise, drifting on noise. There was a woman with a throaty voice giggling about bad karma and an older bloke braying he'd take reincarnation over Dante's *Paradiso* any day.

Something has changed, I thought. I felt calm. I felt absolutely calm. I had no idea what I was going to do, even in the next few hours, whether I was going to stay or go, whether I was due for another conversation with Mrs Harper or Mi Nu, or whether they would never talk to me again. But I was calm. The past was here too. Right here in the dining hall. Jonathan and Carl and Zoë and Mum and Dad, they were all here, in the noise in my head, they hadn't been removed, or buried, or forgotten. I could imagine them sitting at the table behind me, talking together. Like that night in Soho. Or times Carl came to dinner and talked fishing with Dad. They were all here for the day-ten party. But I wasn't upset. I didn't need to chase them away. I was calm. It wasn't the stillness I'd had in the Metta Hall. But maybe it was to do with that.

'So, when do I get my reader's report?'

GH sat down beside me.

'Is it Gary?' I asked. 'Or Gregory or Gordon or George?'

'Geoff,' he said. 'Geoff Hall.'

'I'm Lisa,' I told him.

'Good to meet you, Lisa.'

I asked him about the food and he said too bad he'd never got anywhere near the bananas. 'Those little apples were sour.'

'I thought you'd appreciated the cantaloupes, though.'

'I beg your pardon?'

He didn't understand. He's the kind of guy who says 'I beg your pardon'. And he had a cute line in bushy-eyebrow-raising. Then he got it. 'Oh, right. The canteloupes. Sorry about that.'

We went for a walk around the field. There were people in pairs and knots, moving, leaning on trees and benches. The sky was milky.

'How come you were in my room?' he asked.

'How come you were keeping a diary? You know you're not supposed to.'

He didn't reply. Maybe he was still surprised to be speaking again.

'All day you sit in the meditation hall supposedly dissolving your big ego, then you rush back to your room and start scribbling away and building it up again.'

'It was quite a shock finding you there.' He laughed.

'I was taking some bedding over for a student who was cold. I pushed the wrong door.'

'And just happened to see the exercise books and just happened to sit down to read and just happened to pick up a pen and write me a message.'

I laughed.

'You came more than once. And you tore out a page. Why did you do that?'

'What is this, an interrogation?'

You could see he was excited someone had read his stuff.

'By the way, I really liked what you wrote about your daughter.'

'Oh? What in particular?'

Then I realized that the stuff about adoring his daughter was in the letter. And he didn't know I'd read that.

'Just the way you obviously care.'

He sighed. He had a craggy, troubled look to him, but when he laughed he relaxed.

'Let's cut across diagonally,' I said. We'd finished a first time round the field. 'We can do the bit in the wood.'

We left the path and walked on the wet grass. He was silent.

'Home tomorrow, then?'

'Right.'

'What are you going to do with your famous dilemma?'

'I've no idea. I was hoping the meditation would help me take a decision.'

'It doesn't. It just helps you accept you're a piece of shit.'

He frowned.

'Actually, that's not bad for a start.'

'Have you collected your stuff from the locker yet? You can, you know. You can use your phone if you want.'

He said he'd opened the locker but then shut it again.

'Are you scared?'

'Of course I'm scared.' He thought about it. 'But less than when I came. I feel stronger these last few days.'

'Ah. I haven't read anything since day seven.'

'And I haven't written anything. I stopped.'

'Really?'

He didn't answer. We walked. And as we walked I knew I was getting to like him. I liked his troubledness.

'Why did you stop? Tell me.'

'I had this experience, meditating.'

He waited while we crossed two guys coming in the other direction.

'One of those awful hours of Strong Determination. My ankles and thighs were on fire, but I was determined not to move before the end of the hour. Then I realized how stupid it was. I was holding on so that I would feel proud when I made it, which is exactly the opposite of what meditation is supposed to be about. I don't know how it played out then. I decided to give up, to change posture, not because I absolutely had to, but to avoid this whole endurance-test mentality. I thought it would be better to be humble and accept I was beaten. But instead of uncrossing my legs I leaned forward a bit, leaned into the pain in my knees, my ankles, and let go, mentally. It was such a strange feeling. Like I was diving into a deep pool of pain, giving myself to it. And right when I thought I'd drown, I'd be overwhelmed, it all drained away, ran off like water. That's what it felt like, like hot water running away, and I was fine. I didn't have any trouble at all getting through the hour, even sat on a bit afterwards.'

'That's the experience that hooks everyone,' I said.

'Anyway, after that I really got into it. And I stopped writing. I'm even sad it's over.'

'So maybe you should stay.' I laughed. 'I've been here nearly nine months, you know.'

He asked how come and I told him they always needed volunteers, you just worked for them in return for room and board. 'Aside from the kitchen there's all sorts of maintenance and stuff. Gardening. Plumbing. Electrics.'

'I meant, how come you were here so long?'

I made him wait a moment. 'That's my business.'

'Oh, come on, tell me.'

'Why? Why do you want to know?'

He smiled. 'I'm curious about you.'

'Give me one good reason why I should tell.'

'You've read about my life.'

'Not a good reason.'

He laughed out loud. 'Because I like you.'

What was that supposed to mean?

We reached the corner of the field and moved into the path with the wood chippings, through the trees along the bottom fence where people skive off to the pub.

I said, 'OK. There was a drowning accident. Last summer in France. I was saved by a helicopter, but the other bloke in the water ended up in coma. It was sort of my fault and it started me thinking. Then on the ferry back home someone mentioned this place.'

'Did he survive? The guy in the coma.'

'I've no idea.'

'You don't know?'

'No.'

'But why not? You've got a phone, haven't you?'

'It's been in the locker since I arrived here.'

'Are you scared of phoning, in case he's dead?'

I thought about it. 'I used to be. But not now. The point is, it really doesn't matter whether he's dead or not. I did what I did. My problem is my problem whether he died or not. I hardly knew him in the end.'

He was silent.

'Sorry, it was kind of complicated.'

A little further on he stopped by a tree. 'A couple of days ago I was totally transfixed by this branch.' He pointed at a long twig with thick sticky buds. 'I sort of got stuck looking at the buds about to flower with drops of rain on them.'

'That's a very Dasgupta moment. Day eightish, I reckon.'

'I can't remember.' Then he said: 'Let's go and get our phones. Let's make the calls we have to make.'

'No.'

'Come on. Let's do it. Together.'

'No.'

I started to walk back beside him.

Mum

In my locker I would find the earrings Jonathan brought back from India, Zoë's black swan brooch and the weird amulet with the insect in amber that Carl picked up from the African market in Bordeaux. Jewellery is another thing that is forbidden in the Dasgupta, and makeup, and perfume. Anything bright or smelly. The amulet was supposed to guard against sudden death, Carl said, though it looked more like a bad omen to me. Who wants to be preserved in amber? 'As soon as you get out of here we'll check into a proper hotel and have a fantastic shower,' he said. He was always at my side when I woke in the morning and when I went to sleep at night. It was the last week of August and there was no air conditioning. The note I left said: 'It's over, Carl. I'm sorry. Don't try to contact me.'

Books are also forbidden. I'd locked away a copy of *Jules and Jim* Jonathan gave me. And a band biography of T. Rex. Plus my MP3. Sixty gigs. The battery will be flat. And in my phone. But the charger is there and when I turn it on there will be all the old numbers and all the messages that flew back and forth from New York, and the last message I sent to everybody, I'M AWAY AT A RETREAT. DON'T WORRY.

Can you complain that people haven't come looking for you, when you told them not to? Maybe you can. Nine months is a long time for a retreat. I think if a man cared, or a parent, they'd surely come looking. How many retreats can there be in the UK? I don't reckon it would take the police more than an afternoon to find me. Or maybe people did come looking and some idiot in the office checked through the student list and said, no, there was no Elisabeth Marriot among the meditators, not realizing that I was Beth, the server.

No, I can't turn my phone on, I thought, walking back up the path beside my diarist. I still had that feeling of calm, but the phone was too big a step. Geoff was striding out pretty purposefully. He had a real day-ten, back-to-business walk. As we passed the meditation hall, I said, 'Sorry, there's Mi Nu, I need a word with her.' And I ran.

She was wearing jeans and a loose black cotton sweater. Hair in a ponytail. She was any ordinary Asian woman. That was another day-ten thing. When the silence is broken, the leaders suddenly seem very ordinary.

'Mi Nu, I'm sorry.'

She turned.

'I mean about last night.'

She let her head fall to one side. 'Everything is fine, Beth.'

'Lisa,' I said. 'I've decided to call myself Lisa.'

She looked puzzled.

'Remember you said about changing names? It's sort of Beth, but not Beth, if you see what I mean.'

269

'Ah.' I don't think she did see. 'So, you've decided to leave us.'

'No, no.'

I wanted her to say something but she was silent.

'Actually, I was thinking how *useful* these last few days have been. My equanimity. I'm definitely getting calmer. Another month and . . .'

And what?

'You can always leave and then come back, you know, if you want to.'

I shook my head.

'The Dasgupta Institute will always be here. You'll always be welcome.'

'But I wasn't thinking of leaving.'

If they were going to kick me out, they'd have to say so. Mi Nu put her hands together in farewell. 'Let Dhamma be your guide, Lisa.'

She turned to walk to her bungalow.

I wanted to follow. I wanted to run after her and ask to see her room in daylight. Those faces high up on the wall. I wanted her to tell me whether they were throwing me out or not. I wanted to tell her how important it was to have her as a friend. But I needed to run after my diarist too. It would be good to open my locker with him there. I'd feel safer. Was I really going to do that at last? The key was in the side pocket of my backpack. But why did all the Dasgupta people want me to leave? They had withdrawn completely from the world—Mi Nu, the Harpers, Paul, Livia— they'd given up on sex, given up everything. Why were they so determined to chuck me back into things? As if I didn't deserve to be with them. I wasn't pure enough. Or maybe they saw me as a threat. I threatened Mrs Harper because she was attracted to me.

I began to laugh. More likely they were trying to be kind. Mi Nu was telling me to leave for my sake. The way Jonathan always used to say, 'You're too young for me, Betsy M. Too young for a failed old fartist.'

I got my key but Geoff wasn't in the locker room. Two younger guys were checking football results on an iPhone. Then I remembered there'd be my purse as well. With photos and debit card and cash. Not much. And my passport. Elisabeth Jane Marriot. 'You look like a genie out of a bottle,' Jonathan said. My hair was so wild, big teeth and pop-eyed.

I was getting shivery. I crouched down, pushed the key in the lock and stopped. Hadn't I promised myself I would only get my stuff when I could do it calmly, when the messages on the phone, the photos in the purse, the stupid amulet, the earrings, meant nothing any more? Only open your locker when you're liberated, I used to tell myself. So why now?

Because you are calm, a voice said. You are liberated. Lisa's voice.

The locker was on the bottom row. I squatted down, turned the key and opened the door.

The Pocus demo. I'd forgotten that. *Safe Crash*. And a bottle of Chanel I'd ripped off from Mum before the trip to France.

Then I was on automatic pilot. In a moment I was in the kitchen plugging the charger into the socket for the grinder, turning the phone on. What was the pin? I'd forgotten. Think. Jonathan's age and Carl's. 5229. Pin accepted. Credit? £1.78. I called Mum.

'Elisabeth! Heavens!'

'Hi, Mum.'

Silence.

'Mum?'

'Sorry, love, I'm in traffic, it's tricky. Where are you? I've been so worried.'

'Oh, I'm OK. I'm not far away. At a Buddhist place.'

'Buddhist? You haven't turned Buddhist.'

'Sort of yes and no.'

'Oh.'

What should I say?

'Has Dad been in touch?' she asked.

'What? How could he?'

'You don't know, then?'

'What?'

Ralph slammed a trolley of dirty plates through the swing doors and started to stack them in the sink. I retreated towards the service door, pressing the receiver to my ear.

'Your father left home, Elisabeth. Just before Christmas. Sorry, I'll have to pull over. Hang on.'

When she came back on the line she was crying. Dad had left. After thirty-one years. She'd never imagined it could hurt so much.

'I feel such a failure, Elisabeth. I'm such a terrible failure.'

'I'll come at once,' I said.

'No no, don't do that, love.'

'I'll come tonight.'

'No, Elisabeth. Please.' She'd found a handkerchief. 'It's sweet of you, but I don't want you changing your plans for our troubles. Or rather mine. I'm sure your father's having a fine old time of it. He—'

'I'll be back tonight, Mum.'

His Pack

It was after six thirty, less than half an hour before the last evening discourse, the one where Dasgupta tells you if there's anything you find hard to believe in his philosophy you can leave it out and accept the rest, like the boy who would only drink his mother's soup without the nice crunchy bits, the spicy seeds, the little dumplings. 'If you can't believe in reincarnation, leave it out, doesn't matter, if you can't believe in *sankharas,* leave them out. Maybe later you'll realize what a lovely flavour these nutty bits add, what sense they make. But for the moment all that matters is the practice. Observe sensation, develop equanimity. Keep *sila,* the Five Precepts, work on your *samādhi,* explore the field of *paññā.* Only the practice matters, nothing else. An hour in the morning and an hour in the evening, followed by ten minutes' *metta.* Observe sensation last thing before falling asleep and observe it again first thing on waking. Continuity is the key to success, my friends. Equanimity is purity and purity is liberation.'

Suddenly I thought, If I hear Dasgupta's voice say this stuff one more time, I'll go crazy. I walked straight over to Dormitory A on the men's side, kicked off my shoes and hurried down the corridor. I pushed open his door.

All strictly forbidden.

He was on the bed in his underpants, speaking on the phone. Fresh from the shower.

I leaned against the door and watched. He looked at me, did an eyebrow-raising routine, pressed the phone harder to his ear.

Then the gong began. The ten-minute warning. You could hear it struck somewhere near the bathrooms, then again, getting nearer, in Dormitory B.

'For a while, yes,' he was saying. 'Because the situation is too ugly. You know that yourself . . . I'll file for bankruptcy . . . Where I'll be is my own business, isn't it? . . . Susie is an adult, Linda, she doesn't need us, she doesn't want us to be fussing about her.'

He hadn't drawn the curtains. You could see guys on the path a couple of yards away, heading towards the hall for Dasgupta's last talk.

Then the gong clanged right outside the door. The course manager was in the corridor.

'For the last meditation,' my diarist was explaining. 'It's a gong.'

He started trying to get his trousers on while he talked.

'No, I haven't gone raving religious. It's saner here than the way we live at home.'

He couldn't get his feet into the trousers. One of the legs was twisted.

'No, I'm not chickening out.'

I crouched down, sorted out his trousers and held them open for him to put his feet in. They were loose black linen with a tie-up top. Nice meditation pants. He grinned and stood and I pulled them up his thighs and over his bum. He had a lean, bony body, but the skin was smooth and the pack between his legs plump and solid. I gave it a little pat and tied the trousers off tight.

'It's quite the contrary, Linda.'

I looked around. There was a T-shirt on one of the hooks by the door. Rolling it up for him felt good, it smelt good. He ducked his head for me to pull it over him, taking the phone away from his ear to push it through a sleeve. As he did so I heard a woman's voice saying, 'You don't seem to have thought of that at all.'

'You'll do exactly what you'd do if I was still there,' he shouted. 'In our heads we've been apart for years.'

I rolled up his socks one at a time, pushed them over his toes and unravelled them up his ankles and calves. They were long socks. Clean fortunately. You have to admire a guy who has clean socks on day ten. Without stepping back I stood up. My face was inches from his neck. I smiled.

'Well, come and see if you don't believe me. The last thing anyone thinks of here is sex.'

His eyes looked down at me.

'For God's sake!' He took the phone from his ear and looked at the screen. 'She's rung off.'

Then he turned to the door where his jacket was hanging.

'Don't go to the discourse, Geoff,' I said. 'Come with me. Let's leave now. Take me to London. Tonight.'

He stopped. 'What?'

Now the second gong began. Five minutes.

'Take me to London now. Tonight.'

'I can't.'

'You've got a car here, haven't you? Let's go. This last discourse is a bore. He just drags it out.'

'Didn't you hear what I was saying? On the phone.'

Actually I hadn't.

'I've decided to stay. I asked Harper if they could use some volunteer work for the next few weeks, and he said yes.'

I shook my head. 'After all you wrote in your diary . . .'

'I told you, I started to get into it these last few days.'

'But how can you help your daughter from here?'

'Susie doesn't need my help. The only urgent thing is to declare bankruptcy. And my accountant can do that. At most I'll have to go back for a couple of signatures.'

'You're not coming?'

'No.'

I let my head fall to one side. 'Not for little old Lisa?'

'It's not the right moment.'

'You won't get another chance, Mr Diarist. I don't ask twice.'

He looked confused, but shook his head.

'Maybe just as well,' I said, and walked out.

Deep Deep *Sankharas*

By seven thirty I was gone. No goodbyes. I went back to my room, stuffed my clothes into my backpack and left. Meredith had done her runner this morning. Stephanie was on clean-up, Kristin and Marcia must have gone to the discourse. All the better. I was in no mood for leaving notes. If I was going to get home to sleep I'd have to move fast. The Dasgupta Institute is hardly on the beaten track.

'Goodbye, Mouse,' I said. It was irritating that my diarist, who'd been so sharp about Dasgupta at the beginning, was now preferring the fat guru to Beth. After I'd pulled his trousers up for him and given him a pat on his pack!

You're not Beth any more, a voice reminded me.

Outside, between the Metta Hall and the dining hall, I stopped. I should at least say something to Mrs Harper. No. I hurried through the dining hall, past the kitchen and the office and out.

It was a breezy evening in April. I thought it was April. I hadn't checked the bus times. There was a mile of dirt track to the road. I had to get there before dark. But the backpack was heavy. It was slow going. The hedgerows were high with trees spreading above, closing you in. And as I walked I realized I was full of fear. What of? Every cell in my body was afraid. I could feel it on my skin. A tingling. But I felt confident too, even excited. I was breathing fear, breathing confidence, being alive being afraid. Breathe, Lisa, breathe. I was going to meet fear calmly, happily. There were birds singing too. Evening chirrups. And there were smells. Cut grass, woodsmoke, manure. Too bad about the mud and puddles. My trainers were filthy. Too bad about my period. I'd forgotten to change the tampon again. And too bad the buses only went once an hour. Was I going to start smoking again? I didn't know. Was I going to start drinking? Find a boyfriend, join a band, get a job, go to college finally. Who is Lisa Marriot?

I walked, and at every step along the muddy lane between the high hedgerows I felt more fearful and more confident and more excited. Zinging and calm. Then I remembered: Dad has left Mum. Before Christmas. So four or five months ago. Quite a while. It was something that had really happened. The Thirty Years' War was over. A couple of months without Beth and that was it, they split. Everything falls apart.

Well, good!

Again I had a little fit of fear and bliss. Life really can change. *Anicca*. It was terrifying. I can start again, I thought. Lisa thought. Really st-tart again. I could go home, this evening, and I could leave home, maybe tomorrow. Instead of *having* to live there to keep them on good terms and *not being able* to live there because they were never on good terms. Suddenly I wasn't sure my time at the

Dasgupta had had anything to do with Jonathan or Carl, the beach or the accident. Dad had left. Mum had let him go. I was free.

Darkness came. Then rain. The air greyed and thickened. Damn. I had no umbrella. At the bus stop I let the rain fall on me. My hair would get sticky and tangly. My shoulders were already damp. Don't react. But there was no way I could react. The stop was in the middle of nowhere. A bend in a country lane. Hedges and fields. A gravelly lay-by. The rain fell through a chill breeze. I had left the Dasgupta. Keep the phone off, I thought. And Dad had left Mum. Wait for the bus. It will come. Even in the country the last bus can't leave before eight.

It was almost nine when headlights turned out of the track from the Dasgupta and swept across me. The car shifted gear, accelerating, then shifted down again and stopped a few yards on. The passenger window buzzed down.

'Lisa!'

'Mr Diarist.'

'You're soaking. Get in. I'll stick your bag in the back.'

I wasn't actually sure I wanted this lift now. But I wasn't sure whether a bus would come either. I'd been there an hour. He jumped out, took my bag, and suddenly I was sitting in a car with a man.

'I decided to settle a few things at the office.'

'Fine.'

'And then get back here before the next retreat starts.'

'If you can take me to London, that will be great.'

'London where?'

'Chiswick.'

It was a bit out of his way, he said, but no problem. He'd go and sleep in his office.

'Fine.'

After a few minutes he tried, 'Aren't you freezing?'

I didn't answer.

He drove. I sat and stared. I hadn't been in a car for so long. I stared at the black windscreen, the lights and the rain and the wipers. He turned the heating on.

'If you'd like to change,' he said, 'I won't look.'

We stopped and I got into the back. I fished in my pack for some dry things.

'It's a bit risky,' I told him. 'I've got my period.'

'Don't worry.' He was driving again.

'What will your wife think if she starts seeing stains on the back seat?'

'Just don't worry.'

I lay down on the seat, pulled off my filthy trainers, my socks, and started to wriggle down my soaking jeans. We were still on the back roads before the motorway and the car was swinging this way and that.

He laughed, 'I'm in such a funny mood. I can't decide whether to turn the radio on or not. It's been so nice not hearing anything for ten days and at the same time I feel so tempted. Only I know once I've done it I'll lose something. I'll feel contaminated.'

I kicked off my panties and sat up a bit to get my feet through the fresh ones.

'Maybe we should stop at a petrol place,' I said. 'I need to pick up some tampons.'

'OK.' He kept his eyes on the road. 'Another thing is I can't decide whether to light up or not. It was easy not smoking there, but I always smoke in the car.'

I was busy sorting myself out.

'The funny thing is I'm sure if I turn the radio on I'll light up immediately. Same decision.'

I stuck a wad of tissues in my panties and pulled them up snug. I'd chosen a skirt instead of trousers. It was forbidden to show knees at the Dasgupta.

'You'll have plenty of time for not smoking,' I told him, 'if you go back there.'

'That's true.'

'Bet you don't, though.'

He didn't reply. I reached under my T-shirt and undid the bikini top. Everything was damp.

'Another thing I can't decide . . .' he said quietly.

Knowing I was supposed to say, 'Yes?' I didn't.

'Is whether I want to sneak a look at you.'

'Ha! Don't ask me.'

'You're a funny girl,' he said. He hesitated. 'When you pulled up my trousers, I mean.'

'Be hilarious,' I laughed, 'if you turned the radio on and there was Dasgupta's voice. Sttartt-tagain.'

'I have it tuned to BBC six,' he said.

'Aren't we progressive.'

I peeled off my top, pulled the new one around my waist, a red one, closed the clip, turned it round and worked it up. For a moment I stayed like that, with this red bikini top wrapped round the underside of my tits in the odd light of the car with the yellows and pinks of the road flashing and shifting. There was dead silence from up front. I pulled the top up and at that moment the radio crashed on. It was frenetic rockabilly.

I laughed. 'Too late, mate. I'm done.'

I pulled on a black pullover, climbed over to the front seat and wriggled myself comfortable.

'So, how are you doing, Geoff?'

He sighed, 'Want a smoke?'

Around ten he pulled off the motorway, made a few quick turns, like he knew where he was, and parked about thirty yards from a pub.

'Before closing time,' he said. 'Just one.'

'Why not?'

The place was noisy. He got in the pints while I went to the loo. There was a machine for tampons. I sorted myself out. Walking across the bar between the tables felt very strange and very ordinary.

'Someone's happy.'

He'd already got through half his drink.

'Are you sure you want to go back there? I just can't see you becoming a Dasgupta guy. You're too . . .' I couldn't think of anything.

'Dead sure.'

He was looking me in the eyes.

'*Sila, samādhi, paññā,*' I said.

'Yes.'

'You'll have to keep the Five Precepts. No booze, no smoke, no food after midday, no chat, no sex.'

'Right.'

'Hard to see why you're trying to make out with me then, Mr Diarist.'

He smiled. 'I'm not trying to make out with you, Lisa.'

'Right. Anyway, I'm more or less a virgin again after nine months at the Dasgupta. So be warned.'

What did that mean?

He drank fast. 'What I don't understand,' he said, 'is why you decided to leave now. After so long, I mean.'

I was enjoying the beer too. It felt so bitter and rounded in the mouth.

'Because of your diary.'

'My diary?'

He couldn't decide if I was pulling his leg.

'Another pint?' he asked. 'First hardly touched my throat.'

I watched him at the bar. He had an easy manner but seemed slightly nervy. Carrying the pints to the table, his right hand was shaking.

How wonderful pubs were, I thought then. I was having these sudden waves of enthusiasm. But how wonderful too not to have been in one for so long. Lisa isn't really a pub person, I thought.

'Your wife will never let you leave,' I told him. 'She'll dig her claws in. You'll feel guilty and give way.'

'We'll see,' he said.

'I bet she loves you really. She's just bitter because you make her feel old and useless, with your pretty young girlfriends and your obsession with this scatty daughter.'

He drank his pint, watching me with an absorbed expression.

'Not to mention your fixation with your career. I mean, do you ever re-read what you write? It's all me me me. Jesus!'

He didn't answer.

'I went out with an older guy once who was completely fixated on his career. It was such a turn-off.'

Not true. It turned me on like crazy.

'Why would my diary make you want to leave?' he asked. 'To do what, anyway? What are your plans?'

283

'As soon as you get home,' I told him, 'you're going to be wanting to save your publishing company, or write a book or do something to prove you're not a failure. You'll never go back to the Dasgupta. You'll keep putting it off and then you'll forget it. You'll start a new affair with some new secretary. That's what you're like. Anyone reading what you wrote could see that.'

He frowned. 'You didn't answer my question.' But now he glanced at his watch. 'I suppose we should get moving.' He began to drink up. 'Come on, tell me the truth, why did my diary make you want to leave? If it did.'

I shifted my beer mat to the edge of the table, so it was hanging over an inch, flicked it up in the air with the back of my fingers and caught it on the second somersault. 'Nine months out of a pub and I get it first time.'

'Why? Come on.'

'It reminded me of sex.'

'Sex? I can't remember writing about sex.'

'It reminded me how exciting it is to be anxious and to have decisions to make. There's none of that at the Dasgupta.'

'That's not sex.'

'It felt like sex.'

'Drink up,' he said.

I poured half of my second pint into his and he smiled and drank.

Walking back to the car I took his hand, automatically, the same way I'd flicked the beer mat, the same way I'd poured the beer in his glass, and as we were about to separate to open our different doors, he pulled me round and kissed me. It was a short firm kiss on the lips, nothing adventurous, but as soon as we were in the car I turned to him, he leaned over to me and we kissed again. This time it was a careful kiss that turned warm and then hungry and then busy, really busy. It was a good kiss.

'Oh, God.' I laughed. 'First the radio, the fags, then the booze, now the kiss. What next?'

'All the better for ten days' abstinence.'

'Nearer ten months for me.'

We pulled out into the road and at the first junction there was a police car, lights flashing but no siren.

'Shit,' he said.

I said quietly, 'If you don't think you should drive, then stop. We'll find a place for the night.'

The words hung there. He drove. After a mile or so the police car turned off. Then we were on the motorway and he clicked on the radio and offered the cigarettes again. The car accelerated. The cigarettes glowed. We didn't speak for a while. Then, shaking my head a bit, I murmured: 'Deep deep *sankharas*, Geoff.'

The words just came out. He nodded. He was staring at the road.

'*Sankharas* of craving,' I said softly.

'That's for sure.'

'*Sankharas* of aversion.'

'When I arrive home, definitely.'

'Deep misery,' I whispered. 'Deep deep misery.'

'*Dukkha*,' he said. 'All life is *dukkha*."

'Remain vvery alert, Geoff, vvery vigilant.'

He smiled faintly. 'Start again, Lisa,' he said, 'st-tart again.'

'With a calm and quiet mind.'

'A balanced, equanimous mind.'

'Equanimous mind. Equanimous mind.'

'If you are experiencing, gross, solidified, intensified sensations, Lisa . . .'

'Just observe, Geoff, just observe.'

'If you are experiencing a free flow of subtle sensations all across the body . . .

'Just observe, just observe.'

'Pain, pain, not my pain.'

'Pleasure, pleasure, not my pleasure.'

'Bavatu sava mangelam.'

'Sadhu, sadhu, sadhu.'

I buzzed down the window and chucked out my fag. 'Great kiss by the way.'

He sighed. 'You look wonderful in that skirt.'

'I know.'

We came off the MI on to the North Circular. BBC 6 was playing awful prog rock.

He said: 'We are not masochists. We are not here to torture ourselves. But some discomfort may be necessary in the process of purification. Remember that?'

'Day five,' I said, 'explaining the hour of Strong Determination. You want to be coming off at Uxbridge Road. Then Askew Road.'

And I told him: 'If you do leave your wife, your daughter may change too.'

'Do you think so?'

He turned into Askew Road. It was a question of minutes.

'You know, I envy you, Geoff.'

'God, why?'

'I envy you beginning a long stay at the Dasgupta. Like it was me nine months ago.'

Suddenly I felt tears coming. My chest rose and fell.

'Tell me about it,' he asked. 'I thought you'd had enough.'

His voice was quiet.

'Tell me,' he said.

'Oh, I'll just miss things.' I waited till my voice steadied. 'Like the rabbits in the dew before dawn. Or sitting on my mat with my eyes closed while people come and go.'

'And the gong.'

'The gong. Sorry, take the first right after the lights and it's halfway down on the left. Number thirty-eight.'

'Here?'

'Right. Watch out for the sleeping policeman.'

'Got it.'

I thought and sighed and bit my lip. 'Most of all, though, I'll miss the feeling I always had there that maybe'—but I wasn't sure I knew how to say this—'well, that it might be possible *not to live*, if you see what I mean. Do you? Not to have to live. Like Mi Nu when she wraps her shawl round her and sits on her cushion and is just there. The thought that you could be nothing, but beautifully, for ever. You'd be spared.'

'Lisa!' He stopped the car and switched off. He was smiling and shaking his head.

'Hey,' I laughed, 'I write songs, you know. I'm a deep one. A last cigarette?'

'Why not?'

He handed me the pack and pushed in the lighter. Taking the first puff, I felt absolutely certain that this was the last. Lisa isn't a smoker.

He lit up too.

287

'Now I have to see my mum and explain where I've been all this time. Then there'll be the email, I suppose, Facebook. I'll be up all night.'

He was frowning through the windscreen. 'No more kisses.'

'Kisses, kisses, not my kisses.'

'Want my mobile number?'

'No.'

'Wise.'

'You love your pain too much, Mr Diarist.'

'Right.' He shook his head. 'No sex, no story.'

'No joy, no pain.'

He smiled. 'The tenth day is over, my friends. You have the rest of your life to work.'

'Thanks for the lift, Geoff.'

Anicca

That was two years ago. I exaggerate, eighteen months. A bit more. Now I'm studying psychology in Manchester, share a flat off Oxford Road, sing in a pub Friday evenings. Just me and another girl, all acoustic. I have a pretty nice boyfriend, actually very nice. I'm planning to leave him just before he leaves me. *Anicca.* The universal law of impermanence. I meditate for an hour in the mornings, if I didn't drink too much the night before. I try to take it seriously, to be vvery aware, vvery vigilant. And whenever things get a bit wild, Dasgupta thoughts keep me on an even keel. More or less. One day I'll go back there, I tell myself, and immediately I feel more cheerful. I'll go back and the videos will be the same, the chanting will be the same. *Buddham saranam gacchami.* The stillness. Mi Nu. Mi Nu will be there for ever. I love that thought. Of Mr Geoffrey Hall I have heard and seen nothing, zilch. Philippe is dead. Meantime, the anthropology prof has his eyes on me. Parts of me. He has a nice voice and a sly smile. We'll see. Sometimes I wonder if I couldn't have seduced old Dasgupta himself if I'd ever got to meet him.

In another life maybe.